CW00833244

Death of a Good Woman

Also by Max Marquis in Macmillan

Vengeance

Elimination

Written in Blood

Max Marquis

Death of a Good Woman

MACMILLAN

First published 1998 by Macmillan
an imprint of Macmillan Publishers Ltd
25 Eccleston Place, London SW1W 9NF
and Basingstoke

Associated companies throughout the world

ISBN 0 333 72811 4

1 3 5 7 9 8 6 4 2

A CIP catalogue record for this book is available from the British Library

Phototypeset by Intype London Ltd
Printed and bound in Great Britain by
Mackays of Chatham plc, Chatham, Kent

For Margaret

And in Memory of Ted Hart
(*Canterbury Tales Prologue l.72*)

Chapter One

It all began when the dog barked on a Monday morning. This in itself was not unusual; it is in the nature of dogs to bark. However, this particular dog was very unusual, to the point of being unique. In the course of a long career Sergeant Anthony Rumsden, desk sergeant at Terrace Vale police station, had seen some weird specimens brought into the place, but this one took the biscuit, and could probably have taken anything else it fancied as well. Its owner claimed it was an Irish wolfhound, but it was more like a small hairy mammoth that had been rubbed up the wrong way.

Its name was unusual: Hannibal. Rumsden wouldn't have been surprised to learn its full name was Hannibal Lector because it had a predilection for eating people.

The dog was accompanied by a boy about fourteen years old named Simon Lyons, who had with him a small trolley which he used on his newspaper delivery round.

'Tell me again,' Rumsden said to the boy, not unkindly.

Simon sighed. 'One of the people I deliver papers to is a Miss Mary Docker, Flat 1, Holly Mansions. *Daily*

Telegraph weekdays, *Observer* and *Independent* Sundays. This morning she hadn't taken in her Sundays. They were still on the mat.'

It was a rare model of a statement, concise and to the point, Rumsden noted with admiration. 'D'you always leave the papers on the mat?' he asked.

'I told you. Only the Sundays. They're too thick to get through the letterbox unless I do 'em one section at a time, and that takes too long.'

Rumsden thought he detected a faint edge to the words 'too thick'.

'Then I saw the lights on inside.'

'How did you manage that?'

For the first time Simon Lyons looked ill at ease. 'I looked through the letter-box. Then Hannibal started barking. He never does that.'

'Was it dark outside?'

'Daylight. I came straight here.' He paused. 'Hannibal never barks. I mean, unless there's something. The hairs at the back of his neck stuck up. I'm sure there's something wrong. She's ill, or perhaps she'd had an accident, or something.'

Rumsden was impressed. Unexpectedly he asked, 'What d'you want to be when you leave school?'

Simon Lyons stared at him. 'Architect. Why?'

Rumsden shrugged. 'Oh, you know,' he said vaguely. At least the boy hadn't said he planned to be a detective, or a spy, or a writer, which would have caused Rumsden to have reservations. 'Well, thank you very much. I'll send somebody round to have a look. Better safe than sorry.' Unaccountably he felt embarrassed at having used the cliché. 'If you call in again we'll let you know.'

'It was because Hannibal barked. He never barks,' Simon Lyons repeated as he turned to go out.

Rumsden walked over to the communications room, where PC Phil Clapton was manning the radio. Police work has a weird effect on some people: it drives them to relentless gallows humour. Clapton thought himself a thorough card, but if he was, he was the two of clubs.

Rumsden told Clapton to send someone round to Holly Mansions to check, and dodged out of the room before Clapton could slip into his jokey mode.

WPC Rosie Hall and PC Dick 'Rambo' Wright took the call. In the inverse logic of nicknames – like calling a bald man Curly and a tall man Titch or Shorty – PC Dick Wright was called Rambo because he was small and slight, had fine, gingerish hair and a sharp face with curiously pale eyes. He appeared as menacing as Mary Poppins on Valium. Nevertheless, he had a black belt in judo and karate. These accomplishments he kept mainly to himself. His physical self-confidence made him quiet and unaggressive, unlike his film namesake.

WPC Rosie Hall was christened Rosemarie. The Rosemarie became shortened to Rosie, and most people now thought that was her real name. Although she had spent all her life in a poorer part of London she looked as if she had just come in from milking the cows, and was only partly dressed without a straw in her hair. She was probably the only officer at Terrace Vale who thought it was a fairly peaceful area. Her previous posting had been in a part of southeast London with the highest rate of drugbusts and the busiest hospital casualty departments in the Metropolitan Police area. Any cat with two ears had never left the house.

Rosie put panda car Romeo Juliet 69 – a vehicle known as the Passion Wagon, and other less polite names – on the move just as Rumsden's phone rang back at Terrace Vale.

The call was from Wrappers Ltd, a small packaging firm. They were a little concerned about one of their most reliable office staff who hadn't turned up for work that morning and wasn't answering the phone. Her name was Mary Docker, and she lived at No. 1, Holly Mansions.

Rumsden told Clapton to pass this on to Rosie and Rambo.

'I've got a feeling that this is going to be one of those days,' Rumsden said to a large wall poster about Neighbourhood-Watch schemes.

He was being optimistic. It was going to be more than one day. A lot more.

Rosie Hall parked the panda on a double yellow line outside the front door of Holly Mansions. It was a 1900s four-storey brick-built block of spacious flats with sash windows and high ceilings that meant the rooms were ruinously expensive to heat. On the other hand, the solid construction of the building meant that the flats were almost soundproof and hi-fis could thunder out everything from heavy metal to Wagnerian heavy brass and tympani without disturbing the neighbours.

Rosie and Rambo Wright approached the front door of the block. There was an entryphone system with a small loudspeaker and call buttons for each flat. Just in case it was all a false alarm, Rambo rang twice at No.1 . . . unsuccessfully. He pushed a button marked

'Tradesmen'. The lock buzzed and the door opened a few inches.

'What's the point of having a front-door lock, then?' Rosie muttered.

'It's a timelock, for the postman and paper delivery boy,' Rambo explained. 'Most of them switch off about midday.'

There was no answer to heavy knocks on the solid wooden door of Flat No. 1. Both officers peered through the letter-box. As Simon Lyons had said, the lights were on inside the flat.

They went outside again, to find out if there was anything to be seen through the windows, but the curtains were pulled close without the smallest gap to afford a glimpse of the room inside. All the windows were closed and locked with old-fashioned fasteners of swinging bolts which fitted under a horizontal hasp.

Rosie went round to the courtyard with the block's garages at the back of the building. The curtains and the locks on the rear windows were just as comprehensively shut.

Rambo returned to the block and had a careful look at the front door of the Mary Docker's flat. It had two locks: one Yale-type and a good quality five-lever dead lock. He gently pushed against the door a few times.

From behind him came a weird, banshee mournful howl that modulated into something resembling the honking of an excited seal. He turned, startled. Simon Lyons was standing in the hallway with his extraordinary dog.

'What's your name?' Rosie asked jumpily. 'Baskerville?'

'There's something up,' Simon said. 'Hannibal

never barks.' He explained who he was. Rambo thanked him politely for his interest and shepherded him out. Hannibal shambled after his owner, looking over his shoulder and making small noises like a horror film's creaky door.

'The Yale lock's shut, but not the deadlock,' Rambo told Rosie when she returned. They both thought this faintly sinister. She opened her shoulder bag and took out a credit card. She slid it in between the door and the door frame and jiggled it about for a few moments until she managed to slide back the tongue of the lock.

'At least my card's useful for something,' Rosie said.

As they entered Rambo said, 'Watch where you step,' to Rosie. Lying on the interior doormat was Saturday's newspaper. They were both convinced now that they were going to find something nasty, and at that moment Hannibal gave another of his banshee howls from the pavement outside.

'Hello, anyone at home?' they called out in turn as they advanced into the flat. They slowly went from room to room, calling out as they went. There was something slightly weird about the flat that neither of them could put a finger on. It struck Rosie first. The flat was neat, clean, tidy and polished, as if it were a show flat at an exhibition – almost unlived in.

The last door they tried was to the bedroom. When they opened it it was as if a heavy wave of some evil black ghosts fled past them from the room, making the two officers hesitate.

The interior of the bedroom was oppressively dark, with no light from the corridor relieving the darkness.

'Stay there,' Rambo told Rosie at the doorway. For once she didn't give him an argument.

He could just see the faint outline of a window behind the closed curtains. He made his way warily across the room, barking his shins on a piece of furniture. He swore softly.

Rambo Wright reached the curtains, found the middle, and in one swift movement pulled them apart.

They both stood frozen for what seemed an eternity as they took in every detail of the horror of the scene. At last Rosie turned and rushed into the bathroom where she vomited violently into the lavatory bowl.

Coffee times on Monday mornings in the CID offices at Terrace Vale police station were much like any other morning. 'Coffee time' was an extremely imprecise term. Not only did 'time' cover the entire twenty-four-hour working day, but 'coffee' included the entire spectrum of other liquids from Detective Chief Inspector Ted Greening's cheap whisky, which many of his colleagues believed was principally antifreeze and burnt sugar, to one young detective's skimmed milk, which was about the only fluid he could risk sending past his ultra-sensitive duodenum. He was beginning to admit to himself that he wasn't really cut out for this line of work.

However, some deep-seated, atavistic group-instinct meant that at 11 a.m., the consumption of coffee in the offices reached a brief peak. There was nothing formal or elegant about the ceremony; it simply meant that white polystyrene cups, containing a coffee-coloured liquid dispensed from a machine at exorbitant cost, suddenly sprouted like mushrooms on desks.

Most of the detectives were at their desks, doing two-finger wrestling with ancient typewriters that always won the battles, writing up reports; some were shuffling files of their case loads, wondering which ones were the least unpromising of producing some sort of result. One or two had open files on their desks, reading them while they shaded their eyes. The effect was spoiled when they gave a snore or started dribbling. A few scorned this flimsy subterfuge, and were unashamedly staring into space, their minds turned off, ready to say they were thinking if anyone asked them what the hell they were supposed to be doing.

Detective Chief Inspector Ted Greening was in his office with the door shut, hoping that no one would come in and ask him to make a decision. He had a large stack of files on his scarred desk. They were all 'dead' files, but they looked imposing and gave him an excuse to say he was busy. Occasionally he remembered to wipe off the film of dust on the top one. He reached into his bottom right-hand drawer for a half-bottle of his fiery whisky. Most of the detectives said it was called Old Rot-Gut – 'Not a Drop is Sold, Till It's Three Weeks Old'.

Terrace Vale's senior detective inspector, Harry Timberlake, occupied an office shaped like a vertical shoebox, which he kept moderately tidy. He had been in it since 7 a.m., getting his interminable paperwork up to date. He hated it: but it had to be done, and once it was out of the way he could devote himself to his passion, feeling villains' collars.

On this Monday morning Timberlake was feeling in an uncertain mood, which was making him feel as spiky as a set of railings. He knew precisely what was wrong, not that it did him any good. He was like the donkey in the fable – wrongly attributed to Buridan – that was dying of hunger and thirst. Placed exactly midway between a pail of water and a bale of hay the animal couldn't make its mind up which way to go first, and died.

To put it another way, Miss Jenny Long – as she was known at her hospital – and WDC Sarah Lewis, aka the Welsh Rarebit, were the horns of the dilemma on which he was perched, in a manner of speaking. He had spent a highly enjoyable year with Sarah as a partner, then gone back to his first love Jenny Long, argued with her in a bout of stupid jealousy, gone to bed with Sarah again, then made his peace with Jenny once more.*

To have the opportunity of such a choice was something for which many men would have sent their grandmothers out on to the streets. Timberlake had toyed briefly with the idea of not choosing at all, and remaining intimate with both of them. He soon dismissed the option of keeping them both on the go – if he could – as a solution; not because it would drain his physical and mental resources but because of his innate sense of morality. Harry Timberlake was strictly Old Testament: honesty is the best policy – an unusual precept for an experienced detective to hold – wrongdoing must be punished, and everyone is responsible for the result of his actions. Plus, one man, one woman, at a time.

His mental turmoil was interrupted by the arrival at his door of Sergeant Rumsden and DCI Greening.

*See *Written in Blood*, the third of the Harry Timberlake novels.

Rumsden had informed the DCI that Rosie Hall and Rambo Wright had called in to report what was undoubtedly a murder at Holly Mansions.

Greening came to a decision with unusual rapidity: he handed over the case to Timberlake. 'You take charge on the ground, and I'll organize things at this end,' he said, making it sound as if he were planning the D-Day landings. In fact all he would do was make a couple of phone calls and tell Sergeant Rumsden to detail some uniforms to take care of setting up an information room and murder squad office.

Harry Timberlake set off with his usual initial inquiry team – Detective Sergeant Darren Webb, and DC Nigel Larkin. Larkin's work on the de Gaillmont murders* and Timberlake's recommendation, plus a startlingly good set of results at his detective's course, had got him out of uniform quicker than a ten-quid whore out of her clothes.

When the detectives arrived at the flat, the SOCOs, dressed in their white overalls and overshoes, and the police surgeon were already there.

They were still working in the bedroom as Timberlake arrived at the door. He was half-prepared for what he would see because Rosie Hall was still looking as if she had just landed from a trip round Cape Horn in a sailing dinghy; even Rambo Wright and one or two of the SOCOs had a perceptible greenish tinge about their faces. Timberlake stopped dead in his tracks, and Webb bumped into his back.

*See *Written in Blood*.

What they saw turned their blood cold.

It was the stuff of which the worst nightmares are made. Timberlake clamped his lips shut and breathed deeply through his nose. Darren Webb turned pale, and forced back the bile that gushed into his mouth, threatening to make him throw up. Nigel Larkin raised himself up on his toes to peer over their shoulders, and very quickly let himself down again.

Lying on the bed was a naked young woman. She stared at the policemen in the doorway with dead, blank eyes. The top sheet had been dragged off the bed and used to wipe up some blood. The bottom sheet, which was hardly rumpled, was dark crimson from blood that had soaked into it, but that was not the worst of it. There were splashes of blood on the two walls by the bed, great streaks and spots that reached almost to the ceiling, and had begun to dribble down again before drying. The woman's nightdress was on a chair near the bed. Her body, black-red from her own blood, had deep stab wounds, more of them than the horrified observers could count.

'Where's Dr Pratt?' Timberlake asked.

'Dr Pratt couldn't get here,' Rambo Wright told him.

'I'm the deputy police surgeon,' came a voice from above and behind Timberlake. He turned to see an unreasonably good-looking man about 6ft 4in tall, with prematurely white hair. His practice had a disproportionate number of female patients who were only too ready to take off their clothes to be examined for a mild case of ingrowing toenail.

'Dr Jonah Watkin,' he announced himself. He shook hands with Timberlake. 'Dr Pratt had a big job on.'

'Doing his hair, I suppose,' Darren Webb said softly,

but not too softly to be heard. Dr Pratt was famous for his hair. It was dyed an improbable black and combed carefully from the back into a complex whorl and finally plastered down on his scalp with a perfumed unguent. It was an intricate operation that required the expertise of a Japanese master artist making a patterned sand garden with skilful strokes of a special rake.

There came an explosion of a laugh that rattled the windows. Dr Watkin was leant against the wall, seized by an attack of mirth the like of which Timberlake had never seen or heard before. He was to learn that Watkin was famous for his laugh, and there would be times when Timberlake wondered whether he wouldn't prefer Dr Pratt's excruciating efforts to be funny rather than being deafened by Watkin's foghorn guffaws.

To give his ears a chance to stop ringing Timberlake turned to Webb. 'Start organizing the house-to-house with the uniforms,' he told him. 'Oh, by the way, who reported this?'

'According to Sergeant Rumsden, the paper boy, Simon Lyons. I've got his address,' Webb replied.

'Right, you have a word with him yourself.'

'Is there anything you'd like me to do?' Nigel Larkin asked with his customary eagerness. His eyes were bright and his smooth cheeks looked as if they had not only been shaved but buffed with a chamois leather. He was known, not always affectionately, as the Eager Beaver.

'Yes, stay with me, in case I need a hand.'

Larkin beamed. Harry Timberlake returned to Dr Watkin.

'What can you tell me about the victim?'

'Been dead approximately – approximately – twenty-four to forty-eight hours. More or less,' he added cautiously. 'I haven't counted the wounds yet, but there seem to be about forty. The killer hit a couple of arteries, which accounts for the big bloodstains high up on the walls. Arteries pump out blood: it just drains out of wounds to veins. I wouldn't go to the stake on this, but I'm pretty sure some of the stains on the wall have come from the knife, or from the killer's hand as he pulled it out and raised it again to give her more whacks.' Neither man commented on the mental state of the murderer who had rained blows down on the woman, with blood flying around; there was no need.

'He'd be heavily bloodstained then.'

'No doubt about it. As a matter of fact, if you look at the carpet by the bed, you can see there's an area free of stains. I expect the SOCOs will be able to give you a better idea, but it's almost certainly where the murderer was standing and caught the arterial blood.'

'Or murderess,' Larkin ventured.

Timberlake looked at him. 'Yes.' He turned back to the doctor. 'The weapon?'

'Nothing yet.'

At that moment Sergeant Burton Johnson, in charge of the SOCOs, arrived. He was a broad, rather squat man, who was known as Spence because he had a marked resemblance to the late Spencer Tracy. Although Johnson pretended to be piqued when people remarked on the likeness, he secretly was rather pleased. He never missed a chance to see a Spencer Tracy film, and copied his mannerisms.

'All right to go in there now?' Timberlake asked.

'Yes. We've finished. We're doing the other rooms.'

Timberlake led Watkin and Larkin into the bedroom. He went to the corpse, and lifted the hands to look at the palms, and then the forearms. 'No defence wounds,' he observed.

'No. Are you wondering if the first wound killed her?' the doctor asked. Timberlake nodded.

Dr Watkin shrugged. 'I don't think so. At least two arteries pumped out blood. We won't know until the autopsy, of course, but I suspect she was unconscious when she was attacked. Maybe she was drugged, or something. But for Christ's sake don't tell Professor Mortimer I said so.'

'You mean even if I could get a word in edgeways?' Timberlake said, and immediately regretted that he had, because Jonah Watkin gave another laugh like a roll of thunder.

The timing was unfortunate: the forbidding figure of Professor Peter Mortimer was just entering the room. The undisguised look of loathing that he projected silenced even the ebullient Jonah Watkin for a moment. Mortimer was almost invariably referred to in the Press as 'the eminent forensic pathologist'. A newspaper once incautiously called him 'a modern-day Bernard Spilsbury' and was threatened with a libel suit for their pains, and, under pressure from the most deadly libel lawyer in the country, were forced to publish an apology. 'Spilsbury was dogmatic and arrogant, and made serious errors. I do not,' Mortimer said.

As usual, under his white coat Mortimer was dressed in a dark-grey suit and white shirt with an old-fashioned stiff white collar. He wore what must have been the last pair of Edwardian elastic-sided boots in daily service in England. Mortimer would have been almost as tall as Watkin if he'd ever stood up straight, but a lifetime of bending over dead bodies on mortuary tables had made him round-shouldered. It would have taken a medieval rack to straighten him up again.

Two paces behind him, like a Number Three Chinese wife, was his assistant and secretary, Miss Gertrude Hacker, whose surname most people thought was better suited to her principal. She was about fifty-five years old, dressed in a shapeless tweed suit, woollen jumper and a tweed hat with a totally inappropriate feather in the band. She was carrying Mortimer's black leather bag that could have seen service on the battlefield at Waterloo.

'Good morning, professor,' the irrepressible Nigel Larkin said. Timberlake and Watkin knew better. They just nodded to Mortimer and Gertrude Hacker, and were given minimum nods in return.

Mortimer went straight over to Mary Docker's body and looked at it carefully without speaking for a moment. 'Is the photographer still here?' he asked no one in particular.

Sergeant Johnson, lurking in the background, answered, 'He's already photographed the body and the room.'

'I said, is he still here?'

Johnson admitted that he was.

'Then get him back here with his camera,' Mortimer said.

Johnson muttered something under his breath, and went for the photographer.

Mortimer went through the routine of bagging the victim's head and hands, taking the ambient temperature and the body's rectal temperature, anal and vaginal swabs. Next, he rummaged in his bag and found a sheet of stationers' small sticky-back numbers. Painstakingly he put a number next to each of the wounds in Mary Docker's body.

While he was doing this the photographer waited patiently in the doorway with his apparatus. He knew better than to say anything.

Mortimer next started to fill in his preliminary report. He carefully marked in each of the wounds on the outline body on the second page of the four-page report, numbering each one. When he had finished, without turning round he addressed the photographer behind him.

'Right. Now. I want a photograph of the body with the numbers in place.' The police photographer took them wordlessly and escaped from the room.

'Post-mortem Wednesday eleven o'clock,' Mortimer announced. He exited, followed by Gertrude Hacker, who walked straddle-legged like a Japanese actor playing a tough guy. She hadn't said a word during the whole procedure.

Timberlake's search of the flat produced no indication that Mary Docker had any relatives living, and few enough friends. The only thing of interest to the investigators was a picture of a personable-looking man in a blue uniform with wings, who was obviously an airline pilot. His uniform was not one that Timberlake recognized, and the wings gave no clue as to which airline it was. He handed the picture to Nigel Larkin, the Eager Beaver. 'See if anyone knows who he is. If you have no joy locally, try to trace the airline.'

Darren Webb appeared. 'Guv, she had a daily cleaner, a Mrs Freda Phillips. Lives just round the corner. I've got her address and phone number.' He handed over a slip of paper.

'Right. You get some more troops and start them on the door-to-doors. I'll go and have a word. Maybe she knows who the next of kin are.'

'Guv,' Sergeant Johnson called out from the doorway. 'Come and have a look at this.' He led Timberlake into the second bedroom, a small, irregularly shaped room with a single bed and a small chest of drawers. The floor was covered in worn coconut matting. 'It's the window.' He indicated the horizontal swinging bolt on the old-fashioned fastener. Level with the space between the top and bottom window frames was a bright mark made up of two or three vertical scratches. 'Typical,' Johnson said. 'Someone slipped a knife between the two frames and pushed back the bolt. This style of lock is about as useful as a piece of string. They go back to the last century.'

'It was locked when we got here, wasn't it?'

'Yeah. I suppose he shut it again once he was inside. Thought he'd fool us,' Johnson added with a Spencer Tracy look of contempt.

The window-catch, the surrounding wooden frame and window itself had traces of the grey aluminium powder used for showing up fingerprints. 'No luck there, from the looks of it,' Timberlake said.

'No. No dabs, no fibres. He gave it a wipe with something. Probably a glove. Inside and out. No fibres on the window frames, either.'

A face slowly rose from outside the bottom of the window, followed by a woman's form dressed in white overalls. She silently mouthed 'Nothing,' and moved away.

'She was looking to see if there were any footprints,' Sergeant Johnson explained. 'Didn't expect to find anything. It's a concrete pavement.'

'What about in here? Any luck with the electrostatic mat?' Timberlake asked.

He was referring to the technique where a weak current of electricity is passed through a sheet of foil between two sheets of black acetate. The charge attracts evidence of any impressions on the surface of the mat. Studied at an angle to the light the black surface may show a print too faint to be seen by the naked eye.

'Nothing worthwhile. The carpet pile's too thick.'

Timberlake stood looking at, or through, the window. There wasn't much of a view: a blank side wall of another block of flats to the left, and the courtyard with a line of lock-up garages to the right.

'Guv?' Sergeant Johnson eventually risked.

'Odd,' Timberlake said. He turned away.

Chapter Two

As a cleaner, Mrs Freda Phillips was an almost perfect treasure. She lived what a hack football reporter might call 'a life of two halves'. At home she was a dedicated couch potato who could have been a winner on *Mastermind* with *Coronation Street*, *Neighbours* and *Home and Away* as her specialist subjects. She smoked so much that her home smelt like a locomotive shed in the days of steam trains. There was an upside to this: it concealed the powerful pong of the fortified Algerian red she drank by the bucketful.

Freda's working life was at the far end of the spectrum of human activity. She was just about five feet short, but what she lacked in height she made up for in the circumference of her bust, which was stupendous. She smoked her two mid-session cigarettes in her employers' gardens or on their balconies. At flats which had neither, she stuck her head out of a window. Frequently she would finish her work schedule well within her allotted time. Instead of leaving early or putting her feet up, she scratched around for something extra to clean, polish or iron. As a daily help, she was, as Goldsmith put it, 'the very pink of perfection'.

Or very nearly. She had a nickname which betrayed her one great weakness. She was known by friends, neighbours and clients as The Terrace Vale Gazette; and a simple question like 'How are things?' or 'What's new?' would release a great Niagara of inconsequential, repetitious chatter. Employers who Freda 'did for' soon learned to keep silent or out of her way until the post-work cup of coffee sent her whizzing off to her next job.

When Darren Webb informed Freda that Mary Docker had been murdered, he began with all the standard questions to put her at her ease, but there was no need for finesse: once the initial shock had been replaced by the excitement she gushed like an oil well, without really telling him very much. By condensing and distilling Freda's flood of verbiage Darren Webb was able learn that there had been no change in Mary Docker's attitude or manner recently, that she had received, as far as Freda knew, which wasn't very far, no strange phone calls – 'I wasn't here all that much when she was at home' – nor had got unusual letters – 'The post came before I got here' – and had no enemies, that Freda was aware of.

Webb turned to the man in the photograph. 'You remember seeing it, of course?'

'Course.'

'Do you know who he is?'

'No idea,' Freda replied with a touch of frustration.

'He signed it "M". Do you know his name? Mac? Martin? Max? Michael, or Mike?'

'She never said.'

'Didn't you ever ask her about him?'

'Once or twice, but Mary never talked about him.'

'Never?'

'Never mentioned him.' Freda was clearly miffed.

'Or which airline he works for? What run he was on? Didn't you ever ask her that either?'

'Once. She just said, "Oh, different ones." It was pretty obvious she didn't want to tell me anything.'

Darren Webb framed the next question carefully before saying it. 'Any idea how close they were?'

'No idea.' She looked directly at Webb. 'She always made her bed herself in the morning when she went off to work. She even washed up her breakfast things and put them away, most days.'

'How many times a week did you clean for Miss Docker?'

'At least twice. Usually Tuesdays and Thursdays.'

'So you were last here on Thursday?.'

'No, Friday morning.'

'Why was that?'

'Mary phoned me and asked me to come and do some ironing.'

'Did she let you in?'

'No, I've got a set of keys.'

'Do you know where she'd gone?'

'Work, I suppose.'

Webb made a note to check. Later he found out that Mary had indeed gone to work on the Friday. 'What time were you here?' he asked Freda.

'I got here about half-past ten and left just gone half-eleven.'

'Was there anything unusual about the place when you arrived?'

Freda shook her head. 'No. The ironing didn't take an hour, but there wasn't much else to do, really. On Thursday I'd given the place a thorough do – hoovered, polished, cleaned the kitchen and bathroom, cleaned the windows, put out the rubbish.' She stared at Webb as if challenging him to deny it. 'All there was were her breakfast things – for once she hadn't washed them up herself, but it was a Friday. I did them and put them away.' She began to sniffle again.

'I'm sure she was lucky to have you.' He gave her a reassuring smile, and after a moment said, 'Would you mind letting us take your fingerprints?'

Freda looked startled. 'Whaffor?'

'Just so we can separate them from the other prints we find in the flat, although from what you've told me, I fancy we won't find many. We'll send round a woman officer. By the way – did Miss Docker always pay you promptly?'

'On the dot. She left the money out, regular as clockwork.'

'She had no money worries, then.'

'Not as far as I could see. Always paid me on the dot, gave me my money even when I was on holiday, and a good bonus at Christmas. She kept herself to herself, but she was good to me. I hope you catch the bastard who killed her.'

'We will,' Darren Webb told her with a ringing note of confidence he was far from feeling. As he was about to leave the house he thought of another question. He avoided sounding like Lieutenant Colombo by not pausing at the door and saying, 'Oh. just one more thing.' He settled for, 'How long had she had the photograph?'

Freda thought for a moment. 'About a year, I should think.'

As he left the house with this one meagre crumb of information he found himself wanting to find out the pilot's name and his airline before Eager Beaver Nigel Larkin managed it.

There were not many manufacturing companies in the Terrace Vale area: cafés, restaurants, shops, offices, furtive clubs and brothels of varying qualities were the principal commercial enterprises. Wrappers Ltd, workplace of the late Mary Docker, was a set of plain buildings of the shoebox school of architecture. The manufacture of various kinds of wrappings and packaging was done in a long, depressing two-storey structure that was totally anonymous and could have housed any sort of light manufacturing. The offices were housed in a brick and plaster building that vaguely recalled the German pre-war UFA film studios and had been tacked on to the works as an afterthought. Harry Timberlake thought he'd become clinically depressed if he had to work there for three months. It didn't occur to him that the Wrappers Ltd staff would be even more despondent if they had to spend a fortnight at the Terrace Vale nick.

By the time Timberlake and Webb arrived at the factory the place was already buzzing with rumour. News of a large-scale police activity at Mary Docker's flat had percolated through to the firm, but wild speculation well outweighed facts.

The managing director of Wrappings Ltd was in his office, which could have passed for an Eastern European border police post. His name was Maurice Wellbeloved, which could not have been more inappropriate. All his staff either loathed or feared him, some both. In a couple of sentences he completely established his character. His reply to the news of Mary Docker's murder was, 'Oh, Christ. And she hadn't finished the VAT return.'

A woman of uncertain age, forbidding aspect and a figure that suggested she was wearing a lace-up corset, had a desk in one corner; Timberlake assumed she was Wellbeloved's secretary. 'You'll have to do it,' her employer said. The woman nodded without saying a word, and as Wellbeloved turned his head away she directed a laser look of loathing at him.

Questioning the managing director at length about Mary Docker clearly would be fruitless: it was obvious he knew little or nothing about her, and he seemed preoccupied with the unfinished VAT return rather than with his employee's brutal murder.

'Do you mind if we have a few words with your secretary?' Timberlake asked.

'Well, do it in the next office,' Wellbeloved replied ungraciously. 'I'm busy. And don't keep her too long. She's got work to do.'

'My name is Mrs Cynthia Crossley.' the secretary said in a Cheltenham Ladies' College accent as soon as Webb shut the door behind them. She shook hands formally with the two detectives. 'This was Mary's office.' She looked round it as if seeing it for the first time. The room was as clean and orderly as a nun's cell in a strict convent. The furniture was office hypermarket style and as characterless as a pint of milk, except for some roses in a vase on the desk. They were just beginning to fade, but they had survived longer than Mary Docker herself, Timberlake thought.

'Is it all right for Sergeant Webb to have a look

through her desk and files?' Timberlake asked. 'We're interested only in her personal effects.'

Mrs Crossley stared at him. 'Were you a graduate entry into the service?'

'No. Why?'

'Or were you a school teacher before you became a policeman?'

'No. What makes you ask?'

'You said, "We're interested only in her personal effects". Most people would have said, "We're only interested" . . .'

'Really,' Timberlake replied as politely as he could manage. 'Now, will Mr Wellbeloved complain?'

Mrs Crossley made a noise like a horse preparing to whinny. 'That limp-prick loud-mouth?' she said derisively, losing her stern look. It was a metaphorical loosening of her stays and putting her feet up. The effect was as shocking as the Archbishop of Canterbury singing a rude song in the pulpit. Webb was so startled he nearly knocked over the vase.

Timberlake smiled. 'How well did you know Mary?'

'Not very. She only worked part – worked only part-time, was good at her job – she took care of the invoicing and customer relations – but in the time-honoured phrase, she kept herself to herself.' Mrs Crossley fell silent, but Timberlake didn't press her. Eventually she went on, 'There was something strange . . . guarded . . . *featureless* about her. Almost as if she'd been taken over in the *Invasion of the Body-snatchers*. I once thought deep-cover spies must be like that: absolutely nothing out of the ordinary about them, grey, and with no background. I expect I'm over-stating the case.'

'I wonder,' Timberlake said. 'What about her next of kin?'

'She didn't list any on her personnel-record form.' She stared at Timberlake without expression. There was a heavy silence, broken at last by Webb.

'Nothing here to help us, guv,' he reported, finishing his trawl through the files and contents of the desk. 'All straightforward business stuff, as far as I can see.'

'I didn't really think there'd be anything,' Timberlake confessed. He turned to Cynthia Crossley again. 'Two things. First, you said Mary worked part-time. Were they always the same days?'

'No. We arranged it between us when she would come in.'

'Did she have any particular friends here at the works?'

'Not close ones.' She thought for a moment. 'Not in the office. But . . . she often had her coffee break with Ruth Jameson, lunch sometimes. Ruth's a quality inspector in the cartons section. I'll give her a ring and tell her you're on your way.'

Ruth Jameson was about thirty years old and as spare as Cynthia Crossley was ample. She appeared to be as approachable as a traffic warden with sore feet. Timberlake's introduction of himself and Darren Webb was received with little enthusiasm.

Ruth Jameson met Mary Docker some two years previously at the church they both attended fairly often, she said. At the time they didn't realize they both worked at the same place. For both of them it was the only contact they had outside the factory with any of the other members of the workforce.

During the interview a young woman carrying a

clipboard arrived at the open door. Jameson just said, 'Wait there, Muriel,' and went on answering the detectives' questions. They began with the standard formula about whether Mary Docker had seemed to have something on her mind recently, whether there was any recent change in her manner, whether she had received any unusual letters or phone calls. Ruth Jameson said that she had noticed nothing untoward, and outside the factory only saw Mary at church, sometimes. When Darren Webb asked what sort of person Mary was, even Ruth Jameson came out with the same cliché: 'She kept herself to herself most of the time.' Timberlake wondered if they had signs up in the factory with the phrase printed on it.

'Do you know anything about her boyfriend? The airline pilot?' Timberlake said casually.

Ruth Jameson's mouth tightened. 'No.' She didn't know his name, how long they'd known each other, or what airline he worked for. When Timberlake asked exactly what Mary's relationship with the boyfriend was Jameson looked annoyed. 'I'm sure I don't know. We never discussed him. We weren't all that intimate. All I can tell you is that Mary was a decent young woman, and even if she did . . . have a sexual thing . . .' She seemed to be having difficulty in getting the words out. Her mouth became rigid and lines became apparent above her top lip and at the corners of her mouth. '*If* she did have a sexual association with him, I'm quite sure that didn't make her promiscuous. She wasn't that sort of woman.'

As the detectives left the office, the young woman with the clipboard whispered to Timberlake, 'See you in the back carpark in ten minutes.'

'Reckon she fancies you, guv?' Darren Webb said, rather daringly for a Monday.

Timberlake looked at him, and Webb wished he hadn't opened his mouth. The young woman, no longer carrying a clipboard, came out of the back entrance of the works and looked around. Timberlake stepped out from the shadows long enough for the woman to see him, then returned to the shadows.

She moved towards them with more than a hint of a catwalk sway in the way she walked. She couldn't be mistaken for a virgin at a hundred yards.

'Muriel Seagram,' she announced herself. Webb noted her name in his pocketbook.

'Address?' he asked politely.

She gave it to him, then said, 'You want my telephone number?' Although Webb was doing the writing, she looked directly at Timberlake as she said it.

'We'd better take it,' he said, trying to sound as discouraging as possible. 'Now, Miss Seagram, you wanted to tell us something.'

She briefly studied Timberlake, and then Webb, wondering whether it was worth trying to flirt with either or both, but quickly dismissed the idea . . . for the time being.

'Mary Docker. She wasn't at all like The Acid Drop told you. She was a right raver.'

'Friend of yours?' Timberlake said innocently.

'No. Didn't know her at all. But one lunchtime I was going past her office with some stuff to put on the Dragon Woman's desk' – the two men instantly guessed she meant Mrs Crossley – 'and Mary was on the phone. There was no one else in the place, and she didn't know I was there. I couldn't help hearing her. Bloody hell, she was effing and blinding, talking dirty to some bloke – well, I assumed it was – about how they'd been shagging that night, pardon my French, and how she was looking forward to some more. Actually,' she added confidentially, 'it quite turned me on.'

'And that's it?' Timberlake said.

'Not altogether. I just happened to be going past another couple of lunchtimes—'

'Accidentally, of course,' Webb said, getting a dark look from Timberlake in case it stopped the flow, but Muriel Seagram hardly heard him.

'—And she was at it again. I know she looked like butter wouldn't melt in her mouth, but I bet a lot of other things did. Kept herself to herself? Don't make me laugh! She was a proper little shagbag.'

Chapter Three

The day had started badly for Detective Chief Inspector Ted Greening and he was quite certain it was going to get worse. To begin with, he had got up at 6.30 a.m., with a head that felt as if someone was trepanning his skull with a blunt saw and no anaesthetic; his breath was frankly disgusting and his mouth even worse. This was his usual physical condition when he woke up, but on this particular day his mind, weighed down with unpleasant thoughts, was as ailing as his body. The first thought was that he had to face his wife Marjorie across the breakfast table. She was forty-eight, and could have passed for sixty in a good light. Her mouth was a thin pale red inverted V of disapproval; if she hadn't been strictly religious, she would have divorced Ted Greening years earlier. Instead, she accepted him as Her Cross. Despite her ascetic appearance, Marjorie Greening always ate a hearty breakfast, although whether she did it for nourishment or to make her husband suffer was a moot point. For a man in Greening's condition at 6.30 a.m. the smell of frying bacon and the sight of runny fried eggs was a torture that Torquemada would have admired. There was only one worse conceivable martyrdom that Greening could conceive of: for Marjorie to ask him for sex. The idea would have been even more repugnant to Marjorie herself, who by now probably couldn't tell a penis from a gherkin. In a woman of a different outlook, this lack of recognition could have had serious consequences.

Greening, too, looked older than his age. He was steadily putting on weight, bulging out of his clothes at every gap. In the battle for money, clothing always lost to alcohol. He was a glad-hander, knowing winker and bad dirty storyteller. He was a back-slapper and, when circumstances called for it, a back-stabber of Machiavellian ruthlessness. This was not for spite, but out of fear, because he wanted a life with no waves until his retirement. It was a target his eyes were locked on to like a laser gunsight.

The pity of it all was that once he had been a first-class copper with a good record of major arrests. He had several commendations for his work and bravery. The last one had been a long time ago.

The reason for Greening's depression and concern, the dark cloud approaching inexorably towards him, was the scheduled arrival of the AMIP – the Area Major Investigation Pool team, which Scotland Yard sends to take charge of inquiries into serious crimes, like murder. The mere presence of AMIP in itself would be enough to send Greening's stomach-acid level into the red zone on the dial, what with all the extra activity and organization that it would entail. However, the thunderous, black heart of the cloud was the fact that the team would be led by Detective Superintendent Charles Harkness.

Physically, Harkness was unremarkable: medium height, slender, wiry, clean-shaven, thin-lipped and neatly dressed. Unremarkable, that is, until he looked at you. His eyes, dark for his medium colouring, had stared down some tough criminals and sharp solicitors. It was fairly well known that Harkness was a qualified solicitor himself, and most of the other ones he came up against were left feeling rather less qualified and bright than they thought they were.

In Harkness's first visit to Terrace Vale,* Ted Greening had tried to be clever and had disobeyed a direct order and pursued a theory of his own, and then had done his best to shift the blame on to Harry Timberlake. Harkness hadn't taken any official action against Greening: he gave him a verbal castigation that made him feel that he had been skinned and left out to dry. In subsequent visits, Harkness behaved as if the incident had never happened. Greening tried to forget it, but the old wound throbbed every time he saw the senior officer.

He set off for the Terrace Vale nick with as much enthusiasm as one of the six hundred on their way to the valley, but with a lot less style. His wife didn't try to kiss him as he left the house.

Harry Timberlake whistled cheerfully as he left home in his Citroën BX GTI 1.9, the 16-valve version. He was elated by the prospect of working with Detective Superintendent Harkness again. For the moment he forgot the tragic Mary Docker, whose savage death was the cause of his feeling good. Later, it would unexpectedly hit him, leaving him feeling guilty and rather ashamed.

*See *Vengeance*, the first Harry Timberlake novel.

Timberlake was not the first one to arrive at the Information Room and office for the murder squad, which Sergeant Rumsden had organized. Already sitting in the office was Detective Constable Nigel Larkin.

He bounded up as Timberlake entered. 'Good morning, guv! I've got it.'

Most of the irreverent and coarse members of the Terrace Vale CID would probably have replied, 'Don't worry. Penicillin'll soon clear it up. Next time wear a condom.' Or some other equally brilliant and imaginative remark.

'What, exactly, Nigel?'

'I've got his name, address and the airline he works for. The pilot in the photograph.' He handed over a piece of paper.

As Darren Webb entered he heard Larkin's report with a mixture of grudging admiration and mild jealousy. Keeping a tepid morning smile on his face Webb exchanged greetings with the others.

Timberlake was impressed, not only by Larkin's ability to dig out the information so quickly, but by his readiness to produce it now. There were a lot of coppers who would have waited until someone like Harkness or the Terrace Vale's chief superintendent was present so they could hear of his success.

'Well done, Nigel,' Timberlake said. 'How did you manage to do it so quickly?'

'I took a copy of the picture round the check-in desks to ask the staff if they recognized the uniform. I struck lucky quite early. One of the stewardesses knew it right off. So I went to the airline's main reception desk, where they recognized the pilot, no trouble at all.'

'What, this morning?' Timberlake asked incredulously.

'No, guv. Last night. Heathrow's just the same as the nick. It doesn't close down at night.' He passed a piece of paper to Timberlake. It read: 'Captain Mark Sibley, AirAlbion, Strand, WC2'. There was a home address in Knightsbridge.

'What the hell's AirAlbion?' Webb asked. 'I've never heard of it.'

'It's about the size of Air UK or British Midland. They operate out of both Heathrow and Gatwick. Good reputation, according to the people I spoke to at Heathrow.'

'We'll find out where he is and go and see him this afternoon, after the conference,' Timberlake told Webb.

'He's away at the moment, guv,' Larkin said brightly. 'He's taking a charter flight to the Seychelles.'

Other detectives began to drift into the room, pausing at the door for a last long draw at their cigarettes before the non-smoking Harkness arrived.

Ted Greening had somehow managed to dredge up enough courage to wait for Harkness at the head of the stairs leading to the CID floor and meet him head on. The detective superintendent greeted Greening civilly and without the least hint of any dark undertones. Greening sighed an enormous sigh of silent relief.

'We're rather short of spare bodies at the moment, sir,' he said deferentially. 'We've got a local anti-drugs surveillance operation going on. Still, I've arranged for a team of six detectives for you, sir. Most of them you know. Inspector Timberlake is the senior officer. If you need anyone else . . .'

'Thank you, Chief Inspector.' Harkness entered the conference room, contriving to arrive on the stroke of eight o'clock. 'All right, don't get up,' he said, fractionally before anyone had started to do so. Next time the squad would be much more alert when he entered.

Timberlake introduced the members of the squad to Harkness, who already knew Darren Webb and Nigel Larkin. The three other detectives were Alistair McPhail, a tall, ginger-headed Scot who was as cheerful as a week of Scotch mist, and who hated to be called 'Al'; Bob Crust, a forty-something-year-old with no head hair and a moustache sparrows could have nested in, who had completed the London Marathon on three occasions; and Jeff Waters, who was built on the lines of an All Blacks forward. He was as black as Jack Johnson, had deep-set eyes, a jaw like the prow of a Russian ice-breaker and a nose which had been involuntarily remodelled when he slipped in his bathroom and broke it on the edge of a washbasin. He kept secret the fact that he painted watercolours.

After Timberlake and Webb had briefed Harkness on the situation he questioned them about the case.

'Any immediate suspects?'

'Apparently she had a man friend, an airline pilot named Mark Sibley. He's away for the moment so we haven't managed to see him yet, but apart from him, there's no one, and no obvious motive,' Timberlake replied. Sibley qualified for a mention as a possible suspect because in most murders, the perpetrator is known to the victim. 'From the state of the body, it looks like the work of a psychopath or someone out of his mind on drugs,' Timberlake said.

'The murder weapon?' asked Harkness.

'According to Professor Mortimer a knife approximately fifteen centimetres by five centimetres at its widest point. We still have uniforms searching the rubbish dump at the block of flats, drains and bushes: the usual thing. And the house-to-house enquiries are well under way.'

'I saw the evening news on TV last night. You called for witnesses of anyone who saw a man heavily stained with blood. Any response?'

'Nothing worthwhile.'

'Anything strike you as odd, Harry?'

'Yes, sir. For a man in a frenzy, the murderer seems to have kept a pretty cool head. He got into the flat without waking the victim and took away the knife when he left. He didn't just leave it lying near the body or stuck in it, and he didn't just dump it anywhere where it might have been easy to find.'

'And no one saw him even though he was covered with blood,' Nigel Larkin piped up irrepressibly.

'Indeed,' Harkness said with the faintest hint of a smile. He turned to Timberlake. 'What were you planning to do next?'

'Alistair and Bob are going to call on all the other residents in Miss Docker's block of flats to see what they can find out about her social life, her callers. I want Darren to interview Freda Phillips again – the cleaner – back at the flat and get her to go through the place to see if she notices that something's missing. Jeff can take first turn at manning the office phones and setting up a database on the computer.' He turned to the big man. 'And see if Mark Sibley is on HOLMES* and PNC2.†

'Why do you want Mrs Phillips to check on the flat again? You don't think it might be a robbery that went wrong?' Harkness asked without inflection.

'Hardly. But the killer might have wanted a diary, letters or something that could compromise or incriminate him. I think it's unlikely, in view of the way she was killed, but it has to be checked. I'll be there myself, going through her papers and things.'

'Right,' Harkness said, standing up. 'Meeting back here at five.'

As Timberlake turned to go out, he saw Nigel Larkin looking at him with a mixture of reproach and longing that Bambi couldn't have outdone.

'I nearly forgot,' Timberlake said. 'Nigel, get on to British Telecom, and any other service she was connected up to – cable or Mercury – and get a printout of her calls over, say, the past couple of months. Check on any frequently recurring numbers, very long calls, and any at odd hours: three o'clock in the morning, for example.'

'Right, guv,' the Eager Beaver replied, practically giving off sparks of pleasure.

*

**HOLMES*: acronym for Home Office Large Major Enquiry System – an extension of the old Police National Computer.

†*PNC2*: the second generation Police National Computer, put on line in December 1991. It gives 24-hour almost instant access to information such as fingerprint records, etc. It has five times the capacity of the original computer.

The late Mary Docker's business papers were neat, tidy and up-to-date, which was not surprising considering her job. Her last monthly bank statement showed a payment of £1,000 from Wrappers Ltd, which Timberlake assumed was for salary. He found that she paid income tax as a self-employed person – he remembered that she was a part-time employee – and for the previous year she had declared a total income from Wrappers Ltd of £12,280. Her income-tax return for the previous year, prepared by one of the bank's departments, showed an income from investments managed by her bank's financial services department. She had about £120,000 capital deposited with them, which brought her between £7,500 and £8,000 per annum. Her current account statement showed a credit balance of some £3,000. Timberlake made a mental note to investigate where she got the capital from. Maybe an inheritance, he told himself. Other documents showed that she owned a ninety-one-year lease on the flat.

In brief, Timberlake concluded, she was a comfortably off young woman.

Then came the surprise. There were absolutely no private letters; none from friends, relations – not even from her friend the pilot Mark Sibley.

It was weird.

It was *very* weird.

And there was something else odd about Mary Docker's papers – or lack of them – that increased the weirdness of her lifestyle. He was reminded of Cynthia Crossley's remark: 'I once thought deep-cover spies must be like that: absolutely nothing out of the ordinary about them . . . grey. *And with no background.*'

Timberlake began to wonder seriously if there was something in what she said, improbable as it would have seemed an hour ago. He was shaken out of his introspection when Webb burst in.

'Guv, I think you'd better come in here.' He turned away before Timberlake could ask him what it was about.

Freda Phillips, white-faced and worried-looking, was standing by one of the kitchen units. A cutlery drawer was open.

'Tell the inspector what you just told me,' Webb said comfortingly.

'There's a knife missing.'

'What sort of knife?' Timberlake asked.

'A kitchen knife. You know, a working knife.'

'How big?'

Freda held her hand about six inches apart. 'This big.' Indicating about two inches with her forefinger and thumb, she added, 'And this wide.'

'Fifteen centimetres by five,' Timberlake said to Webb. He looked more closely into the drawer. Wait a minute,' he said sharply, 'what's this?' He picked up a kitchen knife of the size he had just mentioned. 'Isn't this it?'

'No. Mary had two. The other one was older,' Freda said, still worried.

The significance of this find was not lost on either of the detectives. After a long pause Timberlake commented, 'Well, now, just fancy that.' It seemed a rather inadequate observation.

He almost forgot an important question he was going to ask Freda. 'Do you know if Miss Docker had an address or phone book?'

She thought for a moment. 'Funny, that. I can't remember seeing one.'

Timberlake didn't think it was at all amusing.

Detective Superintendent Harkness was going through reports from the Home Office Forensic Laboratory which had just arrived. The first one was about bloodstains.

STATEMENT OF WITNESS

Statement of Percy F. Roth
Age of witness (if over 21 enter 'over 21') Over 21
Occupation of witness Forensic scientist

This statement (consisting of 3 pages(s) each signed by me) is true to the best of my knowledge and belief and I make it knowing that, if it is tendered in evidence, I shall be liable to prosecution if I have wilfully stated in it anything which I know to be false or do not believe to be true.

Dated the 28th day of November 1996

Percy F Roth.

I am a Bachelor of Science and a Doctor of Philosophy. On 25 November 1996, at the request of the Metropolitan Police, I visited. Flat No. 1, Holly Mansions. Terrace Vale, London W.

In the principal bedroom of the flat was a four-foot-wide bed in the corner of the room. The bedclothes were pulled down, and lying on the bed, face up, was the naked body of a woman subsequently identified to me as that of Mary Docker.

There were very many wounds to the neck and body. A considerable amount of blood was on the two walls adjacent to the bed, on a small bedside table, and there were some splashes of blood on the ceiling above the bed.

The bloodstains on the walls were of three kinds. The largest stains were blobs in the characteristic form of 'exclamation marks', showing that they had 'spurted' with some force from the body. The medium-sized stains were similar in form and direction as the largest ones, and were generally at a lower level on the walls. The third kind of stains were light splashes at various heights, and were entirely consistent with having come from a knife or similar weapon as it was withdrawn from the body and raised to strike again.

On the bedside table were some smears of blood which could have been caused by the victim or the assailant brushing up against it.

On the floor beside the bed there were some splashes of blood and drops of blood which had fallen vertically.

The top sheet of the bed had been dragged off and was lying on the floor beside the bed. This sheet was smeared with blood, the marks consistent with it having been used to wipe off some surface. All the bloodstains in the bedroom were Group B, (8 per cent of the population). The victim was also Group B.

In the bathroom there were some small traces of blood near the bases of the taps, and a small quantity, insufficient for grouping to be carried out, was in the U-trap of the discharge pipe.

Harkness frowned. He had expected to find rather more in the report. He was about to turn the page when Harry Timberlake entered with Darren Webb. When he saw their expressions he said, 'Found something?'

Timberlake explained about the knife.

'Sharp of the cleaner – Mrs Freda Phillips, isn't it? – to notice it.'

'I expect she's a Virgo,' Webb said.

'More likely to be a Cancer. They're the home-makers,' Harkness said unexpectedly. '*If* you believe that sort of thing. But that could really be a help. Did you find anything in her papers?' Harkness listened carefully to Timberlake's report. 'Odd,' he observed.

'Is that the scientific officer's report?' Timberlake asked. He usually said 'the forensics report' to most other officers, just to save time, but it went against the grain. Both he and his chief inwardly winced when their colleagues confused the distinction between 'forensic' and 'scientific'. Timberlake often gritted his teeth or said rude words loudly when he heard TV and radio reporters referring to 'forensic experts' and 'forensic evidence' instead of 'forensic *science* experts' and 'scientific evidence'. When he was feeling spiky he gave people a short, sharp lecture on what 'forensic' really meant. Timberlake was not only a defender of the Queen's peace; he did his best to defend the Queen's English – or his rather old-fashioned version of it.

'I haven't quite finished it. Have a look at the fingerprint report.'

It was relatively short. The SOCO had found three sets of prints in the flat, in all the rooms. Two sets were either Mary Docker's or Freda Phillips's, the third set were probably those of a man, judging from the size of the prints. They were in the bedroom on a bedside chair and a wardrobe door, and on a tumbler on the draining board in the kitchen.

Timberlake passed the report to Darren Webb. 'It's a bit early for guessing.' he said, 'but I wouldn't mind betting that the third set are the boyfriend's, and that the killer used gloves. We'll soon know when Sibley gets back.' He turned to Harkness. 'Anything interesting, sir?'

Harkness evaded the question. 'Here are the first couple of pages.' He passed them over.

Timberlake, with Webb looking over his shoulder, quickly scanned the pages. As soon as he had finished them he asked, 'Any mention of malachite green?' Webb wondered what the hell that was, or maybe *who* the hell that was, but discreetly refrained from asking.

Harkness turned over the last page of the report. 'Ah,' he said with satisfaction. 'Here it is.' He read from the report. ' "Leuco-malachite green was sprayed on to the tiles next to the bath, the bath itself, the shower curtain and the handle of the shower attachment. Reactions indicated the presence of blood not visible to the naked eye." '

'So now we know,' Timberlake said. 'Narrows it down very nicely.

Chapter Four

Nigel Larkin turned up for the 5 p.m. meeting of the murder squad a good half an hour early, carrying a small folder of papers. From time to time he unconsciously rubbed his left ear, which had been in intimate contact with a telephone receiver for most of the afternoon. Detective Constables Crust and McPhail were also early. This was due less to their desire to look keen than to the lack of success they'd had in interviewing Mary Docker's neighbours. Most of them were hardly aware of her presence in the block before the major upheaval when her body was found. The caretaker, who collected the refuse bags put out by the tenants every night, said that she could have been away for days on end without his being aware of it, she so rarely had rubbish for him to cart away.

There was one tenant who had something to say: Miss Sylvia Parker, a pensioner who lived in Flat No. 2 on the other side of the ground-floor lobby. If ever a woman was born to be nicknamed 'Nosy' it was Miss Parker. She reminded Alistair McPhail of a fox. While she spoke to him at the door of her flat her eyes were everywhere, glancing up the stairs and through the glass panel in the front door of the block. She described Mary Docker as a 'secretive slyboots' who – inevitably

– 'kept herself to herself'. The lugubrious McPhail managed to restrain himself from observing that he would keep himself very much to himself with a neighbour like Miss Parker.

She had occasionally seen a man in pilot's uniform call on Mary. 'And though I go to bed very late, sometimes at three or four in the morning, he hadn't left by then.' She accompanied this intelligence by nodding like a toy dog in the rear window of a car. Then, leaning forward confidentially she said, 'There were times when she stayed out all night. *All night.*' This time she wagged her head so vigorously that McPhail feared for its security on its scraggy neck.

It was then Nigel Larkin's turn to report. 'I checked Docker's phone calls for the past three months,' he said, emphasizing the 'three'. 'All pretty ordinary,' he went on. 'There were fairly regular ones to Mark Sibley's number, a few to her office. The rest were to tradesmen, a couple to her dentist, a few to a garage, some to a hairdresser—'

'Her car!' Timberlake interrupted. He felt suddenly embarrassed that he hadn't done anything about checking it.

'I thought of that when I got through to the garage. I checked: it's in her lock-up garage at the flats. I expect the key's among her effects,' Larkin said.

'Good,' Harkness said, which for him was only two steps down from awarding a medal. Darren Webb managed to conceal a sour expression at Larkin's marking up more brownie points. 'Not much help there, then,' Harkness added.

'Well, sir, I think there are a couple of things that are rather unusual,' said Nigel with an assumed insouciance. 'First, apart from the calls to Mark Sibley, there were none – none at all – that were to residential numbers. They were all – as far as I could see – business calls, none what you might call social calls.' He paused to let this sink in. 'She had a phone where you could store numbers for one-button dialling. There were no numbers stored. It seems that she had no private life, apart from the Sibley person.'

His listeners were duly impressed.

'And,' the Eager Beaver continued, holding their attention as securely as if he were gripping their balls, 'she never made a call after 7.30 p.m.'

'Sir,' Timberlake said at last. 'There's something very curious about this case. I wonder . . . Would you have a word with the Funny People, see if Mary Docker was known to them or to their contacts?' The Funny People was the CID's less than affectionate nickname for Special Branch.

'Interesting thought, Harry,' Harkness replied. 'I'll do it on an unofficial basis. I'm an old friend of the DAC'

Harry Timberlake finished typing his report with a sigh of relief. Darren Webb poked his head round the door. 'Fancy going for a drink, guv?'

Timberlake glanced at his watch. 'No, not tonight, Darren. I think my wife's doing something complicated for dinner.'

'Lucky you,' Webb said with a touch of genuine envy.

'And if I'm late I'll be on Marmite sandwiches for the rest of the week.'

'Give her my regards, guv.'

'Thanks. Er, how are things with you and . . . ?'

'Naomi has stopped talking to me now. I think it was better when she was slagging me off.'

'I'm sorry, Darren.'

'Maybe I should have stayed in uniform. At least you work fixed hours. You can make plans.'

Timberlake said nothing. There was nothing to say.

Not long after they were married Timberlake and his wife sold their individual homes and bought a house in their joint names. It was something of a barn with more rooms than they really needed, and the house agent's description included the cautionary phrase 'in need of some redecoration'. Still, in the first flush of connubial euphoria Timberlake found the energy to paint, plaster and paper-hang, which he did quite skilfully. He was rather proud of his efforts.

By the time he got home Timberlake suddenly became aware that he was quite hungry. He parked his car in the driveway in front of the garage door and hurried into the house. There was a light showing in the lounge.

'Honey, I'm home!' he called out, in an wildly unsuccessful attempt to imitate Jack Nicholson.

At that moment the standard-lamp light went out.

Timberlake whirled round and switched on the main light. The room was empty apart from him, and there was no one in the hall. It took him only a moment, which seemed an age, to remember that the standard lamp was on an intermittent-time switch to give any potential burglars the impression that there was someone in the house.

He walked into the kitchen. There was no food in sight, and it looked neat and tidy enough to satisfy a dragon of an old-fashioned ward sister. This, he realized, was not because his wife was a naturally tidy person – quite the opposite – but because she hadn't been in the kitchen since the daily cleaner had tidied up earlier that morning.

Timberlake went to the fridge and made himself a thick roast beef and pickle sandwich. For once he opened a bottle of lager and drank it with his sandwich. All the time he was eating he was thinking about his marriage. He was aware that his wife had her duties just as he did, but it didn't make the situation any easier to accept. She could have bloody phoned, he thought, and then guiltily remembered a couple of occasions when the situation had been reversed and he hadn't managed to call her. It still didn't mollify him. When he had finished his sandwich and a second beer, he went into the lounge, got the whisky bottle and a glass from the sideboard and switched on the television. He stared at the screen as intently as if it were explaining the Meaning of Life, without actually seeing it. After a while he got up. He was surprised to find that he stumbled a little, and nearly knocked over the small table which the now-empty whisky bottle was on. 'Christ,' he murmured when he saw how much he had drunk without realizing it.

He thought about his marriage again when he woke up next morning, a couple of hours earlier than usual. His wife was sleeping soundly, and he vaguely recalled her coming home when he was in bed. It seemed to him that she had made some remark about the whisky, but his memories of reality and of dreams were confused.

Timberlake managed to get dressed and out of the house without waking her. At least, she gave no signs of waking.

Sergeant Anthony C. Rumsden was having some breakfast to fortify himself for a shift as desk sergeant when Timberlake walked into the station canteen. Rumsden was one of the station characters. One or two older coppers swore that he had been the inspiration for PC, later Sergeant, Dixon of Dock Green. With no disrespect to the amiable Dixon, Rumsden was much more technically aware and proficient.

He preferred to be called Anthony if people addressed him by his Christian name. At a pinch he would respond to Tony, but Tone or Rummy made his aura go bright red. His middle name was Chamberlain. Rumsden senior had been a great admirer of Neville Chamberlain, and felt that Churchill was sneaky to have got him pushed out as prime minister. Locally, Anthony Rumsden Senior was generally acknowledged to be an advanced crackpot. Later in life he also had good things to say about Margaret Thatcher, but this was charitably ascribed to senility.

Sergeant Rumsden kept his middle name a close secret, for if it were found out his life would be impossible, given the Terrace Vale coppers' Neanderthal sense of humour.

Timberlake approached him, carrying a large black coffee and a one-litre bottle of designer water. The large bottle of water was a dead giveaway to Rumsden, who was surprised. Timberlake didn't have the reputation of being a drinker. He regarded Timberlake shrewdly.

'You all right, Harry?' he asked. Rumsden was the one officer at Terrace Vale who had unofficial licence to call senior officers by their Christian names when the circumstances were right.

' "All right" is putting it a bit strong, but I'll manage.'

Rumsden stayed silent for a long moment. 'How are things at home?' he asked with an innocence that was almost completely convincing. Timberlake was sharper than Rumsden, and could hear the sub-text of the question as plainly as if it had been shouted. He was about to tell Rumsden to mind his own sodding business, but managed to stifle the inclination without difficulty. It would have been easier to be rude to the Queen Mum.

Timberlake shrugged. 'Oh, you know,' he said in a tone that was meant to be non-committal. There was another long pause. Timberlake gulped some of his coffee. 'It's the bloody job,' he added.

'Yours, not mine,' Rumsden said. 'Remember when you asked me to let Sarah work for CID? I said that the job could ruin some people's marriages.'

Timberlake said nothing. Rumsden noted that he hadn't said, 'What's that got to do with me?', or 'Who said my marriage's ruined?'

'I told you, didn't I, Harry, that I was CID once? Like I said then, it practically finished me. Out all the hours God and the devil send . . . often not being able to phone to say I wouldn't be home till late . . . falling in the front door smelling like a fire in a distillery because I'd been on a meet with a villain or an informant . . . Well, I don't have to tell you about that, do I?'

'Yeah, I remember. But it's not that bad.'

'With the best will in the world any wife is bound to get suspicious and jealous eventually. And even if she's an understanding saint with unlimited trust, she'll get pissed off with the life. If I'd stayed another month in CID Joannie would've walked out on me. So I had to decide: the "glamour" of CID' – he said it with an ironic smile – 'or the life of a human being. So I chucked it.'

Sergeant Anthony C. Rumsden got up and walked away, leaving Harry Timberlake in a very dark mood indeed. But what Rumsden seemed to have overlooked was that *Mrs* Harry Timberlake worked all hours, didn't always phone to say she would be home late, and often was too tired to say more than 'Hello'.

Autopsies aren't much fun, not even for the vast majority of pathologists, clinical and forensic. There are a few hyper-eccentrics who turn up for work with a spring in their step and actually whistle or hum when they're carving a cadaver, but they are very much in the minority. Nor are most forensic pathologists noted for their sense of humour. Such gallows-humour witticisms they utter raise chuckles only in other pathologists and puzzled looks in laymen.

One of the least entertaining of forensic pathologists imaginable was Professor Mortimer. It is true that at first sight the tall, cadaverous Mortimer and his well-fleshed assistant Gertrude Hacker had the air of a comedy duo, a sort of reverse Laurel and Hardy.

However, between them they had all the humour of a public hanging, and a morgue that is their stage is one of the most cheerless settings imaginable.

Timberlake was already feeling melancholic, and looked like a first-class professional mourner. Attendance at a Mortimer autopsy was the last thing he wanted. Detective Superintendent Harkness had his usual politely attentive, but detached air. Darren Webb was slightly apprehensive: Mortimer always seemed to enjoy humiliating him publicly for his lack of medical knowledge.

One person seemed as out of place as a whore at a first communion. Eager Beaver Nigel Larkin was almost humming with energy and expectation.

Timberlake was made to feel even more dispirited by the sight of Mary Docker's corpse on the dissection table. The body had been cleaned up, and the fatal wounds looked hardly serious enough to have killed her; her face did not have the usual leaden tinge of death. Curiously, it had a strange, translucent quality. She looked, Timberlake admitted to himself with a pang, beautiful. For once he felt almost nauseated by the thought of what Professor Mortimer was going to do to that defenceless body; it was almost as if Mary Docker was going to be killed again. He had never felt this affected before, and he wondered what had come over him.

Mortimer entered with the style of an old-time actor–manager who knew he was running the show and was its star as well. Gertrude Hacker followed him at a respectful distance, like someone who was playing A Messenger. Mortimer wasted no time on niceties like 'Good morning'. The detectives all murmured greetings, which he acknowledged with a sound which could have been a cough. Gertrude Hacker remained impassive, a bit player who knew her place.

Before he started the dissection Mortimer launched into one of his unnecessary introductions, playing Chorus as well as the lead. 'Incised wounds are divided into two main types, apart from the weapons used, that is. First, where the length of the wound is greater than the depth, one may use the description "slashed wound". Second, where the depth is greater than the length, the wound is characterized as a "stab".'

Totally uncharacteristically Timberlake felt a sick rage mounting against Mortimer's self-important, condescending attitude towards his audience. Normally the old man's pontification left him wryly amused, but not this time. Blissfully unaware of Timberlake's feelings Mortimer continued.

'There are a number of features which can be of importance in stab wounds; some ten or more. However, I shall not discuss them all now.'

'Thank God for that,' Timberlake breathed.

'In this particular case there were some forty-three wounds, all – *all* – of considerable force. This is evident from the fact that there is bruising on the skin surrounding the incisions. It is almost certain that this was caused by the handle of the weapon as it was plunged into the body.'

The old bastard's enjoying this, Timberlake thought furiously, but he was doing Mortimer an injustice. The pathologist was merely being thorough, as usual.

'Four of the blows severed arteries. As a result, the blood spurted under some considerable pressure, which accounts for the bloodstains high on the walls.

As far as I can tell the victim was still alive when three of these wounds were inflicted, any one of which would have rapidly proved fatal on its own. The heart had stopped beating by the time the fourth artery was severed.' He gave them this information like he was handing down stone tablets.

'Could you tell how many of the other wounds were inflicted before and how many after death?' Timberlake asked.

'No,' Mortimer said flatly.

'Is it possible to say whether the victim was actually conscious at the time the fatal blows were struck?' Timberlake said, suddenly alert.

'No. She could have fainted or collapsed at any time during the sequence of the blows.'

Harkness turned to Timberlake. 'You're thinking of the fact that there were no defensive wounds on the hands or forearms.' Timberlake nodded.

'There is the possibility that the subject' – That word again! Timberlake thought – 'was already unconscious from alcohol or drugs,' Mortimer pointed out. 'I shall provide you with the results as soon as the tests are completed. Of course.' He added heavily.

The detectives stirred, ready to leave, but Mortimer hadn't finished. He still had to deliver his usual excruciatingly dreary anecdote. 'Apart from the number and ferocity of the blows, there is, as far as I have seen so far, nothing unusual about them. Not like a case I saw reported when I was a student.

'A man was stabbed with a large pen-knife one centimetre below the level of the left nipple and half a centimetre to the left of the midline. The knife penetrated the sternum and broke off at the outer surface of the bone, leaving the point projecting some eight millimetres through the bone. The wound pierced the pericardium and also the underlying anterior wall of the heart, which showed a very irregular, excavated, lacerated wound some two centimetres in length.' He paused for effect. 'Although the wound passed deeply into the muscle, it had not effected entry through the endocardial surface.

'So how had this come about?' He paused again, then said like a conjurer producing a large rabbit from a small hat, 'The wound was caused by repeated contact between the point of the broken end of the knife embedded in the sternum, caused by the action of the heart and breathing.' He demonstrated by placing the tip of an index finger on his sternum pointing inwards and breathing in heavily a couple of times.

'No need for you stay,' he told the detectives after his performance. 'I prefer not to be distracted while I perform an autopsy.' This was massive mendacity. There was nothing he enjoyed more than showing off.

Back at Terrace Vale the murder squad reviewed the case in the light of Professor Mortimer's preliminary information. Detective Superintendent Harkness ran the informal conferences like a tutor with senior students, encouraging them to think and express themselves rather than overtly dictating to them.

'What's the first thing that strikes you, Harry?' he asked.

'Well, two things actually. First, the ferocity of the murder, and the lack – for the moment – of any discernible motive. Docker seems to have been a quiet, inoffensive young woman.'

'Which might suggest it was a psychopath's random killing,' Darren Webb said.

Timberlake shook his head. 'With respect, I don't think so, Darren. The way the killer got in and out without being seen and without leaving any traces, rules out its being spur-of-the moment crime.'

'And there's the murder weapon – the kitchen knife,' Nigel Larkin ventured.

'Yes . . . that does have implications,' Harkness said. Larkin manfully managed to control any outward signs of smugness or pleasure at the implicit praise.

'There's the other possibility,' Webb said, not ready to be outdone by the youthful Larkin. 'It could be a punishment killing as a warning to others. I mean, we're assuming that Docker *was* an inoffensive young woman who went to church on Sundays and all the rest, but there's something rather funny about her lack of background. We've not managed to turn up any relatives or other next of kin. She *might* have been involved in something dodgy. Have you had any luck with the Special Branch mob-people, sir?

'Well done, Darren, to remind us of that,' Harkness said, while Timberlake nodded approvingly. It was Webb's turn to feel agreeably puffed up. 'No, my friend hasn't got back to me yet.'

'When's her boyfriend due back?' Someone asked. 'Whassisname – Mark Sibley.' This sudden intervention surprised the others as if a waxwork dummy had asked for a light.

'Tomorrow,' Larkin said quickly. Timberlake had to admit there were times when the Eager Beaver was off the mark sharper than an Olympic sprinter gold-medallist.

'I'm rather looking forward to meeting him,' Timberlake said.

He still hadn't learnt about making that sort of statement.

Chapter Five

Timberlake was annoyed for the rather complex reason that he had no right to be annoyed. *That* really annoyed him. His wife had managed to entice him – if that was the word – out of the house as successfully as if she had him on the end of a dog's choke chain. She had got him into *L'Orée de la Fôret*, an extremely expensive restaurant that was as good as it was over-priced. This outing was a tacit apology for her failure to come home in time for dinner the previous evening. He couldn't even resist on the grounds that the restaurant's prices were exorbitant, and added 15 per cent to the already inflated bill for service, whether the customer got it or not. Before he could draw breath to argue, she said, 'My treat,' and then played a dirty, underhand trick. She gave him her brilliant, pure-sunshine smile against which he had no defence whatsoever, and she knew it. That was yet another reason for his annoyance.

In his mind Timberlake conceded that the expensive dinner was a genuine conciliatory gesture; but at the same time he was aware that she was taking him to the restaurant because he couldn't have a serious, raised-voice argument with her there. It was a woman's downright sneaky stratagem, which exacerbated his annoyance.

One of the conceits of the restaurant – apart from the shameless plagiarism of the name of the celebrated Parisian establishment – was its menus the size of a broadsheet newspaper, printed on something that looked like Egyptian papyrus. Timberlake studied his wife of six months while she gave the menu her full attention. He wondered how on earth he had at last become a married man. For three years he had enjoyed successful affairs with Dr Jenny Long, then WDC Sarah Lewis, aka the Welsh Rarebit, then Jenny Long once more, with an aberrant temporary diversion along the way with an actress named Lucinda Fordham, who couldn't stop acting off-stage even when she was asleep. Even then she gave a performance.

He wondered, for the umpteenth time, not only how he had become a married man, but whether or not he had married the right woman anyway.

By the time they got home from the restaurant the tensions of the previous days were almost all forgotten, although there were still residual uncertainties in Timberlake's mind about his choice of a spouse. They were soon dissolved away by some *fine champagne* brandy, which succeeded in provoking the desire without taking away the performance, as Shakespeare put it. The sex was as good as ever it had been, and not for one second did Timberlake think of the act as anything other than what it was: a demonstration of love, not part of a making-up process.

The next morning he felt suprisingly clear-headed and euphoric. He slipped quietly out of bed, set the coffee going, and took two glasses of orange juice back into the bedroom. His wife was awake, and was easing her way to a sitting position. He sat on the bed beside her. Despite the exhausting activities of the previous night he was aroused by the sight of her naked torso emerging from the sheets. She was not unaware of it. She thanked him for the orange juice and asked him, 'What are you going to do today, inspector?'

'Going to meet an airline pilot due back from the Seychelles. And what about you, Mrs Timberlake?'

'Wrong name.'

'*Doctor* Timberlake.'

She put on a censorious expression, but ruined the effect by drawing herself up further from the bedclothes and exposing more of her splendid bust. '*Miss Jenny Long*, if you please. I Am a *Consultant* Surgeon.' She spoke with mock severity in capital letters. 'Show some respect. Stand up when you speak to me, inspector.' She glanced down at him. 'Not like *that*, you copper. Oh, well, if needs must . . .'

So everything between them was fine again. For now.

Harry Timberlake and Darren Webb stared through the triple-glazed window of an office at an enormous aircraft coming in to land at Heathrow.

'Is that it, guv?' Darren Webb asked.

Gus Tennant, an AirAlbion public relations senior executive, answered. He was a man with a Rubens-like face and figure, dressed in a dark-blue outfit that was something between a uniform and a business suit. He looked as if he could sell double glazing in a cellar.

'No, AirAlbion don't run to aircraft that size, I'm

afraid. Captain Sibley will be bringing in an Airbus. That one just landing is a 747. Two hundred tons. There's a version that can take five hundred passengers.'

'Five hundred?' Webb said with some awe.

'But they hardly ever put in that many seats.' Tennant paused. 'D'you know, the Wright Brothers would have had room for their first flight, take-off and landing, inside the fuselage of one of those 747s.'

'Fancy,' Timberlake said, trying not to sound bored . .

Tennant was unfazed. 'When you think some people who were alive when Blériot made that first Channel crossing in a string and spit aircraft are still alive today . . .'

'Maybe they've found his luggage by now,' Timberlake said.

The PR man took the hint and abandoned his image-polishing of aviation. 'Er, what exactly is it you want to see Captain Sibley about? He's not in any trouble, is he? No, I'm sure he's not. He's not the sort of chap to be in trouble with the police.'

Timberlake said he hadn't ever met any sort of chap who was still breathing who couldn't be in trouble with the police, but no, Captain Sibley was not in trouble.

Tennant gave a lips-only smile that didn't get as far as his eyes. 'Can I get you a drink?' he asked with a professional bonhomie that sounded badly off-key.

'Coffee would be a good idea, thanks,' Timberlake answered for Webb and himself.

Tennant spoke into an intercom. 'Bring in some coffee, will you, Lucia.'

Lucia was a short-skirted, would-be Michelle Pfeiffer who entered as if she was on a Versace catwalk. The ground coffee was in a silver pot on a silver tray with delicate china cups. Timberlake guessed that other, non-public-relations executives in the company had to manage with Marks and Sparks crockery, and not even Gold Blend. Lucia gave the three men a meaningless smile of a front-row chorus girl and set down the tray. She looked as pleased with herself at performing this difficult operation as if she had just got a row of sixes for artistic impression. As she turned to go out Timberlake caught the briefest glimpse of a glance between her and Tennant that spoke volumes of their relationship outside office hours.

They drank their coffee in near silence while they waited for Mark Sibley to turn up. Webb wandered round the office, dividing his time between looking at photographs of old aircraft on the walls and real aircraft outside the window. Timberlake just sat.

When Sibley finally arrived Timberlake had to admit to himself that he was an even more impressive-looking man than in the photograph at Mary Docker's flat. That two detectives were waiting to meet him did not seem to worry him at all: he was quite calm. Timberlake thought his self-possession was admirable and, in his experience, almost unique. Nearly everybody who found two detectives waiting to see them would look more or less apprehensive. Maybe it was that aircrew were more in control of themselves than most people. Maybe . . .

Policemen learn many different ways of breaking the bad news of death to people, and choose what they think is the best form of words for each particular person. Timberlake had already decided the best way to tell the composed Captain Sibley. After the introductions he said, 'I'm sorry, but there is no easy way for me to tell you this, and for you to hear it.' In these few words Timberlake had told almost half the story. He looked at Sibley, whose eyes widened. He held one hand in the other but showed no other sign of strain. 'It's bad news about your friend, Miss Mary Docker.' He paused. 'I'm afraid she's dead.'

Sibley's mouth tightened into a thin line. Eventually he said, 'How? How did? . . . Did she have an accident?' His voice was almost steady.

'No, Captain, she was killed.' He avoided the harsh word 'murdered' for the moment.

'Oh no! Oh God, no!'

The PR man Gus Tennant half rose from his seat and was preparing to say something, but looks from Timberlake and Webb stopped him like a punch between the eyes before he could utter a syllable.

The news was beginning to hit Sibley. 'Who? . . . Why? . . . Was it a robbery?'

'It was someone who broke into her flat.'

'Have you got him?'

'Not yet. Captain Sibley, we're very sorry.'

They did what they could to comfort Sibley, and Tennant offered to get the company doctor to see him, but he refused; nor did he want Darren Webb to drive him home in his own car. After they had made sure that Sibley would be all right to go home alone Timberlake brought the interview to an end with a standard formula.

'We'll want to see you again, as soon as you're up to it, of course,' Timberlake said. 'We need to know all you can tell us about Mary and her friends and acquaintances.'

'Tomorrow,' Sibley answered, hardly moving his lips.

Timberlake nodded. 'I'll ring you tomorrow morning.' He paused. 'Forgive me, but I have to ask you. Can you tell me where you were on the night of Friday the 15th?'

Sibley stared at him blankly, then his brow furrowed as he tried to concentrate. Eventually he said, 'I was in Glasgow. I stood in for another pilot who reported sick. I got back the following day.' Realization dawned. 'Was that when . . . ?'

Timberlake nodded. 'I'm sorry. I had to ask: it's routine.'

Sibley nodded in his turn, and made an indeterminate gesture.

Timberlake and Webb walked back to the great echoing horror of the Terminal 3 carpark, breathing in car exhaust fumes and kerosene vapour.

'He took it well, I thought, guv,' Webb said. 'Must have been a shock.'

Timberlake remained silent while they walked fifty yards or more. 'You a betting man, Darren?'

'Not really. National Lottery, sweepstake ticket on the Derby and the Grand National. Why?'

'Because if you were, I'd give you ten pounds to a fiver he did it.'

'*What?* But he was in . . . he didn't say anything . . . How can you . . . ?'

'He killed her. I'm sure of it.'

Chapter Six

The working day in police stations starts early in the morning, and lasts until the same time the next day. No matter what the calendar said, in the Terrace Vale nick early mornings were always Monday mornings. Even weekends had a nasty Monday morning feeling. Normally Darren Webb would have preferred to be at home at this time of the day, but his relationship with his wife was going through one of its increasingly frequent periods of sullen, silent hostility, broken by occasional shouting matches. He sat at a table for two in the crowded canteen, preparing for the day's work by staring into a cup of tea with an expression that was enough to curdle the milk.

'Is this anyone's seat?' Sarah Lewis asked him, and repeated it when he didn't appear to hear her.

'No,' he said neutrally, and looked up. When he saw who it was his expression lightened a little. They exchanged some shop talk before Sarah said unenthusiastically, 'Well, I suppose we'd better be getting upstairs.' She looked at Webb. 'You all right?' She took a guess. 'How are things at home?'

He shrugged. 'You know.' He was almost certain that Sarah had had an affair with Timberlake, and because of that he paused, uncertain if he should go on. Then he jumped in with both feet. 'I'm a bit worried about my guvnor.' The fleeting expression on Sarah's face banished any slight doubts he might have had about her and Timberlake.

'I've got a nasty feeling he's made up his mind too quickly about this case,' Webb said quietly, making sure he wasn't being overheard. 'He saw her pilot boyfriend for just about five minutes and decided right away that he did it,' adding quickly, '*and* the man's got an alibi. Maybe it's because he *has* got an alibi. I think the way he broke Newman's cast-iron alibi* has warped his judgement.'

Sarah looked grave. At last she said, 'Keep an eye on him, Darren.' She managed to stop herself saying 'Keep an eye on him *for me*.'

On his way up to the conference room Webb passed by the main desk. Sergeant Rumsden was speaking to a young woman caller whose dress for an early morning visit to a police station was idiosyncratic in the extreme. She had a shiny black plastic topcoat draped over her shoulders and left open in front. Under it she wore a silver dress that reached about a centimetre below the V of her knickers – if she was wearing any, which appeared no better than an even-money bet. The wide décolleté plunged towards the bottom of the dress, revealing on its way two bulging breasts thrust upwards and together by an engineering masterpiece of a bra. Out of sight behind the bottom of the counter she was wearing shoes with six-inch heels. Her hair – a glittering wedding cake of a wig – crowned a face that was made up to look invitingly sexy in a

*See *Elimination*, the second Harry Timberlake novel.

half-light. It was clear that she had called at the station immediately after a hard night's work. As he passed behind Sergeant Rumsden, she caught Darren Webb's eye, but there was no flicker of recognition, even though they knew each other well.

There was a faint air of general discouragement at the daily conference on the Mary Docker murder. Everyone was aware that the longer they went without a solid lead the colder the trail became and hopes of an arrest lessened. Timberlake was still convinced that Mark Sibley was the killer, but he kept this to himself for the time being, almost as if he had read Darren Webb's mind.

The detectives and the uniforms who had been doing door-to-door enquiries had come up with nothing worthwhile. Furthermore the lab report had come through and was no help. There were no drugs or alcohol in Mary Docker's system. The detectives couldn't make up their minds whether this was good news or bad.

'What's next for you?' Harkness asked Timberlake.

'Darren and I are interviewing Mark Sibley at his place today, sir.'

'Why there?'

Timberlake shrugged. 'He's probably feeling rather low. He might be more forthcoming at home than in an interview room here.'

Harkness gave him a look that even Timberlake found uncomfortable. 'Yes,' he said without expression. He glanced at Darren Webb, then turned back to Timberlake. 'D'you think it could be worthwhile for Darren to go back to the factory, have a word with some of the people there, see if anyone has remembered something?'

'Certainly. I'll take someone else with me to see Sibley.'

Nigel Larkin gave a gentle cough, which managed to draw as much attention to himself as if he'd sent up a rocket. Timberlake waited for a moment to consider the other detectives. Alistair McPhail was too gloomy to invite confidences of a possible sexual nature, he decided, and Jeff Waters was too intimidating, even if he could give some women *frissons* of excitement.

'Bob Crust can go with Darren, and, er, Nigel can come with me.' The two detectives looked pleased: Nigel wanted to learn everything he could from Timberlake, while Bob was slightly relieved he wasn't going. Grammar was not one of his strongest points, and a day with Timberlake could be wearing if he was in one of his critical moods.

As the detectives left the conference room to go to work Darren Webb took Bob to one side. 'Wait for me in the carpark, will you?' he said. 'There's something I want to check on before we push off.'

Webb then went to find Rumsden. 'That tom you had in here earlier, Sharon Lester. What did she want?'

'Oh, you know her, do you?'

'Yes,' Webb replied flatly.

Rumsden waited for him to elaborate, but Webb remained silent. Rumsden went on, 'She was worried about one of her friends, another tom, who's gone missing. Named Vicki Stevens. I said working girls were doing that all the time, going off with someone for a few days. She'd probably gone off with some rich punter for a weekend, but Sharon said that it definitely wasn't the friend's style.'

'Have you done anything about it yet?'

'Just a quick check with the CRO, in case she's got any known dodgy associates, but they don't have anything on a Vicki Stevens. There's nothing in our own files, either.'

'Leave it for a bit, Tony,' Webb said. 'I'll have a word with Sharon myself this afternoon.'

'I see,' Rumsden said heavily.

'No you don't.' Webb stepped closer. 'She's one of my snouts,' he said quietly. 'You can make it official after I've seen her.'

'OK, Darren, as it's you. But don't leave it too long.'

Webb knew he'd have to leave it till the afternoon. Sharon Lester always slept late. After all, she was a night worker.

Captain Mark Sibley lived in a two-bed flat in a Knightsbridge street with a view of the back of Harrods. It was not large, but it was expensive. There were two good imitation Louis-XIV settees in the carpeted, plant-decorated entrance hall, which was probably sprayed on a regular basis with the unmistakable odour of money. The whole package came with twenty-four-hour porterage and punitive service charges. Nevertheless, Sibley could well afford to live there. It's true that he wasn't on the pay scale of an American 747's captain – when that aircraft first came into service it was said that the bump in the fuselage above the flight deck was to give the pilots headroom because they were sitting on their wallets – but he was doing very nicely, thank you.

Sibley received Timberlake and Nigel Larkin wearing cream pyjamas and a dark-blue dressing gown with a silk foulard.

'I hope you'll forgive my being dressed like this, but I got up rather late – what with jet lag and . . . Well, I didn't get to sleep very easily,' he said apologetically.

'Of course,' Timberlake assured him.

'I'm sure you'd like some coffee,' Sibley said. He went into the kitchen and switched on a coffee percolator.

Timberlake let them all get quite settled and as relaxed as possible. He felt that if Sibley was going to give himself away – *if* he had something to give away – he would be more likely to do it if he was at ease and not totally concentrating. Nigel Larkin took notes while sitting just out of Sibley's eyeline to help maintain a sense of informality.

'Where did you meet Miss Docker?'

'At church. We saw each other a couple of times before we spoke, and then it sort of went on from there. We became friends.' He smiled sadly.

'Did the relationship go beyond friendship?'

'Yes. We became very close.'

'To the point of intimacy?'

'Eventually. It was some time before we . . . The relationship developed rather slowly, by modern standards. Anyway, we didn't see each other all that often.' He compressed his lips as if to stop them trembling.

'Captain Sibley, was Miss Docker also seeing someone else at the same time that you were her lover?'

'Not to my knowledge, and I think it highly improbable. You will have to take my word for it that she wasn't a very experienced young woman.' Abruptly he got up and took his coffee cup into the kitchen. It was a moment or two before he returned.

'I'm sorry to have to pursue this line of enquiry,' Timberlake said, 'but I'm sure you understand. What about before she met you?'

'She never mentioned anyone, even casually. Even so, I suppose there must have been someone, at some time.' He shrugged. 'Perhaps she avoided the subject so as not to upset me. She was very considerate, thoughtful . . .' He turned his head away ostensibly to look out of the window. He blew his nose. 'If you're looking for jealousy as a motive, I can't help you. As far as I'm concerned, there just isn't anyone.'

His face was suddenly drawn, his eyes dead. For a moment he seemed oblivious to everything around him. Timberlake gave him time to pull himself together.

'Captain, the firm where she worked couldn't give us any help with her next of kin. Do you know if she had any family?'

'Now I come to think about it, she hardly ever mentioned her parents, and when she did it was always in the past tense. Funny. it never occurred to me before. I suppose I must have assumed they were dead.' He sat up a little straighter in his chair. 'Inspector, I don't know who I should see about it, but I'll pay for all the funeral expenses, whatever's necessary.'

Timberlake said thank you and rose. 'I think that's all for this time, Captain. We may need to see you again. In the meantime, if anything occurs to you that might be a help, no matter how unimportant or trivial it seems . . .'

'Yes, I'll call you.' Sibley shook hands with the two detectives and saw them out.

Before Timberlake started the engine of his Citroën he slipped a tape into the cassette player. It was a recording made from one of Timberlake's collection of classic jazz records, 'Riverboat Shuffle' on the Okeh label.

'Ever heard this before?' Timberlake asked Nigel Larkin, who shook his head. He looked a little pop-eyed as he listened to the cornet solo.

'That could only be Bix Beiderbecke,' Timberlake said. He listened reverently for a while. 'He was the best, better than Louis Armstrong . . . better than anyone. What did you think of Sibley?' he asked in the same breath.

Larkin was thrown. For a few seconds he wondered if Sibley was another musician he'd never heard of. 'Well, I couldn't really see his face properly, but he seemed straightforward enough. Obviously a bit . . . cut up.' He gave an embarrassed cough.

Timberlake was silent for a while. 'Did you notice there was one particular word he didn't use?'

Larkin turned to look at Timberlake. 'Actually, there were quite a lot he didn't use, guv.'

'He never used the word "love".'

'Well, he's English,' the Eager Beaver said. 'I thought he kept his self-control rather . . . well,' he went on. 'Pretty impressive, really.'

'Very,' said Timberlake heavily. He paused. 'Nigel, I want you to check – discreetly – that Sibley *was* on the flight to Glasgow that night. Although I'm practically certain he was. And what hotel he stayed at.'

'OK, guv. Anything else?'

'Yes. What time his flight back was the next day.'

Larkin looked startled. 'You don't think *he*—' He choked off the rest of what he was going to say as Timberlake turned his head and looked at him.

'Yes,' Timberlake said, his voice like breaking glass. 'I do.'

Darren Webb pushed the button next to the initials SL on the entryphone. After a pause there was a neutral-toned 'Yes?' from the loudspeaker.

'Darren Webb,' he announced. He didn't need to say he was a detective sergeant from Terrace Vale. The doorlock buzzed and he entered the hallway of a large house converted into small flats.

Sharon Lester was unrecognizable from the pavement-whore who had visited the Terrace Vale nick earlier in the day. Her face was without makeup except for a trace of lipstick, which made her unexpectedly young-looking, although Webb told himself it would be stretching things to say she looked innocent. Still, she didn't look like a slag. Her skin was good and after a moment he realized that she wasn't wearing lipstick after all. She wore a plain dressing gown and worn slippers. Instinctively she kept the dressing gown closed. The transformation from the prostitute he had visited in her working premises to the nice-girl-next-door was total.

Sharon's flat was plain but comfortable, barely more than just adequately furnished, and was clean and tidy enough to pass a Sandhurst general's inspection. It was another world from her cushion- and tassel-stuffed working premises with its permanent miasma of air-freshener. Sensible prostitutes had long since learned that men wouldn't visit rooms with heavy scents they would take home with them on their clothes. Suspicious wives have a better sense of smell than a bloodhound.

She offered him a drink, which he refused, and a coffee, which he accepted. 'I hope I haven't got you up too early,' he said.

'It's all right.'

'It's about that friend you said has gone missing. Vicki.'

Sharon looked up. 'Why are CID interested?'

He ignored the question. 'How long has she been missing?'

'Two, three days. Maybe four.'

'That's not long for a working girl.' He tried to avoid using the words 'prostitute' and 'whore' when he was talking to Sharon. 'She could have gone off with some rich punter for a weekend or something.'

Sharon shook her head vigorously. 'No. That's exactly what Sergeant Rumsden said. But she never does anything like that. She's a one-off. She works regular hours, all short-time tricks. She turns up at about 9 p.m., and goes home at about 2 a.m. She wouldn't hang around if the street was full of Welsh rugby supporters. Which is a bit surprising, really.'

'In what way?'

'Apparently she comes like an electric eel when she's being screwed, and she's noisy as hell with it. And it's genuine. Not like that bird in the film; you know, the one who fakes an orgasm in a restaurant and another woman says "I'll have what she's having". Course, the punters love it.'

'How d'you know it's genuine?'

'I walked in on her room one night just after she'd had a punter. She was lying back, all flushed and sweaty, and looked like . . . Anyway, another woman can always tell.'

'Does she do drugs?'

'No, I'm sure she doesn't.'

'I don't know her,' Webb said. 'Is she new?'

'Oh, she's been on our turf for about a year, maybe eighteen months.'

'Well, how the hell don't I know her? She must be on our books somewhere.'

'No: she's never been pulled in. Maybe she's got a personal radar and gets a three-minute warning when your lot are on the way for a roundup, or she's got a good friend at the nick who tips her off. Maybe Ted Greening. He's always after freebies. And she doesn't look like a whore. She doesn't mix with us all that much.'

'If she isn't a friend, why are you interested in whether she's disappeared or not?'

'That's a fucking nice thing to say, isn't it! She's a human being, even if she is only a poor bloody whore. Anyway, we look out for each other. Nobody else will.'

'What about her pimp?'

More calmly Sharon said, 'She hasn't got one. None of our little group have.' Webb was taken aback. 'Our landlord looks after us, the ones who've got rooms in his houses. Big Willy.'

'Are you trying to be funny?'

'His real name's Willy Manley, honest. He's got three or four houses in The Grove, with two or three whores in each of them.'

'He'll get done for living on immoral earnings and running a brothel before long.'

'He reckons not. All our rooms have a kitchen about the size of a phone box and a shower and loo, a flat number and a lock on the door; and we've all got rent books. That makes them separate dwellings. And there are a lot of straight people in the places as well. If your lot try to do him he'd have a good defence. He'd get Wim Sachs' – a local solicitor only too well known to the Terrace Vale police – 'and an expensive QC who'd get him off, no trouble.'

'So what did you really come to see me about, Darren? You know I don't work here, where I live. Though I might make an exception for you. I told you once before, I'd like to enjoy it for a change.'

Darren Webb was tempted. The way things were at home he might as well have been stuck on a desert island with six records and a copy of Shakespeare's works. He and his wife hadn't made love for longer than he cared to think. They hadn't even had angry, punishing-each-other brutal sex.

Sharon Lester stood up and started to loosen her dressing gown.

'No,' he said harshly. Then he astonished himself by adding normally, 'Not this time.'

Sharon sat down again and looked at him quizzically. 'That's a date,' she said.

Darren crossed his legs and tried to look calm. Finally he took a deep breath and said, 'You heard about that woman killed at Holly Mansions?'

Sharon looked startled. 'Yeah. What about her?'

'The man who did it's a nutter. He stabbed her so many times she—'

'All right! I don't want a diagram. And why tell me?'

'I wondered if you or any of the other girls had come up against any real weirdos recently, or heard about one, maybe someone who wanted SM, or wanted to whack them?'

'I'll ask the other girls.' She shuddered. 'Can we talk about something else? Getting caught by some psychopath is my worst nightmare.'

'How d'you know anyway if some ordinary-looking, inoffensive punter isn't going to turn out to be the Yorkshire Ripper's brother?'

'You don't. You just play as safe as you can, trust your instinct and keep to the safety rules.'

'What're they?'

'Oh, always with a condom; never get into the back of a van; don't go off in a car for a trick if you've got your own place - or at the very least, have a mate take the car number and let the punter see she's done it. Men in shiny new cars can be dodgy. If I have to get into one, I always pretend to drop something on the floor so I can feel around to see if there's anything that might be a weapon. Blokes in old bangers are usually all right. What else? Oh, yes: watch out for men with tattoos; make sure there's a maid within reach. We've got one in our place who keeps an ear open for all of us.' Sharon smiled. 'Oh, yes - rule number one: get your money up front and don't let him see where you put it.'

She got up slowly, this time not taking care to keep her dressing gown closed.

'Darren?' she said softly.

His mouth felt dry. He was fully aware of the risks of slipping into a sexual relationship with a prostitute, but his desire was strong. 'Next time,' he repeated, adding 'Maybe' in his mind. He turned to the door, opened it, hesitated, took one pace out, then turned back inside again, shutting the door behind him.

He walked into the centre of the room as Sharon let her dressing gown fall to the floor.

Chapter Seven

Darren Webb was late back to the Terrace Vale nick. By the time he got there the regular conference was over, but most of the murder squad were still in the main office. Webb apologized to Timberlake. 'There was something else I had to follow up, guv,' he explained. 'I called on a snout – a tom. She'd reported one of her friends missing, another tom.'

'Why? What's the connection between her and Docker? *That's* the case you're supposed to be working on.'

'Well, none directly, really, I suppose,' Webb replied apologetically. 'It's just made me wonder . . . I asked her if there'd been any suspicious punters knocking around recently, anyone who might be a nutter on the quiet. She said she'd ask the other girls.'

'If there is one, it won't be our man,' Timberlake said positively. 'Waste of bloody time.'

'Well, it was just in case, guv,' he said, trying to sound casual. 'Anyway, I got down to the works, spoke to the dragon, Mrs Crossley, the secretary. She had nothing new to say about Mary Docker. So, I went into the canteen and chatted up some of the girls. Zero. They all said much the same thing as before – including that Seagram woman, the one who reckoned

Docker was putting it about right, left and centre.' He paused. 'She asked after you.'

'Did she,' he said in a tone which made Webb regret the remark. Timberlake turned to Nigel Larkin. 'What about Captain Sibley?'

'According to the airline's log, Captain Sibley was definitely on the flights there and back. I got the times.' He passed over a slip of paper. 'He stayed at the Royal Lomond Hotel on the night of the 15th, guv,' Nigel Larkin reported brightly.

'Alistair!' Timberlake called out. 'D'you know the Royal Lomond Hotel in Glasgow?'

Alistair McPhail came across the room to sit near Timberlake.

'Aye, I ken it well. Glasgow's de luxe knocking shop.'

'Could anyone staying there walk in and out without any of the staff or front desk noticing?'

'At the weekend there's more traffic than at Glasgow Central.'

'D'you have any contacts with the police up there?'

'Guv, I was Glasgow CID for five years.'

Timberlake thought for a moment. 'I want you to go up there and find out what time Mark Sibley landed there on the 22nd, what time he booked into the hotel, whether he had dinner there, whether anyone saw him going in or out of the hotel – any sightings of him whatsoever and at what time. Check if the chambermaid or any of the staff noticed whether or not his bed had been slept in. Ask the reception desk and cashier what time he checked out. I want to know what time he reported at the airport and what time his aircraft took off. In other words—'

'You want me to check his alibi.'

'With a microscope, forwards, backwards and sideways. I'll leave it to you to call the Glasgow police to let them know you're coming.'

'OK, guv. When d'you want me to go?'

'Tomorrow morning. Fly by AirAlbion. I'll fix everything with Superintendent Harkness tomorrow.'

'Right.' McPhail made a few notes in his pocketbook, got up and left.

'D'you want me any more tonight, guv?' the Eager Beaver asked.

'No. Thanks, Nigel.'

Larkin nodded to Darren Webb and went out.

Webb cleared his throat. 'Er, guv. I don't mean to be out of order, but aren't you going a bit strong on Sibley as the main suspect? I mean, he was in Glasgow the night—'

'That still hasn't been proved,' Timberlake said harshly. 'And he's not the main suspect: he's the only one.' There was an awkward silence.

'Guv, man to man?' Webb said tentatively.

'Of course, Darren.'

'You don't think . . . I mean . . . Could there be a possibility that you . . . I mean, since the Newman case when you broke that cast-iron, stone-bunker alibi, could it be affecting your approach? . . . You know.'

Timberlake stared at him like someone looking over a gunsight. Webb had rarely felt so embarrassed with his chief. 'Sorry,' he mumbled.

Timberlake's regard softened as his anger subsided and he was able to appreciate Webb's motives. 'No need, Darren,' he said with a rather forced smile. 'I know you're only trying to be helpful and stop me developing tunnel vision. But if you go back over the case and think about it for a while you'll see that it *must* be Sibley.'

'Yes, sure, guv,' Webb said, not believing a word.

The two detectives took home with them their frustrations and dissatisfactions at their lack of progress with the Mary Docker murder case.

Darren Webb stopped at his local pub before he went home, which was a major tactical error. He had a few beers, some sausages, a couple of cheese rolls and a piece of ham and egg pie which he would never have inflicted on his stomach had he been fully sober. He regretted going to the pub as soon he walked into his home, his breath smelling strongly of peppermint. This pathetic subterfuge only drew attention to his earlier mild self-indulgence. His wife Naomi had decided to try once again to be more friendly and loving towards him, but Webb's slightly unsteady walk and flushed face transformed her welcoming smile into the expression of someone who had bitten into an apple and found half a large maggot.

What made things worse for Webb was the delicious smell of roast lamb coming from the kitchen. Normally this would have cheered him up enormously; now it made his heart sink: it meant that Naomi had prepared a special, large meal. He didn't dare say he wasn't hungry, but when it came to it he could eat only half of what Naomi served him. He knew what this would cost him. Apart from any other ingenious miseries she could inflict on him, for the next week or more he would get delivered pizzas, Chinese take-aways and

– horror of horrors – chicken legs and chips from a polythene box.

While she was eating, Naomi had a couple of glasses of Piat d'Or, which she thought was classy. It was her favourite wine, and it always made her feel mellow and sexy. By the time the meal was over and it was time for bed she was prepared to forgive Darren for his failings. After all, she told herself, he worked hard at a thankless, demanding job. She had to make allowances.

Webb was unable to pay the price – pleasant as it should have been – for earning her absolution. When she snuggled up against him in bed and moved an exploratory hand, Webb was totally incapable of any response. The combination of red wine and beer had given him a headache. The execrable pub grub and the rich food he had just eaten at home made him feel as distended as a dirigible and as heavy as a bag of cement at the same time. He was the nearest thing possible to a lead Zeppelin.

Naomi's warmth quickly turned to heated frustration. 'What's the matter with you?' she asked sharply.

'I'm sorry, darling. I'm just knackered. I've had a terrible day.' He added, rather unfairly, 'And my guvnor's been riding me all day.'

'Well, no one's riding me these days. D'you know how long it is since you last touched me?' Naomi said sourly, her temper rising rapidly. 'Who're you fucking? You screwing some slag down at the nick?' Naomi half-shouted, sitting up in bed. Occupational jargon soon rubs off on to wives and husbands from their partners.

'Don't be stupid,' he replied.

This triggered a new family row of an illogicality

that was surpassed only by its bitterness. It ended when Darren Webb dragged the eiderdown and a pillow from the bed and stalked to the sofa in the lounge. Thanks to the drink he fell asleep quickly. He snored loudly enough to be heard in the bedroom, where Naomi fantasized about strangling him.

Things were little better in the Timberlake ménage. Since they had begun to live together the fabric of their marriage had become increasingly frayed.

Their present argument was about Jenny's arrival home late, once again. It was one of the two days she operated at a private hospital. He wouldn't admit it to himself, but Timberlake was piqued by Jenny's now enormous income, compared with his own. That day she had performed four operations, two at £500 and two at £750, which was not unusual. It was true that she had large overheads, including a consulting room in Harley Street and a full-time appointments secretary. Even so, despite the best efforts of a shrewd accountant, her tax bill often exceeded Timberlake's take-home pay.

Timberlake didn't go as far as Darren Webb and sleep in the spare room. He and Jenny had single beds pushed together to make a king-size double bed, but they could have been separated by a moat for all the effort they made to approach each other. Whether or not they would have eventually come closer and reconciled their differences was never resolved. A quarter of an hour after they went to bed the phone rang. It could have been for either of them, but Timberlake answered.

'Timberlake,' he announced. He listened for a few moments and answered, 'I'm on my way.'

Darren Webb had added non-stop snoring to his other vices when Naomi stormed into the lounge. 'Answer the bloody phone!' she bawled as she shook him.

He struggled up from the depths of a deep, uncomfortable sleep. The phone was ringing. He struggled off the sofa, falling as he became tangled up in the eiderdown. Eventually he managed to get to the telephone.

'Webb,' he said, and then, 'Right,' before he hung up.

Timberlake drove Webb and himself to The Grove. This was Terrace Vale's red-light district, which was treated very leniently by the police. This was because there was rarely any trouble there, and the few local residents who were not on the game were disinclined to complain to the authorities. As far as they were concerned, the less they saw of the police the better. For the whores' part, there was a tacit agreement with the police that as long as they weren't too noisy or outrageous, didn't nick punters' wallets and kept to the largely non-residential area, they wouldn't be too severely hassled. As a result, The Grove had a very low incidence of the crimes usually associated with red-light areas. The Grove had another amenity which made it attractive to prostitutes' clients. A few dozen yards down The Grove from the main road was an Underground station which served the Central and

Circle lines. A punter, fare or gonk who was looking for a quick diddle without much chance of being spotted by people who knew him, or being nicked for kerb-crawling in a car, could nip out of the station, hurry round into The Grove, spend his money and be back on the train looking innocent in not much longer than it took to pull his trousers down and up again.

At the other end of the Terrace Vale area was another red-light district in a road called Peacehaven Hill, part of the area was familiarly known as The Gut, after the notorious street in Valletta which has more whores per doorway than anywhere west of Suez. It was everything that The Grove was not. There was violence, theft, blackmail, drug peddling and addiction, child prostitution and the devil only knew what. Whores had to be pretty desperate, bullied or suffering from a serious drug habit to work there. Keeping the lid on the stewpot of The Gut – more or less – took an inordinate amount of police time and effort in nicking girls for soliciting and men for kerb-crawling. Local residents did their bit to try to scare off customers by marching around in groups with placards and camcorders, but it was like sweeping up dead leaves in a stiff wind. Clear one area of them and other leaves came swirling in from four different directions at once.

As Timberlake turned the corner into The Grove he was greeted by an old, familiar scene, although not in this part of the Terrace Vale area. There were several police cars parked to block the road on either side of a house where policemen were putting up the 'Police – Keep Out' tapes. Other uniformed policemen were standing about on the pavement or near their cars, trying to look as if they were actually doing something.

The whole location was given a surreal air by the flashing blue lights on the many police vehicles, turning it into a vast outdoor disco with strobe lights.

Timberlake and a slightly frazzled-looking Webb walked up the five steps to the front door of the house where WPC Rosie Hall and PC Rambo Wright were on duty. They both saluted – smartly, which all constables at Terrace Vale did to Timberlake. Ted Greening, on the other hand, got something more like a cab driver's acknowledgment of an inadequate tip.

'Do we know who it is?' Timberlake asked.

'No, sir,' Rambo Wright replied. 'A woman, that's all.'

'Who reported it?' Webb asked.

'A Miss Kettle made a 999 call,' Rosie told him. It seemed that everyone wanted to have their say.

'Is she here?'

'She's waiting at the back. You won't miss her,' she said with a straight face.

Rosie beckoned to someone just inside the house. A tall young woman with striped hair and a lot of makeup came to the door. She was wearing a screaming red plastic cat suit which fitted her like a coat of paint.

'Well done. Oh, have someone keep an eye on my car,' Timberlake told Rosie. He didn't have to say which one was his car. Everyone in the Terrace Vale nick knew it.

'Morning, guv. You're not looking too cheerful,' came a voice from behind Timberlake. It was Sergeant Burton Johnson, the senior SOCO, who was followed by his team.

'3 a.m. isn't my favourite time,' Timberlake said tetchily. He and Webb followed the SOCOs to the open door of a ground-floor bedsitter with a tiny kitchen and a door to what was probably a loo. It was a typical working room for a prostitute: it had a bed covered with a counterpane, bedside cabinet with a pink-shaded lamp that was providing the only light in the room, a washbasin with a mirror, a large dispenser of paper towels, a flip-top waste bin, a couple of easy chairs, table, small chest of drawers and a cupboard. The room was surprisingly neat and tidy, except for one discordant element. Lying on the bed was the naked body of a young woman.

Her face was distorted by the effects of the strangulation that had killed her, but Darren Webb had no difficulty in recognizing her.

It was Sharon Lester.

Chapter Eight

While the SOCOs began laying down the track for the doctor Timberlake and Webb took Miss Kettle into the back of the hall again to be interviewed. She was smoking a spliff that didn't smell like Virginia or Turkish. She was about to stamp it out when Timberlake said gently, 'Don't worry. Forget it.' The young woman's carefully drawn eyebrows shot up, then she relaxed and gave Timberlake a thankful smile. Webb risked a reproving look at his guvnor, making sure he was beyond the edge of Timberlake's peripheral vision.

'Miss Kettle?' Timberlake asked.

The woman nodded. 'Lil Kettle. Call me Whistling,' she said. 'Everybody does.' The detectives made no comment, although both wondered furiously what she did to earn herself that nickname.

'Can you tell me what happened?' Timberlake asked.

'Well, I was coming downstairs with a *friend*' – she gave the word a heavy inflection that translated it to 'punter', 'John' or 'client' – 'as we was going past Sharon's place my friend sort of staggered a bit and bumped against the door. It wasn't shut proper, you know, and it came open. And I saw her laying on the bed. I mean, it was obvious she was dead, you know.'

'Did you go in?'

Whistling shuddered. 'Not bleedin' likely!'

'What about your friend?' Webb asked.

'Christ, no! He legged it very smartish. He's always very quick, is Arnold.' Again both detectives managed to keep any smart remarks to themselves.

'Did you see anyone going out as you came down the stairs? Or hear anything?'

'No.'

'Or when you first came in with your friend?'

'No. I mean, well, most punters try to avoid bumping into anyone when they come here. Some of them sneak out the back door and down the path at the back of the gardens. You know how it is.'

'I can guess,' said Timberlake. Unexpectedly he asked her, 'What's Arnold's second name?'

'Dunno,' Whistling said. 'It was his first time with me. Anyway, he didn't scrag her. He was with me from the moment he came into the house.' She looked Timberlake straight in the eye with an expression of such sincerity that he knew she was lying.

'You said he was *always* quick. So what's his name?' He gave her time to answer before adding gently, 'It's all right; I'm not going to cause trouble for him at home.' His manner changed abruptly. 'The only one I might cause trouble for is you. But I'm sure there won't be any need for that.' He gave her the executioner's smile of encouragement to someone mounting the scaffold.

Whistling Kettle soon told him that her punter's name was Arnold Piper, and he worked as a launderette manager in Southington. 'In Victoria Terrace, Castle Road.'

'Thank you,' said Timberlake politely. 'We'll need to have you down at the station later to make a formal statement.'

Before Timberlake entered the room where the body was lying he glanced at Webb. He was shocked to see how pale and drawn he was He seemed ready to throw up at any moment.

'You all right, Darren?' he asked. 'You look ready for a slab yourself.'

'I'm all right,' he said, and added for emphasis, 'I'm fine,' which was plainly ludicrous.

Timberlake assumed Webb's condition was the result of a major row with his wife, and too much scotch. 'If you say so,' he said, but determined to keep an eye on him.

Timberlake was suddenly aware of a new technician among the SOCOs. At first he wasn't certain whether the androgenous person was a young woman or a youth. The baggy overalls concealed his or her figure enough that it gave no clue to the subject's gender; and the haircut was equally unrevealing. Timberlake didn't see more than a fleeting three-quater back view of the technician's face. He was about to ask someone who this new member of the team was, but he was distracted by the arrival of Professor Mortimer.

The pathologist was immaculately dressed as if he were going to a Victorian funeral directors' dinner. He was carrying his old leather bag. This was unusual gallantry on his part: usually Gertrude Hacker lugged it around for him. Perhaps he didn't trust her for once.

He entered the room, Gertrude Hacker following him as if she were on wheels, being pulled along by a string. He handed her his bag, and she took out a pair of rubber gloves. Darren Webb knew what would be coming next. Mortimer would put plastic bags over Sharon's hands and tie them at the wrist. After he had made a careful examination of the body, he would take the anal temperature, then vaginal, anal and mouth swabs. Finally, he would bag the head. The thought of that aged, desiccated and long-since passionless old man probing Sharon Lester's young body caused an uncharacteristic wave of nausea to sweep over Webb. He turned to Timberlake.

'Guv, I'm feeling bloody awful. Is it all right if I go outside for a while? Get some air?'

Timberlake looked at him in some surprise. 'Sure. You're not really all right, are you?'

'Just too much coffee and not enough sleep.' He grimaced in an attempt to smile. 'And maybe too much scotch.' He went out, while Timberlake stared at his back. Mortimer didn't even look up.

He began his work with characteristic cold efficiency while Gertrude Hacker took notes. 'Death by manual strangulation, between one and three hours ago,' he said eventually. 'Autopsy in forty-eight hours. Miss Hacker will let you know time and place.' He snapped shut his bag like nailing down a coffin lid, turned on his heel and strode out, leaning forward slightly as if he were facing a stiff breeze. Gertrude Hacker exited on her well-oiled wheels.

The launderette where Arnold Piper worked was in a small parade of shops which included a greengrocer's, a mini-super-market, a radio and television shop, a dentist's surgery and two estate agent's offices. Much more interesting was a recording studio which was once a theatre where John Gielgud, no less, had appeared as a callow juvenile.

Arnold Piper was a man of medium everything: height, weight, colouring and age. When he had to fill in an application form for a passport, for example, he was hard put to it to write something in the box marked 'Distinguishing marks'. He could lose himself in a crowd of three.

When Webb introduced himself and asked if Piper was the manager, he replied instantly, 'If a machine damaged your clothes you couldn't have operated it properly.' He half-gabbled it mechanically like a policeman reciting the official caution.

'Is there somewhere we can talk privately?' Webb said.

Piper led him into the laundrette's office.

'You know Miss Kettle, Whistling Kettle,' Webb said. 'I have a few questions to ask you about the other night.'

Piper turned pale. 'How did you know I was . . . It wasn't me. I didn't do it. I *couldn't* do anything like that. I never—'

'I'm not accusing you, Mr Piper. I just want to know if you saw, or heard, anything.'

Piper shook his head so vigorously that Webb heard a splashing sound. He stepped back, startled, which in turn, alarmed Piper even more. Almost at once Webb realized that the splashing was coming from one of the washing machines outside.

Webb composed himself, 'Are you a . . . regular client of Miss Kettle?'

Piper gulped and looked as embarrassed as a man

whose trousers had fallen down at a funeral. 'Now and then,' he finally admitted vaguely.

'And any of the other women in The Grove?'

'Sometimes. You know,' he added weakly. 'When Miss Kettle was . . .' he searched for a delicate way to put it. 'When she was . . . unavailable. Busy.'

'Right, now all I want to know is, on that last night, did you see, or hear, anything unusual?'

Piper thought hard. 'Well, there was a dead body on the bed downstairs.'

Webb breathed hard through his nose.

'Yes. But apart from that? Did you see anyone, or hear anything unusual? Please cast your mind back and try to remember everything as you were coming downstairs and walking along the corridor.'

It was clear that Arnold Piper had been trying his utmost to forget everything about that traumatic night.

'Here's my card,' Webb said. 'If you do think of anything . . .'

Piper took it as if it might explode. 'Right,' he said.

Webb was about to leave when he asked. 'You said you occasionally went with some of the other women. Was one of them ever Sharon Lester?'

Piper took a long time to answer. 'Yes. Once. Why d'you ask?'

'No reason.'

Webb never understood what prompted him to ask that one extra question, and he regretted it for a very long time. Until that moment he had theoretically accepted that Sharon Lester was a prostitute, but now he was faced with the reality of one of her clients, the cipher-like Arnold Piper, and it soured everything he remembered about her.

To Timberlake's considerable surprise he found Alistair McPhail already in the murder-squad conference room when he arrived at Terrace Vale half an hour before the morning meeting was due.

'I got in late last night, guv, and when I rang the nick they said you were out on a case, so I thought it could wait till this morning,' McPhail explained.

'What did you find out?'

McPhail handed over a sheet of paper.

Mark Sibley	
Friday 22 September	
Landed Glasgow Airport	15.23
Left Airport	16.45
Arrived Royal Lomond Hotel went straight to room	17.16
Chambermaid noticed DO NOT DISTURB card on the door	21.30
Saturday 23 September	
Had breakfast	08.30–09.30
Left hotel	10.02
Arrived Glasgow Airport	10.41
Took off from airport	13.10

'He was alone in his room for a long time on Friday night,' Timberlake said.

'When he checked in he told the woman on reception that he was knackered and needed a long rest.'

Anyway, who says he *was* alone?' McPhail said with a lascivious look. 'I checked with the cashier. He had the bottle of champagne from the minibar and two brandy miniatures. And the two beds in the room had been slept in. Or used, at least.'

Timberlake looked at him questioningly.

'The chambermaid was very co-operative.' McPhail coughed, and winked knowingly. His expression became serious. 'Guv, if he put the DO NOT DISTURB notice on the door at half-past nine, he couldn't have got to London that night.'

Timberlake felt cold fingers on his spine. He looked at the report. 'The chambermaid noticed the card at nine-thirty. Could it have been put there *before* then?'

McPhail considered this for a moment.

'Aye. Maybe.'

'Thanks, Alistair. Well done,' Timberlake said, although he was disappointed with the information. He tried to be sociable. 'Did you see any of your old CID friends while you were up there?'

'Aye. But I'll be better by tomorrow.' He grinned.

Darren Webb joined them. He looked less ghastly than he had the previous night, but he was far from blooming.

'Good morning, Darren. How are you feeling?' Timberlake asked mechnically.

'Fair enough, thanks, guv. Had a decent night's sleep. Well, decent morning's,' he said, which was a lie. 'I saw Piper this morning.'

'And?'

Webb shook his head. 'He's a right anorak. He's obviously not involved, and doesn't know anything, unless he's a better actor than Jeremy Beadle.' He meant it as a joke.

The other detectives working on the Mary Docker case, together with others who had been called in the previous night to the Sharon Lester murder, began to drift into the room. As usual, Detective Superintendent Harkness entered on time with the precision of the Greenwich time signal, looking as if he had just been taken out of a box and the tissue paper unwrapped.

Timberlake summarized the long night's activities on the Sharon Lester murder for Harkness. Detectives and uniformed officers had interviewed the few whores who hadn't run for cover when the Old Bill arrived. There didn't seem to be a grain of potentially useful information from any of them who were questioned.

'The uniforms downstairs have got lists of all the other local brasses,' Timberlake said. 'I expect that whoever takes over the case will get round to interviewing them all as soon as possible. Willy Manley, who runs some of the houses where the women operate, wasn't to be found last night, but I expect he'll surface pretty soon.'

'Thank you, Harry,' Harkness said. 'We'll sort out who'll do what on the two cases at the end of the meeting.'

The Mary Docker case was quickly reviewed, but there had been virtually no progress in the past twenty-four hours. Except for one thing.

'As you know,' Timberlake said, 'Alistair McPhail went to Glasgow to establish Captain Sibley's movements. I'm going to check aircraft and train timetables to see if he could have been in London on the night of the murder.'

'I see,' Harkness said non-commitally. 'I glanced at Alistair's report. The indications – drinks, used beds – suggest he stayed the night at the hotel with a companion.'

Timberlake looked at him sharply. 'On the surface of things, Sibley's bright enough to have set it up.'

At the end of the meeting Harkness called out, 'Harry, hang on a moment, please.'

When the others had left the room to go into the main CID office, he said, 'Ask DCI Greening if he can spare me a couple of minutes, please. We'll have a word with him about getting some more troops.' Timberlake began to suspect that something was up.

Ted Greening arrived trailing an unmistakable slipstream of whisky fumes and cigarette smoke. He was assuming an air of nonchalance that was as patently false as a ginger wig on Kojak.

Harkness explained that as there were now two murders to investigate, the AMIP squad needed more officers. If the station was short of them, some detective constables could be drafted in from neighbouring areas. However, what Harkness really needed was another Terrace Vale detective inspector or sergeant with local knowledge.

'We're rather short at the moment, sir,' Greening said ingratiatingly. 'We've got Shearer on leave, Lee is sick . . .' He had a moment of inspiration. 'It's put a lot of extra work on me, personally, I'm afraid, but there we are.' This was to be translated as *Don't ask me to go back to legwork in the field.* He gave what he meant to be a resigned, but brave smile.

'I see. Very well, I shall have to work something out. Thank you, Chief Inspector,' Harkness said with a smile that would have frozen a bird in full flight.

'If anything turns up—' Greening began, but Harkness was already studying a file on his desk. Greening made an embarrassed exit.

Harkness looked at Timberlake with a lack of expression that was more disquieting than a ferocious stare. 'From a professional point of view I hate prostitute murders,' he said. 'They're the most difficult of all to solve. There's no starting point, like relations, lovers, friends, rivals . . . The killer could be anyone, someone who's just walked in off the street, a one-off psychopath . . .' Harkness fell silent. After an age he said, 'What do you think of Darren Webb?'

'A first-class officer. I have every confidence in him.'

Harkness nodded. 'Good. I'd like you to take over the Sharon Lester murder and I'll put Webb in charge of the Docker case, although you'll be in overall charge, reporting to me, of course. We don't seem to be getting very far with Docker for the moment; a new approach might do something for us.'

Harkness was not the sort of man you argued with. And for all Harkness's studied use of 'we' and 'us', Timberlake felt keenly there was an implied criticism of him personally. He guessed that maybe it was because of his insistence that Mark Sibley was the murderer. Even if Harkness agreed with him that Sibley might well be guilty, maybe he believed Timberlake wasn't following different lines of enquiry vigorously enough to eliminate other possibilities. And besides, Timberlake hadn't yet managed to show that Sibley could have got to and from Glasgow in time to do the murder. Timberlake wondered whether preoccupation with his crumbling marriage was affecting his work.

'Make sure Darren Webb has all the information on the case,' Harkness said quietly, ending Timberlake's introspection. 'Now, how do we divide up the teams?'

It was soon decided that Nigel Larkin would stay with Timberlake along with the imposing-looking Jeff Waters. Darren Webb's team would be led by himself, Alistair McPhail and Bob Crust.

Timberlake was not pleased, but both he and Harkness were surprised by Webb's negative reaction to the news that he was going to run the Mary Docker inquiry.

'Something wrong?' Harkness asked without emphasis. Darren Webb remained silent. 'Sergeant Webb?' Harkness prompted with an edge.

'It's just that, er, perhaps I'd be better suited to work on the Sharon Lester case, sir.'

'Why?'

'Well, she was one of my snouts. She didn't give me a lot, but what she did was good stuff. I'd like to get the bastard who did her. I knew her quite well – as an informant, of course.'

Harkness looked at him for a moment before saying, 'Which is exactly why you shouldn't be on the case. By now you should know the importance of objectivity and no personal involvement in an investigation.

Chapter Nine

WDC Sarah Lewis was dressed as she thought female local government officials would dress, which was pretty insulting on her part, because she looked like a 1930s Russian party activist. Norman Meade, who was a real local government official, regarded her with disfavour. To accompany Sarah on a co-operative exercise with the police he was dressed, as usual, like a Tory councillor.

Although the murders were the major preoccupation of the Terrace Vale constabulary, this did not mean that all other investigations there were put on hold until the murder or murderers were nabbed. One of the CID's reliable snouts had tipped them off that some of the older children at Abbot Perceval Secondary Modern – one of the few local schools that weren't breeding grounds for future delinquents – were on drugs. It was generally known that there was a fair amount of marijuana about in the area, but much more worrying was the possibility that some of the older boys were on cocaine. And even if they weren't now, they might well progress from spliffs to sniffs.

Sarah Lewis and a number of different partners had been keeping observation on the school's entrance, and their eye had been caught by the regular visits of an ice-cream van, driven by a black man with dreadlocks.

Norman Meade was an environmental health inspector. He and his 'assistant', Ms Lewis, were on their way to inspect the premises and van of Eric Obekachi, the Rastafarian who sold ice-cream outside the school. They had picked the time of their visit carefully. From observation over a few days Sarah had learned that Obekachi regularly left home for the school at 11 a.m., in time to be ready for business at the pupils' playtime break. So if he was pushing drugs he would have them on his van by then.

Sarah was aware that there might be complications about the validity of any evidence of her finding drugs on the premises while she was pretending to be a council enployee. If she did spot anything she would leave, call up reinforcements and nick Obekachi while the drugs were seized and bagged.

Meade and Sarah drove through streets which looked as if they hadn't been cleaned up since the blitz. Obekachi lived in an end-of-terrace house with a garage attached. This was convenient for Sarah: a jam-butty police car – so called because of its yellow-red-yellow stripes along the side – followed Meade's car and parked in the side road almost within shouting distance to provide any necessary backup.

Norman Meade reluctantly rang the doorbell as if the bellpush might have carried some contagion. When Obekachi opened the door he was taller than Sarah expected because she had seen him only from above while he was standing behind the counter of his ice-cream van. He was wearing black trousers and a white Tee-shirt with the legend 'I'se happy when I'se getting

It'. The 'It' was pretty equivocal, Sarah thought. Obekachi studied them warily. She had an uncomfortable feeling he had already spotted her as a copper.

Meade produced his council identity card and explained that this was a routine health and hygiene check, and could they see the kitchen, please.

The kitchen was small and entirely domestic except for a deep-freezer large enough to take three people lying down. There was no sign of any ice-cream-making machinery.

'I don't make the stuff,' Obekachi explained. 'I buy it in bulk.' He went to the large freezer and opened it. Neatly stacked inside were large, factory-sealed tubs of various flavoured ice-cream. Meade sniffed, and continued to inspect the kitchen as a matter of course. However, there was nothing connected with ice-cream sales in the private, domestic fridge; there were adequate, well-maintained hand-washing facilities, no greasy or cracked working surfaces, no loose tiles, and the floor, as one of the friends of Sarah's parents used to say, was clean enough for the Queen to eat her dinner off of. Meade's failure to find something to complain about gave him the despondent air of a bloodhound with a bad case of nasal catarrh.

'I gotta be going in a minute, man,' Obekachi said apologetically, directing his remark to Meade, 'otherwise I'm gonna miss the playtime trade.'

'It won't take us long to inspect the van, will it, Mr Meade?' Sarah said firmly.

Obekachi sighed dramatically and led them to the van in the garage.

There was the sound of a petrol motor running. 'What's that?' Sarah asked.

'The compressor for the van's fridge,' Meade said, looking pityingly at his new assistant.

'I always start it half an hour before I go out,' Obekachi said. He looked pointedly at his watch.

The van was an old vehicle, clean and apparently well-maintained, but very basic. It took Sarah little more than a glance to see that there was nowhere to conceal packets of drugs – soft, hard or well-done – in the front section. The back of the van had much more potential for hiding illegal substances. Meade, always the health inspector, instinctively inspected it closely, checking that there were handwashing facilities. Meade finally gave a small grunt of something that could pass as approval.

Sarah was indifferent to the possible existence of any enormous colonies of bacilli and other nasties. She looked into small drawers, cupboards where wafers, cornets, bottles of flavouring syrups and small chocolate logs were stored. She took off the lids from the large tubs of ice-cream and peered inside. They were three-quarters full. She had to admit to herself that the possibility of there being any packets of drugs hidden in the ice-cream was virtually non-existent. Getting them into the ice-cream would be easy enough, but getting them out inconspicuously would be another thing.

'What do you do about handling money?' Meade asked, which struck Sarah as a silly question.

'I don't touch the wafers and cornets with my bare hands. I hold them in those paper wrappers.' Obekachi indicated a box of thin, greaseproof-paper squares.

'Quite satisfactory,' Meade pronounced with a tinge of disappointment. 'Just one thing, though,' he added, brightening up. 'The lino on the floor of the van is cracked, and isn't quite as clean as it might be.'

'I'll put down a new strip tonight,' Obekachi said.

'Well, that's that, then,' Meade concluded. 'Unless you have something to say, Miss Lewis?'

The only thing Sarah would have liked to say was short, sharp and Anglo-Saxon. She settled for shaking her head.

As they drove away out of sight of Obekachi Sarah took her personal radio from her bag and stood down the crew in the jam-butty car round the corner. 'Take me back to the nick, if you don't mind,' she said to Meade in a voice that made it plain that it didn't matter whether he minded or not. She was silent throughout the drive, trying to make her mind up about Obekachi. Was his home and van impeccable because he was simply a conscientious and honest ice-cream trader, or because he didn't want to risk any trouble with nosy authorities?

Sarah's gut feeling was that Obekachi was rather too good to be true. He gave her the same vibes of being up to something, as a late-night motorist who drives at a steady 29mph, dead straight, always on the left-hand side of the road, giving correct signals, in a deserted, well-lit street.

'Yes, you're up to something, chummy,' she said out loud.

Meade jumped. 'I didn't do anything!' he said, half an octave above his usual register, edging away from Sarah.

'Sorry. Thinking out loud,' Sarah said grumpily.

*

At the nick Sarah, acting on her own initiative, went to see Detective Sergeant Luke Mawdsley of the Terrace Vale drugs squad, who looked like he slept in a dosshouse, when he was lucky. He was definitely of the school of TV police-series characters, complete with three-days' growth of beard, black tee-shirt, torn jeans and battered trainers. Drugs detectives working the street don't dress like bank managers.

Mawdsley knew about Sarah's investigation into Abbot Perceval Secondary Modern, and was secretly grateful to have someone working on the marijuana end of the drugs scene: he and his under-strength squad were totally occupied with serious drug dealing – heroin, cocaine, Ecstasy and the rest.

Sarah told him about the suspicious behaviour of Eric Obekachi .

'I haven't heard anything about him; he's not on my list,' Mawdsley said, scratching his backside. Sarah didn't know if he really had an itch or was simply keeping in character in the best traditions of Method acting. 'If you learn anything, I'll be grateful if you mark my card. We've got problems with a new dealer operating in the area we haven't identified yet, which is keeping us bloody busy.'

Sarah promised him he would be the second to know if she uncovered anything.

Nigel Larkin bounded into the CID office. Like an Olympic sprinter who has just heard the warning 'Get set!' he would catapult himself into action the moment Harry Timberlake metaphorically fired the starting gun. Within moments he was back at Timberlake's desk.

'What's on for today, guv?' he asked.

'We're going back to The Grove. Darren Webb told me Sharon Lester came in here a few days ago to report another prostitute named Vicki, in the flat next to hers, had gone missing. Well, we didn't take much notice: toms often disappear for a few days. Uniforms made a few enquiries that came to nothing. But Sharon and this other woman, Vicki something, were sort of friends, so—'

'There could be a connection,' Larkin finished for him.

'It's a possibility,' Timberlake admitted.

Although it was only a little after 10 a.m. there were a few whores waiting hopefully for punters at the end of The Grove. They were rather less garishly costumed than the night shift, but unmistakably for hire nevertheless. The day shift on the game is not like the night turn. After dark, in addition to the usual 'normal' customers, out come the weirdos, the creeps, the drunks, the bashfuls, the impulse shoppers, the first-timers and the would-be anonymous johns. The women wear extravagantly titillating outfits to encourage the waverers and outshine their competitors trading on the same pavement.

Morning punters are a different matter. Before they leave home the men have already made up their minds to go humping on their way to the office. Maybe they think a quick screw to start the day clears the mind, relaxes the body or lifts the spirit, thus reinforcing their air of authority. Whatever turns them on. If they are afternoon, on-the-way-home, specialists, they may be looking for a whore so they can pretend they're really screwing the boss, or simply someone they can feel superior to.

So, the women of the day know they won't have to strut and go into a big sales talk. Day customers have already decided, more or less, to buy the product.

When Timberlake and Larkin got out of their car, one or two of the women started to stroll towards them, stopped dead with recognition, turned back, and began to scamper away with a rat-a-tat of high heels on the pavement. The detectives' indifference to them soon restored their confidence, and they cautiously drifted back to their territories.

At the front door of the house a bored police constable stood on guard, presumably against tabloid-newspaper journalists and pervs who would be thrilled to see a close-up of the scene of a murder. As the two detectives mounted the stone steps a small, dapper black man came out of the front door. The effect of his neat and relatively sober clothes was offset by his gold jewellery – fried-egg-sized wristwatch, a bracelet as big as half a pair of handcuffs and rings like carbuncles.

Timberlake didn't need a crystal ball to know who he was. 'Mr Manley?' he asked politely.

'That's me. Otherwise known as Big Willy.' He smiled like a piano lid being opened. Two of his front teeth had small diamonds inset, demonstrating that his choice of personal decoration wasn't limited to gold. 'The way the officer here saluted you, I take it you are members of the Metropolitan Police.'

Timberlake admitted it, and introduced himself and Nigel Larkin.

Manley had a room at the back of the house. It

could have been a corner of a St James's club, with a couple of deep leather armchairs, a small flat-top desk with an inlaid, tooled leather top. The fitted carpet had a pile you could lose a pound coin in.

'What can you tell me about Sharon?' Timberlake asked, getting straight to the point.

Manley shrugged, more Gallic than Caribbean. 'Not much, mister. Good girl, never caused any fuss, paid her rent regular. As far as I was concerned, she was a perfect tenant.'

'Who was her pimp?'

Manley looked at him with a feigned mixture of incomprehension and innocence. 'Don't know what you mean, mister.'

Timberlake sighed. 'Look, we want to get a murderer. We're not vice squad. Other people can worry about anyone living on immoral earnings. So cut the bullshit.' Larkin looked startled at Timberlake's phrase.

Manley studied Timberlake steadily for a moment, sizing him up. 'She didn't have no macaroni, mister. Not many in my places have got one. If any.'

Timberlake was mildly surprised by the answer. 'Macaroni' was Black American slang for pimp, not West Indian. He wondered briefly whether the expression came from the French slang *maquereau*, a mackerel or pimp.

'I run a legit property business. All my tenants pay reasonable rents and have got rent books to prove it.'

'And the rent in the book is the same amount they pay you, of course.'

'You bet. And they all tell me they've got good jobs. So . . .' He shrugged. 'Maybe – *maybe* if controlled brothels were legal, I'd be out of business.' He smiled slyly. 'Or in a different one. But right now you'd have a real hard time in court trying to get me on an immoral-earnings rap with all the witnesses I'd have. Know what I mean? I got all sorts of tenants. Single girls, sure . . . but I got genuine university students, too . . . *And* a solicitor. If I catch anyone misbehaving or breaking the law, out they go, man.' Manley gave his Gallic shrug again. 'Mister, off the record, you fellers should thank me. In my places nobody don't get mugged, rolled or cheated. Here, girls don't get whacked or their faces razored by pimps for holding back money. Nobody's hooking girls on shit so they have to take all sorts of rough trade to pay for their habit . . .'

'All right, all right. I'll put you up for the next Honours List,' Timberlake said. Then, heavily, 'But Sharon Lester was killed here.'

Manley was silent for some time. 'There's always that risk, man, whoever, wherever you are. People even get blown away in churches. I'm sorrier than you are. If I could help you, I would, but right now I don't know shit.' He eyed Larkin suspiciously. 'Is he regular?' He meant reliable.

'Yes.'

Manley nodded. 'If you say so. OK, I'll ask around and let you know. People are going to talk to me easier than they would to you. But you keep coming here and my cred's going to be zilch.' He took out a visiting card and wrote a telephone number on the back. 'That's my private number. If you want a meet, call me on that. But no jerking around, man. It's got to be heavy.'

Timberlake nodded, and handed over a card of his own. 'If you've got anything for me, that's my direct number at the nick, and my home number. If you can't get me on either, ask for DC Larkin at the station.'

The Eager Beaver remained impassive, but inside he was practically pregnant with pride.

'Now, there's something else,' Timberlake went on. 'A few days ago Sharon Lester called into the nick to report that her next-door neighbour, a girl named Vicki Stevens, had gone missing.'

'You know women,' Manley said. 'It's a pound to a pinch of poop she's gone off with some loaded fat cat.'

'But she and Sharon were friends. There might be a connection,' Nigel Larkin said, encouraged by Timberlake's show of confidence in him.

'So we'd like to have a look in her flat,' Timberlake said. 'Just to make sure.'

Manley understood the implication. 'No sweat, man.' He rose, went to his desk, and unlocked a drawer. There were a heap of door keys with tags on them. He rooted around, and found the one he was looking for. He took it out, closed the drawer and locked it again. Timberlake silently approved his caution. Manley handed the key to Timberlake.

The three men went into Vicki Stevens's flat. 'Thank you, Mr Manley,' Timberlake said politely. 'We'll take it from here.' Manley went back to his office.

Timberlake opened the door. He waited briefly, then breathed in hard through his nose. Relieved, he said 'Well, at least we don't have a stinker.' He entered, closely followed by Larkin. The place was dark, with the curtains pulled. He went over and opened them.

Although there was no piece of furniture in the main room that was outrageous or overstated in itself, the sum total of the parts made its purpose as obvious as a room with a dentist's chair or a billiard table. The bed was never meant for sleeping, the lights not for reading. And yet . . . Paradoxically, although it was a whore's working address, it was neat and tidy, almost prim. The only luxury item was a small television set.

The room produced an odd feeling in Timberlake which he could not identify at first. When he identified it, the more he tried to resist it, the more insistent it became. There was no mistaking: he had a strong sense of *déjà vu*.

But from where?

The two detectives searched the small flat, but they found nothing that told them anything at all about its tenant, Vicki Stevens. There were no papers, no tickets, no bills; only a rent book in the name of Vicki Stevens.

Timberlake looked in the wardrobe. It contained the working clothes of a whore: a wig, a short sheath dress with a deep décolleté, so-called sexy underwear and shoes with absurdly high heels that must have been hell to stand in, let alone walk. There were no costumes to wear for kinky customers: no nurse's uniform, nun's habit, Gestapo uniform or schoolgirl's gym slip. Nor were there any whips, chains, handcuffs or masks. Vicki Stevens clearly didn't cater for punters with special tastes.

There was nothing unusual or thought-provoking to even the smallest degree in the alcove that passed for a kitchen. The equally compact bathroom – loo, bidet, shower, washbasin – had makeup on a shelf beneath the mirror. There was an industrial-size box of condoms.

'What do you make of the place, Nigel?'

'Weird, guvnor. It's ordinary enough on the surface, but . . . there's something weird about it, something not quite right.'

Larkin felt embarrassed at what he had said, until Timberlake nodded agreement. 'Not quite right,' he said slowly. 'And there's the big question.'

'Where is she? What's happened to her?' Larkin suggested.

'That's two questions. Important enough, but not the *big* question.' He didn't elaborate.

'You think there might be a connection with her and Sharon Lester?'

'They were friends, colleagues, lived next door to each other; one was murdered; the other has disappeared. I make that too many coincidences for them not to be connected. We'll continue doing everything by the book: house-to-house calls, interviewing all the local tarts, appealing for punters who knew Sharon to come forward, total anonymity guaranteed - and all the rest. For a start, we'll see if the CRO and the collator have got anything on her. Maybe some sort of connection may show up.'

'But if we don't know who she really is, how—?'

'We'll have the place fingerprinted - there should be enough on the makeup jars and the kitchen stuff. And *maybe* if - when - we find out who she is, it'll open up another line of enquiry on both her and Sharon.'

It would not so much open up a new line of enquiry as lob in a massive bombshell.

Darren Webb should have been flattered by having been given charge of a case that had been taken away from his guvnor, but he didn't exactly feel that his cup runneth over; and what was in it had a bitter taste anyway. Even if Timberlake sometimes treated him as less than brilliant, Webb had a strong sense of loyalty to him, and his advancement to fill the place left by Timberlake's shift sideways to the Sharon Lester investigation seemed a rather hollow prize.

There was also a less altruistic reason for his misgivings. Webb had a foreboding that he wasn't going to win any brownie points for a burst of inspirational deduction and leadership.

Added to this was the niggling suspicion that maybe Timberlake had got things right again and Captain Mark Sibley was the perpetrator after all. But Darren Webb couldn't see why Timberlake insisted that it *had* to be Sibley; insisted that it was *obvious*, when it was clear that he had no possible motive.

Deep down in his subconscious was yet one more reason for his despondency, but it hadn't come to the surface yet.

His last major row between his wife Naomi and himself had not been totally forgotten. When he got home this particular evening Naomi had decided to make one of her heroic attempts to try to repair their relationship. After all, she did love him, she told herself, and she knew he was a copper when she married him. He wasn't a bad sort of man, really.

The only trouble with her good intention was that the effort she was making was as obvious as veins standing out on her forehead.

In any case, Webb wasn't inclined to react to Naomi's mood. All he wanted was peace, quiet and no need to dissimulate. When Naomi asked solicitously,

'Are you feeling tired, darling?' he instantly felt the way the wind was blowing.

Naomi did her best with a good meal, but with no perceptible success. She played what was going to be her last card. 'Darren, what is it? Something's upset you, it's obvious. Tell me what it is? Maybe I can help?'

'No I don't think so, thanks. It's nothing you can do. It's work.'

'Getting it off your chest is better than bottling it all up inside you. That'd help.'

He reflected for a long moment, then took a step over the edge and into the abyss. He told her.

'I'm taking over the Mary Docker investigation from Harry. I don't think the super's satisfied with the way he's doing it. I'm running it now.'

Naomi was taken aback. 'But that's good, isn't it?'

'He's got my case. I wanted to keep it. I was doing all right with it.' This, of course, was a wild exaggeration.

'What case was that?'

He wanted to bite his tongue, but he had to answer. 'The Sharon Lester murder.'

'But she was only a prostitute! That other woman was—'

' "Just a prostitute"? She was a human being. Oh, I know, no one worries much if a prostitute, or a . . . burglar, or a child molester is murdered. It's a case of "slag on slag".'

'If you were doing so well why did he take you off the case'?'

His bad mood made him careless. Unthinkingly he said 'He reckoned I was too personally involved.'

'*Personally* involved?'

Darren Webb was aware too late, far too late, that he was in free fall to disaster. He tried vainly to clutch on to something. 'She was one of my snouts.'

'That's not all she was, was she? I knew it! You were fucking her!'

'Don't be bloody stupid! Of course I wasn't!' If he had been telling the truth with total sincerity and a clear conscience she wouldn't have believed him anyway; but as it was, she sensed from his tone that he was lying. The only thing she got wrong was that it had been a one-off.

'If you've given me anything you've caught from that whore I'll *kill* you! You hear me?'

'I should think half the sodding street has heard you!' His mental reactions were sharp now after his first faux pas; he didn't make the mistake of saying 'I wore a condom.'

'I want you to have a blood test. Tomorrow!'

'*You* have one. There's nothing wrong with me.'

'I can't get over it . . . screwing a filthy whore . . .'

Again he resisted the impulse to say 'She wasn't filthy.' Instead he said, 'I see. So I suppose it would've been all right if I'd shagged one of your girlfriends.' People can say stupid things when they're angry. And when they're not, come to that.

Naomi knifed him from head to foot and back again with a look, turned and shouted over her shoulder, 'You're not sleeping with me again, ever! You can come into the bedroom for your clothes, but that's it. I don't want to see you in it, you hear me?'

'I bloody heard you the first time,' was the best Darren Webb could muster.

She went into the bedroom briefly, then threw into

the lounge blankets and a pillow which lay in an untidy heap on the floor. Darren Webb stamped out of the flat, slamming the door behind him on his way to the pub.

Poppy Monroe was a whore, and amiable enough with it for someone of her profession. As a result she had quite a few regular clients. Inevitably she was known to all her friends and customers as Marilyn; inevitably so because she was blonde and big-boobed.

One of her most recent regulars was a man she knew as Simon, but she guessed that he had as much right to that name as she had to Marilyn. Not many punters – at least, of the married ones – give their real names to prostitutes.

Marilyn closed the door of her tiny flat – one of Willy's in The Grove – as Simon took off his rather special light-coloured raincoat and put it neatly over the back of a chair. This was his fifth or sixth visit and he had been a model client. He handed over her 'little present' in advance without demur, and didn't ask for anything he hadn't paid for, unlike some punters who paid the lowest rate and then asked for a complete strip or a bout of French halfway through. Marilyn's response to this sort of liberty-taking was a short, sharp, 'You haven't paid for it, you can't have it.' Giving freebie extras wasn't her style. Besides, she didn't care for fellatio, even for money. Trying to sound American but with a magnificent lack of appreciation for what she was saying, she told her friends, 'Fellatio sucks.'

For all that Simon was quiet, clean, had no tattoos or weird habits and didn't ask for sex without a condom. Marilyn had a tiny, niggling sense of unease about him. Although punters come in many shapes and sizes, Simon didn't seem to fit any of them. 'Maybe it's me old age,' she told herself. She was twenty-nine.

'How are you, darling?' she said automatically. 'I've missed you. Nobody makes me feel like you do.' She walked away from him towards the bed, taking off her blouse as she went, he came up behind her.

'Really?' he asked. He put his hands round her, gently, and held her breasts.

'Honest.' She made what she thought was a sexy, purring sound. For a moment she didn't realize that he still had his gloves on.

Without warning, before she had time to react, his right arm came up and his forearm pressed cruelly against her throat as he pulled her close to him. His left hand grabbed his own right wrist to increase the already fatal pressure. Marilyn had time only to try to scratch his hands – vainly, because of the gloves – before everything started to go black. She died, silently, with horrifying suddenness.

He held her body upright, his forearm still pressing against her throat with crushing force for half a minute before lowering her noiselessly on to the bed. He took off a glove and felt for a pulse in her neck. There was none.

Simon put his glove back on before going to the top drawer of the small dressing table where Marilyn always put the punters' money and took it out. He retrieved the notes he had just paid her from the wad, and put them into an inside jacket pocket. Next, he picked up his reversible light-coloured raincoat and turned it inside out, transforming it into a dark-blue coat. He put it on, stuffed the rest of the money into one pocket, and took out a dark cap from the other. He pulled the cap well down and turned up the collar of the raincoat.

Simon opened the door a few inches and peered out. Even if someone had seen him, the gesture would not have looked out of place. Punters often slunk out, trying to avoid being recognized. Satisfied, he came out of the flat. The door closed behind him with a soft click from the Yale lock.

He left the house by the back door, passed through the small, dark garden to the pathway. No one saw him walk swiftly towards its far end and into the next street to The Grove.

Two streets further on he crossed to the kerb, looked round quickly, bent down and pushed the money from Poppy's flat through the bars of a drain.

He smiled faintly as he thought of some lucky sewer worker who would see the money come floating towards him.

He had one last task to perform. When he got home he undressed, carefully cut out all the labels from his suit, and put it into a bin bag. Next morning, on his way to work he dumped the bag, unobserved by anyone, into one of the tall wheelie bins standing in an alleyway by the side of a large office building. It was never seen again. The murderer was an intelligent and thorough man. He was making sure that fibres he had left on Poppy Monroe's back could not be matched up with any of his clothes.

Chapter Ten

Despite appearances, life had taken a small upturn for Sarah Lewis, for a couple of reasons. It was nothing to write home about, but there was no one at home to write to anyway. She was back on observation in the suspected drugs-dealing case, but on this occasion it was at a different time of the day and at a different location. This surveillance was just after the last class of the day at Parkside Comprehensive School.

Opposite the school, set back from the roadway, was a line of decrepit lock-up garages clinging to a high wall running alongside a railway line. Anyone trying to get in or out of the garages had to thread a way through, or around, the cars and commercial vehicles in all stages of decay parked in the street opposite the school.

One of those vehicles was a plain dark van containing Sarah Lewis and her temporary partner. Sarah had discovered that Obekachi also sold his ice-cream at the end of the scholastic day at Parkside Comprehensive. After the mid-morning stint at Abbot Perceval Secondary Modern, Obekachi drove round residential streets to make a few casual sales, before making a brief trip home at lunchtime, presumably to stock up again. By keeping him under observation twice a day she reasoned that she had twice as much chance of catching him doing something nefarious.

Her partner in the van was DC Benny Holmes. Any detective named Holmes is inevitably called Sherlock, which can become wearisome after the first ten years. Benny Holmes was even more unfortunate than all the other Holmeses in the Met. He was a third-generation English Jew. His great-grandparents had escaped from a Russian pogrom, and when they eventually arrived in England to settle in Whitechapel, they changed their name from something virtually indecipherable and unpronounceable to Holmes. Why and how they had settled on this name nobody knew. The irreverent and coarse members of the Terrace Vale nick – especially the racially inclined ones – instantly nicknamed him Shylock Holmes. He took their jibes and excruciatingly feeble quips philosophically and equably. He laughed at some of them, especially at one detective constable's almost daily enquiry of how the little grey cells were working.

Benny Holmes had a very sharp mind and an acid wit that went over the heads of most of the constables and quite a few sergeants. He was forty-five years old, large, round and bald, built on not generous but extravagant lines, and he affected an Old Bill moustache – the Bairnsfather Old Bill, that is, not the Metropolitan Police version. Although he was in daily contact with thieves, muggers, drug pushers and the rest, he was a cheerful and optimistic person. Maybe he thought coming up against thieves, muggers, drug pushers and the rest was a definite improvement on his grandparents' existence.

He was a good detective, even though he was still

only a detective constable. Like most men he had a secret, unfulfilled ambition. When he was taken to the seaside as a small boy he had a couple of pony rides. From that moment on he wanted to ride horses. When he joined the force as a beat copper he was going to apply to be transferred to the mounted police but incautiously mentioned it to his father, who nearly exploded. 'My son wants to be a Cossack, coming home every night with the blood on his hands of innocent peasants he's crushed under his horse's hooves? Why not a Nazi, maybe, riding a tank?' It was useless to point out that the blood would hardly be on his hands, and in any case, innocent peasants were thin on the ground in the Metropolitan Police area. His mother simulated a heart attack with a dramatic power that would have left Sarah Bernhardt grinding her teeth with jealousy.

Benny Holmes was in the driver's seat of the van, a newspaper open on the steering wheel. Anyone who knew him would have spotted at once that he wasn't reading the paper because he wasn't wearing his glasses. His long sight, though, was excellent. He was dressed in a work shirt and overalls. Behind him, sitting on a bench, Sarah was in old jeans and a baggy black sweat-shirt.

They were a little early at Parkside Comprehensive and sat, unspeaking, until the raucous chimes of the ice-cream van made them sit up. It parked right opposite the gates. A few minutes later pupils jetted out of the school, some to go home, some adventurous ones to go to pubs . . . and some to buy ice-cream. Sarah watched from inside the police van, peering through the viewfinder of a 35mm camera with a

500mm telephoto lens aiming at the adults in the vicinity, while Holmes studied the children who had stopped ostensibly to buy ice-cream. Unfortunately their vantage point was not good, and they could get only a three-quarter rear view of the ice-cream van. They waited until the last customer had been served and the van set off with a last jangle of chimes and a short burst of 'The Sound of Music'.

Holmes started the engine and began to move off. 'Zilch,' he said. 'Did you see anything?'

Sarah shook her head. 'To tell you the truth, Sherlock, I don't think Obekachi is involved. He doesn't strike me as the type.'

'Oy! Famous last words. Haven't you got any leads from some of the kids, or their parents?'

'Not a sniff. That's one of the odd things about all this. Anyone who might possibly know something is too scared to talk. One family found some pot in their son's bedroom. He was from Abbot Perceval Secondary Modern. The mother came and tipped me off. I saw the boy but all he'd say was he found it in the street and he hadn't tried it himself. I couldn't budge him. I asked him which street he'd found it in, but—'

'He couldn't remember,' Holmes finished for her.

'Take me home, Sherlock.'

Mrs Jenny Timberlake, or as she preferred to be called, Miss Jenny Long, was feeling tetchy. In another woman her mood might have been put down to PMT, but Jenny didn't believe in it. Even if she had, any drugs she might have wanted were readily at hand as she was a consultant surgeon. It had been a long day and she had a headache. Surgery can be murder on the feet, too. She had come home to find Timberlake sunk in a chair staring at nothing. The day had been just as long for him, and a lot less satisfying. All the routine enquiries, house-to-house calls and interviews with local prostitutes in The Grove had produced nothing new in the Sharon Lester murder inquiry. He had come home to an empty house and had prepared bacon and eggs for himself, indifferent to anything Jenny might say about the cholesterol.

Harry Timberlake's and Jenny Long's backgrounds were very different. He was the son of a general labourer and hospital cleaner who lived in the docklands area of London. At school he sailed through all his examinations: because of what he called his facility for learning he got seven O levels and three A levels – English, sociology and history. He could have got a fourth in political science if they'd let him take it. His headmaster urged him to try for a university place, but the prospect had no attraction for him whatsoever. When he left school and started looking for a job, without thinking about it too much, Timberlake joined the police. It was an instinctive decision, and it was the right one.

He grew into a striking-looking man with a face of strong planes and deep-set eyes under thick eyebrows, which gave him a disconcerting, penetrating stare when he turned it on. Timberlake could have improved his east-London accent if he had wanted to, but he didn't bother.

Jenny Long had always had what the police sometimes call 'an educated accent'. She was the daughter of a hospital consultant physician with a lucrative private practice in the Surrey stockbroker belt. She went to a private school and on to Cambridge University where she began by reading law and switched to medicine after a year. Now a consultant general surgeon, she was tall, blonde and elegant. When Harry Timberlake first met Jenny she strongly reminded him of Joanna Lumley in her early *Avengers* days.

Initially they appeared an ill-sorted couple, and their relationship once broke down completely for a year, as each of them found other partners – in his case Sarah Lewis, an arrangement they managed to keep secret from everyone at Terrace Vale. However, Timberlake and Jenny eventually returned to each other and he finally made the commitment to marriage that Jenny wanted. To his surprise, he found he enjoyed the arrangement. At first.

The marriage, which began with such bright promise, became dull and tarnished. Both of them were aware of it, but neither knew why. When Timberlake reflected about the reason – which was not often, he accepted the fact like bad weather and taxes – he thought that it was because they were seeing more of each other than when they were just lovers. Or maybe it was just the opposite: because of the demands of their work they were together less than they expected to be as a married couple.

Probably Jenny didn't mean to appear superior to her husband, but often these days she succeeded in thoroughly infuriating him. The first poison dart into his sensibilities on this occasion was her reaction to one of the letters, which had arrived after she left for hospital. It was in a thick cream envelope, which looked as if it cost more than the first-class stamp. The letter itself had an embossed heading with a list of offices in some thirty major cities worldwide.

'Oh, damn. Damn, damn, damn,' Jenny said.

Timberlake didn't ask her what was wrong: he had his own problems. He simply acknowledged he had heard her with, 'Uhuh'.

'It's from my accountant. He says the tax inspector is querying some of my expenses for the past year. He's increased my assessment by . . . *what?* . . . five thousand-odd! God, I pay the bloody accountant two and a half thousand just to do simple arithmetic. Why can't he deal with it?'

'Yeah. Tough.' Timberlake said, trying not to sound cynical. His early upbringing was in a society where the man was the breadwinner and the master of his home. If the woman went to work it was in a menial position and for low wages. Lately he had become increasingly aware of how his wife's income was much greater than his own, even though she was careful to avoid underlining it. Her skilful skating around the subject managed to pique him more than if she had boasted of it.

Jenny casually threw the letter on to the table. 'God, I'm starving. Darling, make me a sandwich or something.' She sat in an armchair and kicked off her shoes.

Timberlake was a hairsbreadth away from making a brutal answer. Instead he bit his tongue, got up and walked towards the kitchen.

Suzanne Oliver lived in the Hillside district of East Porton, a couple of police areas from Terrace Vale, although the only hill in the area would hardly make a pensioner get off his bike. Nevertheless, the name Hillside sounded fairly posh and suited the upper-middle-class homes of the neighbourhood, which didn't have anything as vulgar as a bus route running through the tree-lined, well-lit, residential streets. Her home was a first-floor flat with spacious rooms in a rambling, converted Edwardian house. There wasn't much of a view, particularly in summer, because the front garden had two flourishing cedar trees. It was a pleasant flat nevertheless.

Suzanne was a woman about thirty years of age, tall, with dark auburn hair, green eyes and a pale skin. She would have been beautiful were it not for her mouth, which was just a little too thick-lipped and slightly slack.

She usually wore the sort of plain suits favoured by off-duty solicitors and barristers in court. Some of her neighbours thought this was rather pretentious for someone who worked as a dealer in a Knightsbridge casino, even if it was the sort of place that supplied free smoked-salmon sandwiches and champagne to its seriously wealthy clientele. She rarely spoke to her neighbours, principally because her job meant that her life operated twelve hours out of synchronization with theirs. Casino staff are night workers, like most people in the live entertainment business. She was now returning home at her usual time of between 5 and 6 a.m.

Suzanne was lucky; there was a parking space very near her own house. She parked her car, carefully locked it and set the alarm. She walked through the wide front gate and down the path to the side door of the house, which opened on to a staircase that led directly to the upper floors. Suzanne sometimes felt that the dark pathway, although only fifteen yards long, was creepy, and she instinctively quickened her pace, her front-door key ready in her hand. She unlocked the door and stepped inside.

A man who had been waiting for her, hiding in the bushes along the pathway, silently followed her into the small hall at the foot of the stairs before she realized it, and slipped a thin nylon noose over her head from behind and pulled it murderously tight round her throat. Her unseen attacker lifted her off the floor, pulling the cord tighter so that it cut into her neck, breaking the skin. She had neither time nor breath to call out, nor could her feet drum against the floor in her all too brief death throes. The killer was not surprised how quickly Suzanne stopped struggling. After he let her body slide noiselessly to the floor he removed the nylon cord and felt for a pulse in the carotid artery. There was none.

He was about to leave the house when a thought struck him. He considered it for a moment, then nodded with satisfaction. He brutally jerked open her jacket, pulling off a button as he did so. Next he ripped her blouse, and broke a bra strap. He pushed her skirt above her waist, tore away her tights and knickers, and pulled up her knees.

Silently he exited, closing the door behind him. No one saw him leaving the house.

Chapter Eleven

Neither Harry Timberlake nor Darren Webb looked as if he was enjoying life. The morning conference had been as dull as an Icelandic weather report, with no one able to announce any sort of significant development in the murder inquiries. Nigel Larkin was as bright-eyed as ever, though, and even managed to hum cheerfully until Webb shut him up with a look.

Ten minutes after the meeting broke up Detective Superintendent Harkness called Timberlake into his office. He gave him time to sit down and said quietly, 'Everything all right, Harry?'

Timberlake was surprised. 'Yes, sir.'

'Because you're not looking a hundred per cent today.'

'Oh, too much to eat last night, I suppose. I'm in my slow-start mode.' He smiled unconvincingly. 'Nothing wrong, really.'

'Good,' Harkness said.

They both knew that there was a lot unsaid, and that each knew that the other was aware of it.

'I've just received a report from the fingerprint technician about the flat of the missing Vicki Stevens,' Harkness went on. He looked at a sheet of paper in front of him. 'She says she lifted some prints from the makeup jars and tubes that are very probably Stevens's, and a lot of others from various places in the flat. One of them was very interesting.'

Timberlake perked up.

Harkness went on, 'It was a print of a right thumb with a small star-shaped scar, which meant it was easier to identify than an ordinary print.' He paused. 'It's of a man named Dimitrios Ionides, aka. Dimi the Greek, date of birth 7th of August 1951. Obviously he's known to us.' He handed over the paper. 'You'll want to get his record.'

Dimitrios Ionides was, in fact, a Cypriot, born in Limasol. The photograph showed him to be a good-looking man who would have been almost handsome, albeit in a vulgar way, had it not been for his nose, which was two sizes too large. He arrived in England in 1966. He had an impressive criminal record which included wounding, demanding money with menaces and living on immoral earnings. Of his thirty years in England, nearly half of them had been spent in jail. His last known address was near the Peacehaven Hill area.

Dimitrios Ionides's flat was in a modern block just beyond the invisible boundary line between the vice-ridden slums of Peacehaven Hill and a relatively respectable middle-class area of Tory voters. Although there was no spill-over of the licentious activities of The Gut into the adjoining Abbey Gardens ward, there was practically visible hostility between the two areas. Abbey Gardens residents wrote letters to the police, the local newspaper and to the council about the disgusting goings-on at the bottom of their road, and even campaigned to have a wall built between them and the neighbouring vice-traders. For their part, the pimps and drug dealers sounded the horns of their large American cars and dumped rubbish as they drove through Abbey Gardens late at night. The prostitutes didn't do anything other than just stand about, smoking and squawking, within sight of their enraged neighbours.

There was no answer when Timberlake and Nigel Larkin knocked, rang and hammered on the door of Dimitrios Ionides's flat. The standard door had been replaced with a tasteful, custom-made bronze affair, with a Bramah lock, the one that even MI5 specialists can't pick. Timberlake tried to peer through the letter-box, but it was blocked off by what he guessed was a steel box.

The caretaker and general factotum of the block of flats was a tall, ruddy-faced man who looked like an ex-military policeman or naval Master-at-Arms. He announced himself as Charles Whatmore. 'Mr Ionides?' he said, investing the simple 'Mr' with a whole wealth of innuendoes. 'Haven't seen him for the last couple of days. Hasn't put his rubbish out, either.' 'Rubbish' carried as many shades of meaning as 'Mr'.

Timberlake turned to Larkin. 'Well, we'll have to try his women, see if any of them has any idea where he is.'

If they did know anything, they successfully kept the information to themselves. The Gut's tarts, and other creatures in the illegal underclass of the local society, and Dimitrios's neighbours in his block of flats either had no idea where he was, or claimed they didn't. In any case, no one seemed very concerned at his absence.

Dimitrios Ionides, aka. Dimi the Greek, had disappeared as completely as Vicki Stevens.

Sarah Lewis had dirty-grey hair poking out from under a woollen stocking hat, a shapeless duffel coat, torn jeans and battered trainers. She was in the Fox and Duck – a pub whose name led itself irresistibly to a deliberate spoonerism by its patrons – situated well away from the Terrace Vale area. She didn't seem out of place, for the public bar didn't have sawdust on the floor only because the landlord considered it an unnecessary extravagance. She sat at a table in the corner of the bar with half a pint of Guinness in front of her. On the seat next to her was an old shopping bag crammed full of God knows what, with a pile of magazines on top. Prominent among them was a copy of *Hello!*. Even when she was in a near-meltdown temper as she was now, Sarah's sense of humour survived.

The first moment his mother saw Jocko McLeish she wondered how quickly she could get him adopted, but no one would have him. Time did not improve him. Now he was a nondescript man with a razor scar on his forehead which gave one eyebrow a quizzical curl. He didn't look trustworthy enough to tell you the right time

Jocko took a single pace into the pub, stood in the doorway and looked round the bar. As soon as Sarah caught his eye she summoned him over with a movement of her head.

'You're fucking late,' she hissed at him.

'Sorry. Business,' he said out of the corner of his mouth. 'You know.' He had the gravelly voice of a long-time meths-drinking, forty-a-day smoker. The man was one of Sarah's snouts.

Sarah slipped some coins across the table top. 'And get me another Guinness,' she said.

He looked at the coins reproachfully, but didn't dare to say anything before he turned to go to the bar.

'Well?' she asked when they were sitting down together with their drinks in front of them. 'Any word on who's dealing at the school?'

McLeish evaded the question. 'Haven't any of the kids said nothing? Or the parents?'

'From what I can find out the kids either don't know or are too scared of what'll happen to them if they say anything.'

'I did hear a wee something.' Jocko was always a stage Scot. He waited for Sarah to react. When she didn't he rubbed his forefinger and thumb together in the universal gesture meaning money.

'I'll see what it's worth first,' Sarah said flatly.

'They reckon it's the spade who sells ice-cream from a van.'

Sarah snorted. 'Bollocks,' she said audibly enough for people round her to hear, to help reinforce her persona as a young bag lady. Then, softly, 'We've been watching him. It's not him.'

McLeish was not put off. 'You just haven't seen him do it, is all.' In a wheedling tone he said, 'Look, Sarah, I—'

'I've told you! Don't call me Sarah.'

'Oh, sorry. Look, miss, I'm right skint. Couldn't

you manage a wee something on account?' He looked desperate.

'On account of what?' But Sarah, despite acting tough, had a soft centre. Under the cover of the table she passed him a ten-pound note. 'You'd better earn it, and come up with something hard.' She could see that Jocko McLeish was about to risk a dirty reply. She gave him a stare that froze his tongue. 'Right, I'm off. Don't come out with me.'

She got up and shuffled away. Outside in the street, keeping well back, she peered into the pub through the dirty window. McLeish went straight to the bar, bought a double vodka and twenty cigarettes, which cost more than half of the money Sarah had given him. However, he didn't speak to anyone except the barman and didn't go to the telephone. He had given her a few fairly good tips in the past, but she still didn't trust him farther than she could spit into a Force Seven wind.

Nigel Larkin, accompanied by the physically imposing Detective Constable Jeff Waters, continued fishing in the dirty waters of The Gut for news of Dimitrios Ionides's whereabouts, but didn't come up with as much as an old boot. It was an education for Larkin, whose first experience as a uniformed constable had been in a middle-class residential suburb so well-ordered that the empty milk bottles put out for collection were always thoroughly rinsed and sparkling. Terrace Vale was a few steps down the social ladder, but even there somehow he was never sent to patrol the more lively sections. Now he was suffering something of a culture shock. He concealed it manfully.

Timberlake decided to continue the search for Dimi the Greek from the other end of the trail, at The Grove. He picked a hell of a night for it: all London was shivering under a sleeting rain with an icy wind that had come straight from Spitsbergen. There were only a couple of pavement princesses visibly on duty at The Grove, and Timberlake had to admire them for their ingenuity as well as their fortitude. They both had transparent umbrellas and transparent plastic raincoats over their normal working outfits that would have got them arrested on a Spanish beach.

They were stationed outside a café called The Jack in the Box. The window sported a small logo of a traditional jack-in-the-box, although the shape of the jack was highly equivocal. In the warm, well-lit and surprisingly clean interior were half a dozen prostitutes grouped round a table. In a corner of the place a couple of elderly men were chomping away slowly on sausages and chips. They weren't bothering to look at the women.

As Timberlake walked in one or two of them started to get up to slip away, but he said genially, 'Don't worry. This isn't a bust.'

Whistling Kettle said something quietly to the others at the table, and they stayed seated, but remained wary.

Timberlake sat down next to Whistling. 'Hello. Got over the shock of the other night?' he asked kindly.

'More or less. I get a funny feeling when I go past that door, though.'

Two of her working companions laughed coarsely.

'You ought to make 'em pay extra for that,' one of them said.

Timberlake ordered tea all round and offered cigarettes, although he never smoked himself.

'You know what I'm after,' he said at last.

This set off some more vulgar giggles. 'As the weather's keeping the punters at home with wifey you can have three for the price of two tonight,' Carmen, the self-appointed wit of the group, said. Timberlake felt he should be flattered.

'It's about Sharon Lester and Vicki Stevens. I suppose none of you have heard from Vicki?' He waited, but no one spoke. 'We know Dimi the Greek was in her place, but we can't find him either. Any of you any ideas?' He waited for a moment. 'I know you don't like talking to our lot, but this is for one of your friends, and there's always the possibility he was involved in Sharon's killing.'

Again, Kettle was the first one to speak. Timberlake's sympathetic treatment of her on the night of Sharon Lester's murder was bringing its reward.

'That bastard,' she said viciously. 'He's been trying to put the frighteners on some of us.'

'I always said it was too good to last,' said a young woman no more than twenty years old. She looked fresh and bright-eyed, and was dressed conservatively by local standards. She identified herself as 'Emma'.

'How exactly?' Timberlake asked

He was answered by a black girl of unidentifiable age, wearing a pair of micro-shorts and a bolero jacket fastened with a ribbon tied in a loose bow.

'I'm Patti,' she said. 'It used to be peaceful round here, with no macaronis causing no grief. Well, not much. But now . . . ponces are trying to move in. Dimi tried to put the frighteners on me. I told him to get stuffed.'

'Willy told me there aren't any pimps at all round here,' Timberlake said.

Carmen, the oldest one of the group, a raw-boned woman with a leonine head, wearing an almost-see-through blouse and tight trousers, gave a muffled snort of derisive laughter. 'Willy wouldn't know if his balls had caught fire if somebody didn't tell him.'

A meek-looking teenager, sporting a gold-coloured crucifix at her throat and dressed soberly enough to go to church, nodded vigorously. She rejoiced in the name of 'God-botherer'. Her punters fell into two groups. There were some timid men who didn't want to be seen walking ten yards with an obvious prostitute. The majority were weirdos with fantasies about having sex with the vicar's daughter, and with novices in mufti.

'Dimitrios tried it on with me,' she said in a Louisa M. Alcott voice. 'I dunno whether I want to stick around here much longer if we're going to have pimps harassing us all the time, particularly after Sharon Lester was murdered.'

'And what's happened to Vicki?' Carmen said in a throaty contralto. 'And the others?'

'Others?' Timberlake said sharply.

'Red Janie and Marilyn, for a start. They haven't been around for a while.'

'Marilyn told me she was thinking of packing it in here,' Whistling said. 'I wouldn't be a bit surprised if she decided to find another pitch. I'm having second thoughts myself.'

'Then the sooner I can find Dimitrios the better,' Timberlake said. 'Any ideas?'

'There's a working girl over at Peacehaven called Big Bertha Cannon. Have your lot spoken to her?'

'I don't think so,' Timberlake said. 'I'll check. Why would she know?'

'She loves him, the silly cow. She'll know if anyone does.'

'But whether she'll tell you . . .' Patti said.

'By the way,' Timberlake said. 'I thought that these days you pick up most of your punters by telephone. Why do you have to work the pavements?'

Carmen looked at him with a wry expression. 'You don't use public phone boxes much, do you?'

'Hardly at all.'

'Well, the local council are a right pain in the arse load of busybodies. After all, phone boxes don't belong to them, but they've got Christ knows how many teams going round taking down our cards. As soon as our carders stick 'em up, the sodding clean-up squads are round taking them down again. And BT are putting the block on our phone numbers.'

'I've got cards put up in Southington, where they aren't so fussy,' Whistling Kettle told him, 'but punters won't drag their arses all the way over here when they can get laid five minutes away from where they're phoning.'

One of the two girls outside the café put her head round the door. 'It's stopped raining,' she announced.

The women at Timberlake's table pushed their chairs back and prepared to go out on patrol. The last one to leave was Emma, the fresh-faced young woman in the modest clothes. Timberlake stared at her curiously.

Emma smiled. 'Go on, say it,' she said.

'Say what?'

'What's a nice girl like me doing whoring in a place like this?'

'I was thinking it, but I wasn't going to ask.'

'I'm at university. I can't cope on my student grant, and I can't get a decent part-time job, so . . .' She shrugged. 'Two or three nights a week here and I can manage comfortably. And have time for study.'

'Studying what?'

She smiled. 'Medicine. And my speciality won't be venereology. Definitely.'

As Timberlake and Nigel Larkin entered the Terrace Vale station to type up their reports they passed Sergeant Rumsden, who was preparing to log off for the day. Before he had finished tidying, the phone rang. The two detectives were halfway up the stairs to the CID offices when Rumsden called out after them.

'Guv,' he said. 'There's been another one.'

Willy Manley had found Poppy 'Marilyn' Monroe's body. Uncharacteristically she was nearly a week late in paying her rent, and with some of the girls leaving the area, Willy decided to see if Poppy had done a moonlight flit as well. He knocked on the door of her small flat a couple of times before opening it with his master key.

It took him only a few seconds – which seemed like minutes to him – to see that Poppy was dead. He slammed the door shut and ran back to his own place where he drank a triple scotch to steady his nerves before phoning the police.

Timberlake was suffering another sensation of *déjà vu* – no, it was something more bizarre than that, bordering on the supernatural. It was as if he were caught up in a film loop which was repeating the same scene over and over again. The personnel of the SOCO team examining Poppy Monroe's flat were exactly the same as the one that dealt with Sharon Lester's murder, and the uniformed police keeping back the public and the media representatives were all too familiar. The undertakers with their plain black van who came to take the body away to the morgue – contrary to television and film drama, ambulances don't take bodies – were the same crew as last time. As for Professor Mortimer, it seemed to Timberlake he had known the pathologist all his life.

Mortimer, inevitably accompanied by the tweed-covered Gertrude Hacker, was as taciturn as usual. 'Death by strangulation, of course. From the marks on her neck it is most probable that her assailant attacked her from behind and killed her with pressure from his forearm. Death occurred rapidly.'

'How long ago?'

'More than forty-eight hours, less than a week. I may be able to narrow the time span after the autopsy.'

PC Brian Pegg very rarely wore his uniform jacket, and almost never wore his helmet. The only time he wore the full rig was at ceremonial parades and funerals, although he did wear his jacket on duty twice in the office when the central heating at Terrace Vale failed. In shirtsleeves he could have been mistaken for a second-hand car salesman, or a rather dodgy financial adviser. In fact he was a rather pleasant young man, although he wasn't as witty as he thought he was, and even less irresistible to women.

Pegg's prodigious memory made him a brilliant collator – a sort of intelligence gatherer. His files were an absolute treasure trove of arcane and apparently trivial information which could often prove to be priceless but was not to be found on official computer files.

Brian Pegg was the obvious person for Sarah and Benny Holmes to turn to.

The three of them sat at a table with a great pile of still photographs and photographs lifted from the video tapes. Sarah and Benny had just about given up hope of Pegg finding any possible suspects when he stared at one photograph for a long time.

'Have you got a copy of this one, or can you get one?' he asked.

'Sure. Why?' Sarah asked.

'Do you remember seeing this chummy?'

Sarah looked at the picture. 'Yes,' she said flatly. If Pegg was going to play mysterious, so was she.

Pegg took a black marker pen from a drawer and very carefully drew a beard on the man's face, then darkened and added to his sparse grey hair. Still remaining silent, he went to his files and eventually found the one he was looking for. He put it on the table before the two detectives.

The subject was one Alfred Herbert Gunter, date of birth 23rd of June 1942. His height, weight and general description was given followed by a list of convictions. The first one was the important one.

> 17.11.67. Sentenced at Inner London Crown Court to four years for possession of 2.5 kilos of cannabis. Released from Parkhurst 10.6.72.

There followed a few further convictions after 1972 until 1982, all for minor offences: drunkenness, disturbing the peace, things of that nature.

Studying the photograph of the man on the record, Sarah said, 'I wouldn't have recognized him if you hadn't drawn the beard and done the hair on our photo.'

'Yeah, well done, Peggy,' Benny Holmes said.

Brian Pegg hated to be called Peggy, but he managed to keep his resentment to himself. 'Thanks, Shylock,' he said with an innocent smile. 'Anyway, do you know who he is?'

'Oh, yes, we know who he is, all right,' Sarah said darkly.

Chapter Twelve

Since the murder of Mary Docker, Mrs Freda Phillips, the treasure of a cleaning woman, had become something of a local celebrity. For once her various employers were keen to listen to her as she milked her relationship with poor Mary Docker to the last drop. Each time she coloured and extended her version until she was practically painting a garish picture of how she was the one who found the body, and narrowly escaped being murdered herself as the crazed assassin brushed against her as he made his escape.

Quite soon she half convinced herself that this is what had actually happened, and she worked herself into a state of major jitters. As a result, she had been taking medication for her nerves: a minimum dose of benzodiazepine prescribed by her doctor, and a powerful extra dose of her favourite Algerian red, contrary to her doctor's strict instructions. Fortunately she drove nothing more dangerous than a vacuum cleaner, and the heaviest machinery she operated was a corkscrew. So nowadays she was a little slower than usual, but her anxiety attacks were diminishing.

Suzanne Oliver, like all Freda's clients, trusted her with keys to her flat. As Freda opened the street-level door to Suzanne Oliver's flat she kicked against newspapers and letters on the mat. Puzzled, she bent down to pick them up. Not until she straightened up did she see the obviously dead body of Suzanne Oliver sprawled at the bottom of the stairs.

Freda Phillips gave something like a whinny and took a deep, shuddering breath to scream, but she fainted before she could make another sound. She fell motionless, close to Suzanne Oliver's corpse. It was an even bet which one of them looked the worse.

Two young Americans were the unfortunate persons to come on the scene. They were Jehovah's Witnesses who were prepared for most of the receptions they were given in the course of their missionary work, but two dead bodies – as they thought – taxed even their self-possession. It was made even more fragile when Freda Phillips sat up with a jerk and finally managed to scream.

The River Thames is, of course, a tidal river as far as Teddington. At Mortlake, where the Boat Race ends, the difference between a very low tide and a very high one can be over twenty feet. Depending on the state of the tide when a floating object falls, or is thrown into the water, it could be tossed up on the river bank almost anywhere. Or even not at all, if it goes drifting out to sea.

The naked body of a male of about fifty years of age came ashore on the mud near a bend in the river near Fossefields – so named because bodies from the Great Plague were buried in mass graves there, although not many of the modern residents realized that. Where this cadaver had gone into the water was anyone's guess. There were two unusual features about it. The first was that the feet were tied together with rope, which had a trailing length of some three or four feet. The end was frayed as if it had rubbed against some hard surface, or perhaps been chewed up by the propeller of a motorboat. The second peculiarity was the presence of four bullet holes: one in the back of the head, the others through the chest, including one in the heart. When the river police fished the corpse from the mud, without difficulty they rapidly deduced that death was not due to suicide or accident. It also seemed highly probable that when the victim had originally been thrown into the water, there was a weight attached to the rope.

The body was taken to Fossefields mortuary. This area was on the other side of the Thames from Terrace Vale, and in another AMIP area. The local pathologist here had a problem with fingerprinting the corpse because the skin of the hands and other parts of the body was macerated; that is, white and wrinkled. First he injected the bulbs of the fingers with glycerine from below the joint. Next, he manipulated the finger tips between his thumb and index finger. With great care he cut around each joint below the bulb, then gently removed the skin like a finger-stall, and slipped it over his own finger in its thin surgical glove. Then he was able to do the fingerprinting in the normal way.

Identification of the fingerprints was quicker than usual. The search to match the prints with a set on record was made simple because of one peculiarity: the right thumb had a distinctive star-shaped scar.

A detective superintendent arrived from Scotland

Yard the next day and began putting together a murder squad.

The murder of Suzanne Oliver in East Porton was about to seriously disrupt the professional lives of most of the coppers, and the private lives of some of them, in Terrace Vale. This was because East Porton was in the same AMIP area. Although there was no obvious connection between the Suzanne Oliver murder and the goings-on in Terrace Vale, Detective Superintendent Harkness had to take charge of this case as well. It was more convenient to centre both investigations at Terrace Vale because the nick was large enough to accommodate the murder squads investigating the Mary Docker and Sharon Lester murders, and the disappearances of Vicki Stevens and Dimi the Greek. The top floor of the grim pile normally housed only dust, some mice and a lot of spiders. East Porton seconded some officers to Terrace Vale, but this extra investigation put a strain on Terrace Vale's human resources.

One of the victims of the overload was Sarah Lewis. For some time she had been having very little contact with Detective Chief Inspector Greening. This was not really surprising, for he tried to avoid contact with anyone who was doing any work in case he had to make a decision. As far as the operation involving Sarah and Benny 'Shylock' Holmes was concerned he simply said Shylock could run it: he was an experienced detective and he had every confidence in him.

When Sarah was told that Greening wanted to see her, she knew from long experience it was going to be for something unpleasant.

'You're on your own for the surveillance at Abbot Perceval and Parkside schools,' he said. No 'sorry', no 'hard luck'.

'They want Shylock in with the murder squads,' he added.

'But we've just got a good lead on the probable dealer,' Sarah said angrily. 'We might need two of us on it if something breaks. At least two.'

'Pity,' Greening said with massive hypocrisy. 'But it's out of my hands. And don't start looking for any overtime.'

Sarah stamped out, angry on principle, her brow like storm clouds over Snowdon. When she had calmed down a little she became aware of strongly conflicting emotions. She was going to have a tough and almost certainly boring time on her own, but at the same time she was relieved that she hadn't been taken off an inquiry where she thought there was a good chance of getting a result. She was still discontented because she would also have liked to be involved in the inquiry into the serious, major crime of murder. She said some very rude things in Welsh, which somehow was more satisfying than in English.

Three detectives of the East Porton area – an inspector, a sergeant and a detective constable – reported for duty at Terrace Vale the next morning. First, they had to brief Detective Superintendent Harkness on the Suzanne Oliver murder at the daily conference with the other members of the murder squads. The immediate question the meeting had to decide was whether there was a connection between the recent prostitute murders – and maybe the disappearances – and Suzanne Oliver's killing.

The Mary Docker case, it was rapidly agreed, was not linked with the murder of Sharon Lester or Poppy Monroe, nor the disappearance of Vicki Stevens. These three women were all whores, and an unmistakable pattern was emerging of a serial killer with a grudge against prostitutes. In fact one or two newspapers were already bandying about the name Jack the Ripper II.

Suzanne Oliver did not fit the general pattern, either. She was not from The Grove area, and she had a regular job. On the face of it, she was the victim of an attempted rape that had been interrupted before it was consummated.

The East Porton DI reported on the preliminary investigations into her murder. So far they had turned up practically nothing: Suzanne Oliver's neighbours had almost nothing to say about her. They saw her go out to work in the evening and once or twice early risers and a milkman had seen her returning home. During the day she might have been the Invisible Woman as far as they were concerned.

'What about her workplace?' Harkness asked.

'We don't know where that is, yet. All the neighbours could say was that she worked as a croupier in a West End casino. There's nothing in the flat to tell us. I planned on phoning round the casinos as soon as we're settled in here, and can have a go at the local National Insurance office, if that's all right with you, sir.'

'Good idea,' Harkness nodded. He turned to Darren Webb. 'Are we any further with the Mary Docker case?'

'Not yet, sir,' Webb replied, trying to sound optimistic.

It was not one of Terrace Vale's better days. Progress on the inquiries into the other murders – Sharon Lester and Poppy Monroe – and the disappearances of Vicki Stevens and Dimi the Greek were no more promising. The general feeling among the detectives was that they were all thrashing about, treading water in Army boots.

However, the general sense of frustration was lightened a little by a message that came through just as the morning conference was about to break up. Harkness gave a small cough, which was nevertheless loud enough to silence the chatter from the detectives.

'The body of a man taken from the river near Fossefields has been identified as Dimitrios Ionides,' Harkness announced. 'He had been shot four times.' He looked at Harry. 'That makes it our investigation, the body is being taken for autopsy tomorrow, nine-thirty, at Professor Mortimer's hospital. I'll come with you.'

Timberlake didn't let it worry him too much that his spirits were raised by the news that a waterlogged body had been dragged from the Thames, near the site of an ancient mass grave full of plague victims. He took the positive view that perhaps this was a breakthrough that would open the way to finding a murderer. He was getting up from his desk to go out when his phone rang.

'It's me,' said a familiar voice which he couldn't identify for the moment. 'Whistling. Whistling Kettle.' She sounded badly stressed.

'Hello. What can I do for you, Whistling?'

'Can we have a meet?'

'Sure. When and where?'

'My place. Not my working flat. I don't want anyone round there to see us.' She gave him her home address.

'All right to bring my DC?'

'Does he look like the Old Bill?'

Timberlake glanced at Larkin. If anything he looked like a theology undergraduate bursting with faith.

'Hardly.'

She thought for a moment. 'No, better not. This is just between you and me. I'm not saying anything in front of a witness. And I don't want *anyone* – round here or at The Grove – to know I'm talking to you lot. So for Christ's sake don't come in a police car. Better leave it at the end of the street in White Cross Road. Some bugger may come along and block your way out.' She added, mysteriously, 'And bring a big briefcase with you.'

Lil 'Whistling' Kettle lived in Southington, in Gateway Street, a road of what were once cottages for railway workers. Now they were 'town houses', which is house-agent speak for 'tiny and expensive'. Most of the locals were employed in the media or some branch of the arts, although there were a few civil servants as well. Railwaymen of the time when the cottages were built didn't have cars, of course, so there were no private garages. Cars were parked nose to tail on both sides of the road. If a delivery van had to visit Gateway Street, the street was totally blocked until the driver deigned to move his vehicle. One of the local amusements was to watch the arguments when two vans arrived in Gateway Street from different directions. Timberlake was grateful for the warning. He left his car where Whistling had suggested.

Mrs Kettle, as she was known locally, lived in one of the two up, two down cottages, with nothing about it to give the least hint of how she earned her living. The few people in the street who knew her thought she was a despatcher for a large minicab firm, who preferred to work nights because the pay was better.

When Timberlake arrived at her front door, she greeted him loudly, for the benefit of the neighbours, 'Oh, you've come to see about the television.'

Timberlake nodded and held up the briefcase. 'Clever stuff,' he said as he walked in. The small house was neat, tidy and comfortably furnished, but there wasn't room to swing a kitten.

'Always dealing with bastards who think you're fair game makes you keep your wits about you,' Whistling said. She looked awful. She lit a fresh cigarette from the stub of the one she was smoking. An ashtray was full to overflowing, and an empty glass stood next to a half-bottle of scotch. Timberlake gave her time to recover. She indicated the bottle as an invitation to Timberlake, but he shook his head. She poured a hefty one for herself and took a gulp. It didn't seem to have any effect on her.

'Can I trust you?' she said suddenly.

'Would you expect me to say no? You've got to make up your own mind, Kettle.'

She let out a great, shuddering sigh. 'I've got to tell

someone, for God's sake. But this is between you and me. If you tell anyone I'll deny I ever said it.'

'Which is why you didn't want a witness.'

'Right.'

Somehow this seemed to steady her a little. She licked her lips. 'Last week, one of my mates came over to see me at The Grove. Big Bertha. I was walking along with her, towards that café, the Jack in the Box, when Dimi the Greek comes up to us.' Timberlake nodded casually, although he was immediately alert.

Kettle went on, 'I think he was going to try to recruit us, you know, when this dirty great car drives up, nearly as big as an American limo, on to the pavement, beside us.' Her breathing quickened, and beads of perspiration appeared on her forehead and upper lip. 'Out of the back jumps this fucking great spade, the most evil looking bastard I've ever seen.' She shuddered and took another swig of the whisky. 'He dragged out a gun and told us – all three of us – to get into the car, or he'd kill us right there and then. I was going to scream, but my throat had gone all seized up and I couldn't make a sound. Then he belted me across the jaw with the gun.'

Kettle turned her head, and for the first time Timberlake saw a long, purplish bruise which she had concealed from him, running from the point of her chin to just below her ear.

'He was stark, staring fucking crazy, Mr Timberlake. His eyes . . . no whites, all red, standing out . . . There was spit at the corners of his mouth . . . Christ knows what he was on – probably that American stuff Angel Dust.'

'PCP,' Timberlake said. 'Phencyclidine.'

'Whatever. He was worse than a wild animal . . .' She was trembling. 'You've guessed who it was, haven't you?'

'I've never met him professionally, but he sounds like Yardbird Charlie.' Timberlake thought it ironic, or something, that this violent criminal had the same nickname as Charlie 'The Bird', or occasionally 'Yardbird', Parker, the incomparable jazz saxophonist.

Kettle gathered herself, and then went on, 'I wasn't going to fucking argue with a madman waving a gun about. Me, Dimi and Big Bertha we all fought to get into the car before he shot the lot of us on the pavement. There were two of his mates in the motor, nearly as wild-arse as him. I'm sure they were carrying guns, too.' She paused again. 'He took us off to his place, terrace house near Peacehaven Hill.' She wiped the perspiration from her face, although it was not hot in the house. 'When he took us down in the cellar I nearly shit myself. I didn't think I'd ever walk back up the stairs. Bertha was crying, and Yardbird clocked her one, too, and told her to shut it. The two who were in the back of the car just stood to one side, watching, but didn't say anything.'

She drank some more whisky, and went on, 'Yardbird forced Dimi the Greek on to his knees and just screamed at him for God knows how long about trying to take his girls from him. "I'm Yardbird, I'm the man here, the man, you get it?" I mean, Dimi wasn't my ponce, I hadn't got one, although Bertha gave him all her money.'

Kettle got up and walked around the small room like a convict in a cell. Timberlake let her take her time.

'Then Yardbird turned and stared at me and Bertha. Jesus Christ, I'll never forget how he looked . . .' She drank the last of the whisky in the glass. 'Then he said, "You tell anybody about this, and this is what you'll get, you grey-meat slags." He dragged out his gun, and shot Dimi, still kneeling there, Bang . . . bang . . . bang . . .' she said, pausing for a second between each word. 'Just like that, right through the chest, taking his time. Dimi fell on his face, and Yardbird leant over him and shot him in the back of the head.'

The whisky glass fell from her hand into the fireplace with a clatter, making Timberlake jump.

'Why have you told me this?' he asked. He very carefully avoided asking her if she'd testify in court. He'd worry about that later.

'Just so you know. I hope to Christ you get him, but don't expect me to help you. If he thought I was going to talk to anyone, let alone give evidence, he'd have me killed like Dimi.'

'What about Big Bertha? I thought she was in love with Dimitrios. D'you think she might give evidence if we give her protection?'

Whistling gave a short bark of cynical laughter. 'Her? She's more bloody scared than me, if that's possible. If Yardbird was lying dead and nailed down she might spit on him, but that's about it. And if you say anything to her, she'll know it's come from me.'

Timberlake nodded. 'OK, Whistling. Don't worry, I won't drop you in it. One thing: can you tell me where Yardbird lives? The place he took you to?'

'Oh, sure. Everybody round The Gut knows his place. It's twenty-three, Cairo Walk. Besides, he's got his fucking great motor parked on the forecourt.' She poured herself yet another whisky. 'Right, I feel a bit better now.' She smiled wanly. 'And you've got the television working perfect, thanks.'

Nigel Larkin was sitting patiently in the car when Timberlake arrived. 'OK, guv?'

'Oh, yes. I'll tell you about it in a minute.' He took his mobile phone from his pocket and dialled Detective Superintendent Harkness's direct line. 'Sir? Timberlake. If it's not too late, I think we ought to keep it secret we've recovered a body from the Thames. If the Press have got it already, at least keep it from them that we've identified it. It's quite urgent. I'll explain when I get in.'

Nigel Larkin practically buzzed with energetic curiosity. It would have taken a harder heart than Timberlake's to keep him in suspense, and he explained his interview with Whistling Kettle.

'So why keep it quiet we've found Dimi the Greek's body?'

'If it's made public we've found Dimi's body with bullet holes in it, the moment we pick up Yardbird he may well suspect someone's been talking. But if we nick him on some other pretext our informant's not at risk. Well, not much.'

The firearms expert dealing with the Dimitrios Ionides shooting was named Bert Petch. He greeted Timberlake and Larkin with all the sympathetic gravitas of a Californian funeral director.

'You've come about the body in the Thames,' I suppose.

Timberlake admitted that was so.

'The bullet's in good condition,' Petch said, showing the first signs of any enthusiasm. 'Yes, well, it's a conical-nosed bullet, weighing 125 grains, and .615 inches long, approximately. Maximum diameter, .355 inches. Cross-section area, .0989 square inches. Would you like those in metric?'

Timberlake politely declined.

'So, it's a bullet from a nine-millimetre cartridge.'

Eager Beaver Larkin began to ask what sort of gun it came from, but Timberlake nudged him. He always let experts have their say, when there was time. It was one of their few pleasures.

'Did you say something?' Petch asked Larkin.

'No, no. Just trying to stifle a cough.' Larkin coughed unconvincingly.

'Since I was able to discover what make of gun fired these bullets, I have a fairly shrewd idea what the cartridges were. How did I know what make of gun they came from?' he asked rhetorically. 'This particular bullet shows the gun had six grooves with a right twist. That narrowed it down to about fifty per cent of all the automatics in existence. However, the grooves had one complete twist in sixteen inches. The groove diameter was .356 inches.' He looked at both men in turn. '*Now* any guesses about the cartridge?'

He waited a moment before going on. The two detectives were irresistibly reminded of Professor Mortimer doing his dragging out the drama act.

'Nine-millimetre Luger, or Parabellum,' Petch announced. He stood like a conjuror who had just performed a difficult trick.

'Bravo,' Timberlake said. He felt he could say no less.

Petch beamed. 'These cartridges have a muzzle velocity of 1,150 feet per second, and at fifteen feet they will penetrate ten soft pine boards, each one seven-eighths of an inch thick.'

Timberlake felt it was a mistake to congratulate Petch earlier.

The guns man continued. 'It was fired from either a Browning High Power Model 1935, made in Belgium, or a Browning BDA9 or BDA 380. The 380 is really a Beretta 84 look-alike, first in service in 1980. The BDA9 is a modification of the High Power, first brought out in 1993. There's a different lock mechanism, and it has a de-cocking lever instead of a safety catch.'

'Fascinating,' Timberlake said, but the irony still didn't get through.

'You want to be careful if anyone's shooting one of those at you. Don't make a grab for him just because he's fired seven shots, or nine. The magazine carries thirteen or fourteen cartridges, according to the model. You can actually get a special magazine that takes twenty bullets, but it sticks out and makes the gun look unwieldy. The Dunblane killer had two like it.'

'Well, thanks very much.' Timberlake took Larkin's arm and moved to leave.

Sarah Lewis was seriously pissed off. As she stamped up the stairs to the CID offices at Terrace Vale, she said quite audibly, 'I'm pissed off.' Fortunately there was no one within earshot to hear this unladylike remark. In the circumstances it was a relatively mild expression. She had been on surveillance outside Abbot Perceval Secondary Modern and Parkside Comprehensive

Schools on her own, which was as mind-rotting a way of spending time as watching a late-night ITV 'sexy' programme for young morons. Perhaps not quite. Nevertheless, she gritted her teeth and tried to reassure herself that it would all be worth it in the end when she caught the miscreant. Tomorrow would be another day. What she didn't know yet was that tomorrow would be worse. The first intimation was when Benny Holmes came up to her and said, 'Old Bag of Guts wants to see you.' She didn't have to ask who that was.

'You wanted to see me, guv?' she said to Detective Chief Inspector Greening.

He suppressed an incipient belch, not from any considerations of politeness, but because the uprushing gust of hot gas would make his long-abused œcsophagus feel it was on fire.

'Oh, yeah. We're shutting down the surveillance on those two schools for the time being. We need you in here to go on the computers. AMIP need more bodies to operate them for records and God knows what shit. They're scraping the barrel for people to work on them.' Sarah could have strangled him for his casual, thoughtless insult. 'The super's bagman, whassisname, Sergeant Braddock, will tell you what to do.'

'But I've got a suspect!'

'Tough. Sergeant Braddock. And shut the sodding door.'

Everyone interested in the Dimitrios Ionides case – which meant a sizeable proportion of all the murder squad detectives at Terrace Vale – was at the morgue for the autopsy, all dressed in the protective gear that

Professor Mortimer insisted on. Dimi, naked as the day he was born but a lot less lively, lay on the dissection table. He was a very hairy man, and the black body hair on his pale skin somehow made him look untidy.

Of the principals in this grisly drama Gertrude Hacker was the first to appear. Wrapped in a white laboratory coat and a protective long green apron she was as shapeless as a half-inflated hot-air balloon. She wasn't wearing her famous hat with its inappropriate feather, and with a shock Timberlake noticed she had streaks of grey in her ginger-mouse hair. All at once he felt an unaccountable tenderness for her. This sentiment died like a burst light bulb when he noticed her staring directly at him.

Mortimer arrived with an impeccable sense of timing – keeping everyone waiting just long enough for them to wonder if he'd got lost or had a heart attack, and arriving just before they decided they didn't give a damn.

Mortimer switched on the tape recorder for his report. Getrude Hacker also took down his notes in shorthand, acting as a sort of backup disk in case of a tape-recording fault. Mortimer was the sort of man who wore both braces and belt.

Timberlake put his brain on automatic pilot while Mortimer went through the standard procedure of describing the body and the outward signs of damage. Once again he wondered whether Mortimer really had no sense of humour whatsoever, or whether he was quietly sending up all the police officers there.

'There are three entry wounds from the bullets in the front of the torso all to the left of the centre line, in an area of approximately five to eight centimetres in diameter. There are two exit wounds in the back, which strongly suggests that one of the bullets is still in the body,' he said with a perfectly straight face. 'A fourth entry wound is in the occipital area of the skull. The bullet penetrated the occipital lobe of the brain, continued in a straight line through the supramarginal gyrus and the front lobe, emerging from the skull through the supra-orbital foramen one centimetre to the left of the centre line and some five centimetres above the eye socket.'

Mortimer straightened up from studying the corpse and stared at the detectives standing on the other side of the table, as if inviting questions. There were none.

'The two bullets which are not still in the body penetrated, first, the aorta; second, the superior vena cava. The third bullet glanced off the sternum, which caused it to tumble and cause severe damage to the right atrium, the right lung and a dorsal vertebra. I have been able to fix the position of this third bullet from X-rays, and after I have removed the lungs I shall retrieve the bullet.'

Mortimer removed the lungs with the rapidity and ease of decades of experience. He deposited them into the spring scales as unemotionally as a shopkeeper weighing a bunch of bananas. As he did this he observed, 'Although the body was discovered in the river, there was no water in the lungs, so the subject was dead before immersion.'

'Fancy,' an unidentifiable voice commented.

Mortimer gave no sign of having heard. 'Lungs, one kilo, one hundred and forty-two grams,' he said, sounding like a talking weighing machine.

He took a pair of long forceps, and slipped pieces

of rubber tubing over the serrated ends of the instrument so there would be no risk of scratching the bullet and possibly vitiating identification of it. After a moment of delicate probing he carefully withdrew the forceps, holding a bloody bullet. He dropped it into a kidney dish with a sharp metallic clang. Gertrude Hacker took the bullet from the dish and wiped it clean with a piece of gauze, then handed it over to Detective Superintendent Harkness. He scratched an identifying mark on the base before putting it into a plastic envelope, which he handed to Timberlake.

The message came into Terrace Vale just as the morning murder squads' conference was nearing its end.

Sarah entered the conference room with it and made her way to Harkness, followed by the hot and lascivious eyes of a score of police officers. Timberlake, the only one of the group who had been Sarah's lover, watched her with mixed feelings, one of which was jealousy. Fortunately Detective Superintendent Harkness was the officer in charge of the meeting, otherwise Sarah would have been greeted with a series of whistles and very rude remarks.

Harkness took the message from her. He was the sort of man who would give no clue as to whether he was looking at his winning lottery ticket or an income tax demand. He waited for a long moment, then nodded slightly as if coming to a decision about something. The entire room held its breath.

'Suzanne Oliver has just been identified by her fingerprints as Red Janie Hanson, a prostitute with an address in The Grove,' Harkness announced. He let this sink in before continuing. 'Well, now there's little doubt that her murder, too, is associated with the other murders of prostitutes in this area, which reinforces our theory that we are dealing with a serial killer – as if that self-evident fact needed any confirmation. I think it almost certain that the missing Vicki Stevens is dead – perhaps in the river somewhere like Dimitrios Ionides.'

He was right about her being dead, but not in the way he thought. Not by a long way. In a manner of speaking, Vicki Stevens was going to surface again and cause a massive re-think.

Chapter Thirteen

Timberlake had been trying to decide the best way for the murder squad to follow up Whistling Kettle's information about Yardbird Charlie's murder of Dimi the Greek. Timing would be everything. If they raided Yardbird's house while he wasn't there they might well find physical evidence to support Whistling's story, but Yardbird could fly the coop, in a manner of speaking, out of reach of the Metropolitan police – back to the Caribbean or some of the more pestiferous bolt-holes for criminals in Europe or North Africa.

On the other hand, if the police left things too late Yardbird could remove all traces of his murder of Dimi.

The problem was solved for Timberlake with an anonymous telephone call. The caller was obviously disguising his, or her, voice: it was pitched somewhere between a full contralto and a light tenor. Maybe Professor Higgins could have identified the accent, but Timberlake wasn't sure whether there were very slight traces of West Indian rhythms or even London cadences. Nevertheless, there was something faintly familiar he couldn't quite place.

The message was simple. 'Yardbird Charlie's going to be at his place in Cairo Walk tonight with his bodyguards and their women. They'll be having a piss-up to celebrate some deal he's pulled off. But watch it if you turn over his drum. There'll be shooters all over the place.'

'Who is this?' Timberlake asked, not expecting an answer.

He got one: a sarcastic chuckle.

Timberlake pondered the value of this anonymous tip. On the plus side was the fact that Yardbird Charlie must have a small army of enemies who would be delighted, relieved or both to see him removed from the scene. These enemies would be too afraid or powerless to take action themselves but would risk an anonymous call to the police if they knew something. But *who*? For a while he wondered if it was Willy. No: more likely some tart who'd been roped in against her will to provide services for Yardbird and his guests.

Timberlake could think of no motive for the call being bogus other than its possibly being purely mischievous: his gut feeling was that it was genuine.

He reported the call to Detective Superintendent Harkness. They discussed it carefully before Harkness finally said, 'I'll go along with your instincts about it, Harry. They've been pretty reliable so far.'

Timberlake felt a surge of pride at the compliment, but this almost instantly turned to foreboding when he realized the massive amount of egg he would have on his face if he was wrong.

'We've got something of a safety net in case the call is spurious,' Harkness added, and explained. Timberlake's spirits rose again.

There was no difficulty in getting a search warrant for Yardbird Charlie's home: Terrace Vale's chief superintendent, master of the funny handshake, knew exactly which magistrate to approach

The briefing for the task force who were going to turn over Charlie's drum was held in the station's conference room. There were eight Terrace Vale detectives there, including Timberlake, Darren Webb, a serious-looking Nigel Larkin, the massive Jeff Waters, Alistair McPhail and Bob Crust. In additiion there were a dozen local uniformed officers plus another twelve-strong, uniformed, group of Territorial Support Group officers.

Timberlake was addressing the squad. 'You may think that we're going overboard with the troops in this operation. Well, the target is Yardbird Charlie, who is known to be armed and dangerously unstable. Two days ago we had information from a reliable informant, and subsequently backed up by intelligence from our vice squad, that there is most probably a considerable quantity of arms in the house. He has a number of criminal associates who won't hesitate to use violence. The only reason they haven't been charged before now is that we've had no reliable information that arms are kept in the house, and their victims won't give evidence against them.

The house we're going to search is in the Peacehaven Hill district. You all know its reputation. Any police activity risks sparking off some reaction up to an actual riot.'

Timberlake pointed to a large-scale map of the immediate area. 'Cairo Walk will be sealed off here, and here. During the search, no one will be allowed in or out of the street. Other units will be stationed here, and here, on adjoining streets. It's possible to get from Cairo Walk through adjoining back gardens into Alexandria Street, so we'll be able to cut off anyone doing a runner out of No. 23.' Timberlake looked round the room, but there were no questions for the moment.

'Now,' he said heavily, 'five officers will be armed. Myself, DS Webb, Bob Crust, Jeff Waters and Alistair McPhail. I don't have to tell those officers again about the rules for using weapons. It's Cairo Walk, not the O.K. Corral. Any questions so far?'

'Yes, guv,' Darren Webb said. 'What's the warrant?'

'Oh yes. Daylight to dusk. Sunrise tomorrow is 5.07 a.m. We go in at 5.07 a.m. and thirty seconds.'

Timberlake continued with the briefing to cover the details of the proposed operation.

Detective Superintendent Harkness had the final word. 'I'll remind you of the purpose of this operation. It is to find any evidence in the murder of Dimitrios Ionides. That is the principal objective. However, it seems highly probable that there will be evidence of other offences in connection with drugs and illegal weapons. I don't want us to miss anything.' He waited to make sure he had everyone's attention. 'I shan't re-emphasize the importance and the delicacy of this operation. We run the risk of being accused of heavy-handedness and of racial harassment however careful we are. So, there will be two police cameramen, one inside and one outside, during the entire operation, and I have invited a camera crew to cover for the BBC, ITN and Sky News. They have not been told where or what the operation will be. They will be escorted to the scene from a rendezvous chosen by me.' Then, deliberately and slowly, 'You should see that these arrangements are a demonstration of my confidence in your professionalism, and for your own protection.

'One more thing. The final decision whether the operation will go ahead will be made when we reassemble here.'

Jenny Long Timberlake was at home when her husband arrived. She had decided to make an effort to re-establish an atmosphere of married-life normalcy between them; recently they had been almost like strangers living in a cold climate. 'Shall we go out for dinner?' she asked, managing to check herself from saying, 'My treat.'

'Thanks, but I've got to go out again at half-past three.'

'Oh, God. Something important? Silly question; of course it must be. Do you want to eat?'

'I'm not sure.' He made a wry gesture with his clenched fist of a knotted-up stomach. 'I suppose I ought to.'

'We'll eat in the kitchen,' Jenny said brightly. 'Scrambled eggs and smoked salmon?'

'Yes, all right,' he said, adding, 'Sorry if that sounded ungracious. I'm just a little wound up.'

'Of course. Don't worry.' They did not notice that neither of them had said, not even automatically, 'Darling'.

Timberlake ate some pasta and then the eggs and smoked salmon, surprised that he had felt hungry after all. 'Thanks. That was great. Look, I'll sleep in the spare room so I don't wake you up when I go out.' He smiled wryly. 'I don't suppose I'll sleep much anyway, and I don't want to keep you awake by tossing and turning.'

'Whatever you think best,' Jenny replied. Both of them felt a further drop in the temperature of the relationship, which could hardly be called warm, anyway.

Timberlake lay on his bed, unable to sleep, but schooling himself to relax as much as possible before he had to set off for the dawn raid. He reflected that when he was a young beat constable any murder got big headlines on the front page, as did the use of a firearm in the commission of a crime. These days some murders – maybe most – are worth only a couple of paragraphs on an inside page. Gangland and drug dealers' use of guns is commonplace.

For no particular reason he thought of Nigel Larkin, and with a shock he realized that he knew nothing of the young man's private life – whether he had a girlfriend, whether he lived with his parents or shared a flat with friends . . . nothing. He resolved to get to know him better once the present case was over.

An insistent double-buzz startled him. At first he had no idea what it was, but then he became aware that it was his alarm. He must have slept after all. Silently he got up and went to the bathroom where he shaved and took a lukewarm shower.

The coffee percolator was still switched on, with half a jugful still on its hotplate. As he took his first sip Timberlake mused that it was a perfect example of Talleyrand-Périgord's recipe for coffee: 'Black as the devil, hot as hell.' Well, that was at least half the recipe, he thought. It wasn't pure as an angel and sweet as love: he never took sugar. And as for love . . .

Four o'clock in the morning is an awful hour for normal human beings, but Timberlake was as wide awake as if he had enjoyed his normal seven hours' sleep. He drove to the nick with the car window down, and the fresh air and the caffeine in the coffee jolted his system into overdrive. By the time he walked into the conference room he was almost indecently lively. Everyone was on time; Harkness looked as immaculate as usual.

'First, the operation is on,' Harkness announced flatly. There was a murmur of satisfaction from the officers. 'The house has been under covert observation during the night. Yardbird Charlie is definitely there with a number of associates and young women, and they have had a noisy party. So, the first part of our information has been proved to be accurate. Everything has been quiet for the past hour or so.'

The plan of the operation was gone over again, meticulously, while the news cameramen recorded the scene. They were given two simple directives: 'Don't get in the way, and don't try to be heroes.'

The last part of the preparations was the issue of firearms, ammunition and flak jackets. If anyone had not fully appreciated the seriousness of the operation, putting on the body armour and picking up the ugly weapons brought it home to them.

The convoy moved off unfussily and quietly, led by unmarked cars with the police vehicles following. Everyone appeared calm enough on the surface, although anyone who knew the men well would have detected slight signs of edginess. When Darren Webb said to Timberlake, 'When we get there, with a bit of luck Yardbird Charlie'll be laying in bed spark out.'

'What'll he be *laying*? Bricks? Eggs?' Timberlake replied, more sharply than he realized. 'You mean "lying".'

'Right, guv.' Others in the car exchanged long glances.

The convoy divided into two sections before arriving at Cairo Walk, which was approached from opposite directions. As soon as the unmarked cars entered the street, vans blocked the roadway behind them.

The vehicles pulled up without squeals of tyres. Quietly the officers got out, being careful to shut the car doors silently. They didn't want to wake anyone with a fusillade of door-slams. Timberlake, Darren Webb, Bob Crust and Jeff Waters approached No. 23; Alistair McPhail was standing by in Alexandria Street, much to his disappointment, with uniformed officers in case anyone tried to leg it out by the back way.

Two large uniformed constables soft-footed it up to the front door. One of them had a sledgehammer, the other a special one-man battering-ram. Timberlake and the other armed detectives were just behind them. The men's heavy heartbeats were almost audible. Timberlake looked at his electronic watch, then nodded.

The sledgehammer and battering ram thundered alternate blows on the front door, which gave way with a splintering crash and hit the floor with the sound of a small explosion. Timberlake led the charge of his group up the stairs, thinking furiously, 'I hope to Christ nobody falls over and baulks us . . .' Behind them other officers were checking and securing the downstairs rooms.

A bar of light appeared under the door of one of the upstairs rooms. Timberlake gestured to Darren Webb to go to the room next door and to Jeff Waters to follow him into the room where the light was on.

By the light of a bedside lamp Timberlake could see Yardbird Charlie beginning to sit up in bed, his eyes half-closed. With him in the bed was a naked red-headed girl.

'Armed police!' Timberlake shouted in a voice that could be heard outside the house. 'Stay where you are! Don't move!'

Yardbird sluggishly moved his hand under his pillow. Timberlake pushed his gun against Yardbird's forehead. 'Take your hand out, slowly, with nothing in it,' he shouted.

On the other side of the bed the young woman moved more quickly than Yardbird, and managed to pull a small automatic from under her pillow. Jeff Waters closed a massive fist over her wrist and twisted it. She yelped with pain and dropped the gun but tried to scratch his eyes. With his spare hand Waters pushed her down on the bed. By now two uniformed Territorial Support Group officers were in the room. 'Get some clothes on,' he told the girl. As she climbed out of bed, her face twisted with rage, a line of needle punctures on her left arm was clearly visible. Waters and one of the uniformed men watched her dispassionately as she put on a track suit, screaming obscenities as she did it. Yardbird Charlie was nearly as loud, but incomprehensible. The arrival of a TV crew with powerful lights on their camera did little to calm them down. When the woman was dressed, she was handcuffed.

The other TSG officer went round to Timberlake's side of the bed and helped him keep watch as Yardbird got dressed in his turn before being handcuffed.

Timberlake lifted his pillow. Underneath was a menacing looking gun.

Timberlake was ready to bet a week's leave it was a Browning BDA9 or BDA 380. He picked it up with a pencil through the trigger guard and put it into a plastic bag, which he sealed.

The task force brought back a highly satisfactory haul from 23 Cairo Walk in both men and materiel. Sergeant Rumsden and Sergeant Dick Bush, the young custody sergeant, gazed glumly at the tatty-looking gang of Yardbird Charlie and five male accomplices – plus the girl in Yardbird's bed, three others much like her, and two girls who looked both disgusting and pathetic at the same time. They were a squalid crew, but no one is at his best when he has been rousted out of bed by police at soon after 5 a.m. after a late night of over-indulgence in sex, drink and drugs.

There was a quantity of marijuana, plastic bags containing white powder, hypodermic syringes – which were handled with extreme care – and other drug addicts' paraphernalia. Sergeant Bush was puzzled by some odd-looking and even odder-smelling cigarettes.

'What the hell are they?' Bush asked Sergeant Rumsden, who was more experienced.

'Sherm,' Rumsden replied. 'They're ordinary

machine-made fags that've been steeped in embalming fluid.'

Bush stared at him with a mixture of astonishment and horror. 'You're kidding.'

'Honestly.' Rumsden assured him.

There were enough drugs to keep the gang in Yardbird's house happy, but not enough to suggest that they were dealing. Much more sinister were the arms found in the house. In addition to the two in Yardbird's bedroom, the Browning and the woman's Austrian OWA .25in. – a neat little weapon which would hardly stop a rhino but could give someone a nasty headache – were another Colt automatic, a couple of .38 Smith & Wesson revolvers and a terrifying Uzi sub-machine gun. Plus a hand grenade.

'Who's first?' Sergeant Bush asked at last.

Darren Webb put Yardbird Charlie at the head of the queue. He was charged with having in his possession firearms without holding firearm certificates in contravention of the Firearms Act of 1968. He was also formally warned that there might be further charges to follow, which, Sergeant Rumsden observed, was a better bet than Crewe Alexandra not winning the FA Cup. The young woman, an oddly-named Pepper Birch, was charged with the same offence. Other men in the house at the time were charged with a variety of offences.

When all the prisoners had been fingerprinted and tucked away in cells, and the physical evidence tagged and locked up, Webb gave a deep sigh of relief. 'I reckon we got that lot just in time. Christ knows what might have happened otherwise. It would have been like Dodge City. As far as we could tell, only Yardbird's gun has been fired recently. The guvnor wants that one fingerprinted and sent to the firearms expert a.s.a.p.'

'Where is H.T.?' Rumsden asked. 'I didn't see him come back with you lot.'

'He's still at the house, with the SOCOs. They're digging round in the cellar.'

Timberlake, Jeff Waters and Sergeant Burton Johnson with his team of SOCOs had struck gold. They had dug a nine-millimetre bullet from the plaster-covered wall and it was in good enough condition to be checked against the bullet that had been taken from Dimi the Greek's body. A second bullet was embedded in a floorboard, which was stained with blood. One of the forensic scientists with Sergeant Johnson carefully removed the bullet, taking care not to scratch it as he dug it from the wood. It was almost as smooth as if it had been fired into a water tank. Next, the bloodstained floorboard was removed. 'I should think the lab'll be able to get enough of that blood out to do a DNA,' Johnson said cheerfully.

It was Timberlake's big day. Almost immediately another SOCO came into the cellar carrying a coil of a greenish coloured rope. 'I found this in the shed, guv,' he reported to Timberlake. 'I think it's the same sort that was wound round Dimi the whatnot's legs. I had a good look at it.'

'Well, he's given us enough rope to hang himself with,' Timberlake said.

The massive Jeff Waters giggled. He actually giggled, which was as incongruous as Shirley Temple singing bass.

*

When Timberlake returned to the nick he began the interrogation of Yardbird Charlie himself, with Nigel Larkin and a uniformed PC in the interview room. In an adjoining room Darren Webb and Bob Crust were questioning one of the other men found in the house.

Timberlake switched on the two-track recorder. 'Interview of Charles Stewart Windsor King at Terrace Vale police station.' He added the date and time. 'I am Detective Inspector Harry Timberlake. Also present are—' He signalled to the Eager Beaver.

'Detective Constable Nigel Larkin.'

'And PC 279 Peter Calver,' the uniform said.

Timberlake went on, 'Charles King, I am charging you with being in possession of a Browning nine-millimetre automatic pistol without a valid firearms certificate. You are not obliged to say anything, but if, when questioned, you do not say something that you later rely on in court, it may harm your defence. Anything you do say will be taken down in writing and may be given in evidence. Do you understand?'

'Yeah, I understand you're going to fit me up, right?'

'I repeat, do you understand the caution I have just given you?'

'Yeah, pig. You think I'm some dumb nigger?'

'I am also arresting you on suspicion of the murder of Dimitrios Ionides.' Timberlake added the date of the murder.

Yardbird Charlie half rose from his chair.

'Sit *down*!' Timberlake said. 'I remind you, you have been properly cautioned.' Then, less tough, 'We'll start with the gun. Is it yours?'

'No, man. I don't do guns.'

'Then how did it get under your pillow?'

'I don't know. Hey, one of you pigs planted it.'

Timberlake smiled contemptuously. 'Oh, come on. You know better than to try that one. I thought you said you're not some dumb nigger.'

'Hey, don't you call me "nigger"! That's racial prejudice and harassment!'

'*I* didn't call you "nigger". You did. I was quoting you. It's on the tape. For the second time, how did that gun get under your pillow?'

'I don't know nothing about it.' Then, with a burst of inspiration, 'That fucking bitch must have slipped it under there. Yeah, that's it.'

'Which woman is that?'

'The one that was in bed with me, what d'you think? Pepper Birch.'

'Why would she do that?'

'I don't know, man. She's a stupid bitch, might do anything. Maybe she was scared of burglars.'

Timberlake laughed before saying, 'But she had her own gun, a .25 automatic under *her* pillow.'

'I tell you it's not my fucking gun, man! I never saw it before this morning.'

'So you say,' Timberlake said with heavy irony, using a phrase popular with advocates trying to disparage a witness. 'Well, we'll have to see what Pepper has to say about that, won't we? And those other people who were in your house.'

'They won't tell you nothing, man. Nothing. Cause they don't know nothing.'

'Maybe,' Timberlake said casually, ignoring Yardbird's predilection for double negatives. 'Though Pepper might find it a strain on her loyalty when her last fix starts to wear off. When was that, by the way?'

Yardbird Charlie looked at Timberlake with ferocious hate, but there was a faint hint of anxiety in his eyes. Timberlake returned his gaze, smiling faintly. 'You know we can tell if a bullet has come out of a particular gun? Well, maybe that one that appeared from nowhere under your pillow has been used in the commission of a crime.' He let this sink in. 'If it has, that job'll be down to you.'

Yardbird Charlie licked his lips.

Timberlake studied him for a few moments, then said, gently. 'Of course, you might have an out even if it has done another job.'

He stayed silent, until Yardbird said, 'Yeah? How's that?'

'I dunno. Why should I help you? You haven't been exactly frank with me.'

'Be fair, man.' There was no bravado in his tone.

Timberlake turned to Nigel Larkin. 'What d'you reckon, Nigel?' The Eager Beaver didn't know what was expected of him, so he settled for a non-committal shrug.

'Oh, all right,' Timberlake conceded. He turned back to Yardbird. 'Look, if you tell me where you bought the shooter, maybe it'll be the guy who sold who goes down for anything tied to the gun.'

Yardbird considered this for a long moment, but came to the wrong conclusion. 'I can't tell you, man.'

Timberlake looked unconcerned. 'It's your skin. Let's go, Nigel.'

'I mean, I can't tell you. I would if I could, honest to God, man. But I didn't buy it. I found it,' Yardbird said hurriedly.

'Where?'

'In a skip down River Road.'

'When?'

'About a week ago. Ten days.' He tried to sound vague.

Timberlake nodded. 'So it is your gun, and wasn't put under your pillow by the tooth fairy.'

Yardbird looked at him with rage at being outsmarted. 'I want my brief!' he yelped.

'Any particular one?' Timberlake asked politely.

'Wim Sachs.'

Timberlake thought, but didn't say, 'I might have guessed it.' Instead he simply said, 'Interview concluded at 9.12 a.m.' He switched off the recorder, and got up. 'Take him back to his cell,' he told Larkin and the uniformed PC

'Brilliant, guv,' Larkin whispered, not trying to be a brown nose. 'You didn't ask him about the keys, though.'

'I don't want him to know we've got them. He might get word to someone to clear the weapons cache out before we get to it. If we strike lucky and find out where it is we might have something unexpected to hit him with.'

In the corridor Timberlake met Darren Webb. 'How did it go with Pepper?'

'Nothing yet, guv, but it won't be long. She's sweating and beginning to get the shakes.'

'Has she asked for a doctor? Or a brief?'

Webb shook his head. 'What about Yardbird?'

'I've put him back in his cell to let him stew and

start worrying. He's admitted the gun is his. He's asked for Wim Sachs.'

Timberlake and Larkin met at Sergeant Bush's desk. 'Dick,' Timberlake said, 'Yardbird Charlie has asked for Wim Sachs. Before Sachs gets here, no one is to question Yardbird. Got it?'

'Right, guv. Er, shall I phone for Sachs, or will you?'

'You do it, please, Dick.' He added heavily, 'When you've got time.'

Sergeant Bush looked Timberlake in the eye for a long moment, then coughed apologetically. 'I've, er, got a lot of paperwork to get through. Might take me quite a while.'

'Two hours?'

'At least.'

'Well, do your best, Dick.'

Sergeant Rumsden came up to join them. Timberlake went on, 'Dick's going to phone Wim Sachs for Yardbird.' He paused. 'As soon as he has time. If Sachs comes in before I get back, ask him to hold on. I want to talk to him.' He stared at Rumsden with wide-eyed innocence. 'I hope he doesn't get the impression I want to do some sort of deal.'

Unspoken messages flashed back and forth between Timberlake and Rumsden. At last the sergeant said , 'I'll make sure he gets the general idea.'

'I'll do my best to get back before he's finished reading the transcript of the interview. Make sure Sachs gets it as soon as it's been properly typed out.'

'You can rely on me, guv.'

Nigel listened to these exchanges like a child who has just been told that there's no Father Christmas. He hadn't realized that Harry Timberlake could be a devious bender of the rules. He didn't know whether he was pleased or disappointed. At first. He soon made up his mind.

'Wait here for me, Nigel,' Timberlake said. 'I've got to see the super first then we're going out.' He was back within five minutes.

'Have you got your car here, Nigel?'

Nigel Larkin nodded.

'Good. Mine's too well known.'

'Where're we going, guv?'

He grinned. 'To see if we can pull a couple of women.'

Chapter Fourteen

Whistling Kettle was not pleased to see Harry Timberlake, and the presence of Nigel Larkin did nothing to ease her annoyance, which turned to alarm when Timberlake explained why he had come.

'We've nicked Yardbird Charlie—' he began.

'Christ, you haven't told him what I said about him shooting Dimi the Greek! You said—'

'He's not been arrested for that; it's for illegal possession of firearms. I'll be charging him with possession of drugs as soon as we get the lab report on the stuff we picked up at his house. I'm holding him *on suspicion* of murdering Dimi the Greek. There'll be a whole sackful of scientific evidence as soon as we get the lab reports. We've got the gun that almost certainly was the one he used to kill Dimi, plus a whole lot of evidence from the cellar. There's absolutely no way he can walk away from it. That's so far. I'll bet you some of the others in the house will start talking when they've had a dose of cold turkey – especially his girlfriend Pepper.'

Whistling seemed a little less scared. 'So why come here?'

'Yardbird is seeing his solicitor in a couple of hours or so. Wim Sachs.'

'That crooked bastard!'

'Yeah. Now, you know Yardbird better than I do. All his men from the Cairo Walk house are inside on drug charges, but you *saw* the murder. What're the odds he'll tell Sachs to put out a contract on you, and what're the odds Sachs'll do it?'

Whistling Kettle went a dirty-grey colour. She got up and went to a side table where she poured herself another large scotch. The neck of the bottle rattled against the rim of the glass.

'Contracts on you *and* Big Bertha,' Timberlake added. He let this sink in for a moment. 'There's one solution. I shan't bullshit you.'

'What?'

'You agree to give us a statement about seeing the murder and—'

'Fuck you, Timberlake!'

'*Listen!* We'll put you in a safe house, keep you under wraps with a twenty-four-hour guard. Your testimony will be like throwing away the key of Yardbird's cell. We'll even re-locate you after the trial, with a new identity if you want.'

Whistling took another big gulp of her whisky. Her hand was still trembling.

Timberlake let her think for a while. Then, 'What's your alternative?'

'You bastard, Timberlake. You let me down.'

'I'm trying to *save* you. Look, pack a bag for a couple of days. We'll have someone come and get anything else you need later. We'll take care of you.'

While Whistling was upstairs, Larkin asked, 'Is that why you went to see Superintendent Harkness? To get authority for a safe place to keep the women out of sight?'

'Yeah. There was one snag. He wasn't in.'

Larkin looked startled. 'Suppose he doesn't give it?'

Timberlake grinned wryly. 'Then I'll have one of them at my place. Have you got a spare bedroom for the other?' He was pulling Larkin's leg. Timberlake knew Harkness would arrange safe accommodation for the women.

Before Larkin could say anything Whistling Kettle came thumping down the stairs, carrying a suitcase. The two detectives escorted her to Larkin's car, keeping her shielded from view as much as possible. 'Keep well down in your seat and cover your face,' Timberlake told her.

Big Bertha was no problem. Whistling's agreement to go along with the plan, and the fact that Big Bertha had loved Dimi the Greek made her easy to convince.

When the group got back to Terrace Vale nick Timberlake told Larkin to drive right up to the back door of the station. 'Make sure that Wim Sachs and any other civilians are nowhere about. And get a couple of uniforms to escort the women up to CID We'll get statements later.'

Wim Sachs was waiting at the front desk when Timberlake and Larkin came back down from the CID office. Timberlake greeted him with a sweet smile. 'I see you have a copy of your client's statement there, Mr Sachs.'

Sachs, a medium-sized man, was wearing a suit which could have been part of a 1946 demobilization outfit, or even made by the pre-war 50-Shilling Tailors. His shirt would have been received with reservations by Oxfam, his tie spurned altogether. His shoes were old and cracked. Sachs' face was pink and puffy with an underlying dark smear of a heavy beard. If he shaved at 9 a.m., at half past he had a five o'clock shadow. The ensemble should have irresistibly suggested a poor, struggling, unsuccessful man.

It was a shrewd act. Some magistrates, the more naive ones, would feel sorry for someone represented by an obvious loser like Sachs. Others would bend over backwards not to be prejudiced against such a transparent shyster. However, there was one feature Sachs could not disguise: his eyes. They were as lively and perceptive as an eagle's – and as friendly.

'Mr Timberlake,' Sachs said with a lips-only smile. 'I've read the transcript of my client's supposed unsigned statement concerning the firearms charge . . .'

'It is not supposed: it was made, under caution, to myself with two other witnesses.'

'Police witnesses, of course.'

'Naturally. He didn't ask for a solicitor.'

'Was he told he could have one?'

'Mr Charles Stewart Windsor King has been interviewed and cautioned enough times to be aware of his rights. But he was told again, yes. By the way, has he given you his cassette recording of the interview?'

Sachs acknowledged that he had. 'I see he's also being held on suspicion of the murder of a Dimitrios Ionides.'

'Enquiries into that matter are still continuing,' said Timberlake, deliberately sounding as stilted as a novice policeman giving evidence. 'You'll be kept informed, of course.'

There was an awkward silence. Tentatively Sachs

said, 'Sergeant Rumsden said you wanted me to wait to see you.'

'That's right. I wanted to give you some friendly, off-the-record advice.' This was comparable with Hitler offering a present for a bar mitzvah. Even the usually poker-faced Sachs was taken aback. 'We've got Yardbird absolutely bang to rights, double-stitched up. Get him to plead guilty so all the evidence isn't produced in court. It may – *may* – get the judge to reduce the sentence. I'm sure you can dig up some mitigating circumstances for the poor lad.'

As he walked upstairs to the CID offices Timberlake crouched and punched the air directly in front of him.

Things turned out better than Timberlake hoped. The science labs had given the Yardbird Charlie case priority, and come up with encouraging provisional findings. The bullets dug out of the cellar at Yardbird's house, were shown to have been fired from the Browning automatic under Yardbird's pillow. The bloodstains on the floor were AB group, the same as Dimi the Greek's – a group found in only 3 per cent of the population. No bookmaker would have given odds against there being a D.N.A. match when the results came through. In the phrase of laboratory reports, the unusual rope round Dimi's corpse 'matched in every detail' the rope found at the house.

Finally, some of the other people arrested at the house already were beginning to crumble and very probably would start making statements soon.

*

'Thank goodness you've wrapped up that case,' Detective Superintendent Harkness said to Timberlake at the daily murder squad meeting, which, for once, was being held in the evening because of the morning's activity. 'It was an unnecessary diversion. Now we can get back to finding our serial killer.' He thought for a moment, then said, 'I suppose you've considered the possibility that Yardbird is behind the murders of the prostitutes? Even if he didn't do them himself and paid someone?'

'To scare the others into working for him?' Timberlake said.

'Possibly.'

'I don't think so, sir. From what I've learned from them, the women themselves don't think he's behind the killings, which they obviously would if the motive was to terrify them.'

'True,' Harkness conceded.

'I've been thinking about Big Willy – the landlord in The Grove. I can't see any motive for his being involved, but he's an equivocal figure. There's something . . .' He shrugged. 'He rings false like a cracked bell. I think I'll give him another call.'

Harkness turned to Darren Webb. 'And the Mary Docker murder. Any progress, Darren?'

'Not really, sir. I was on this morning's operation, so I haven't had a chance to read today's reports yet.'

'Yes, of course. Well, let's all think things over tonight and get off to a good start tomorrow.'

'Can I buy you a beer at Fergie's Bar?' Timberlake called out to Darren Webb as the meeting broke up. 'Fergie's Bar' was the nearby Duchess of York pub, the scene of some fair old police shindigs in its time.

'Sure, guv.'

Timberlake ordered himself a designer water and a pint of Old Peculier ale for Webb. Timberlake was a well-known eccentric about drinking, by CID standards. He never drank alcohol – not even one half pint of beer – when he was going to drive a car. For a very long time other detectives tried to talk him into 'Just one, Harry. One won't hurt.' Some of them occasionally spiked his soft drink with alcohol, but he was never caught out: since he was a non-smoker his nose was too keen.

The two men took their drinks to a table at the back of the saloon bar.

Webb knew Timberlake too well. 'What's up, guv?'

'Just let me finish what I want to tell you without interrupting, and I'll leave it for you to think it over and I won't mention it again. Right?'

Webb nodded. Inwardly he said, 'Oh Christ.' He knew what was coming: Timberlake was going to tell him why Mark Sibley *had* to be Mary Docker's murderer. But Darren Webb was going to be reprieved.

'Is Detective Inspector Timberlake here?' a barman shouted. 'Telephone!'

'Shit,' Timberlake muttered. He went to the phone.

'The nick got a call and told the caller to try here,' the barman said.

Timberlake nodded. 'Timberlake,' he said brusquely into the phone. He was surprised by the voice that replied. It had an unmistakable, bred-in upper-class accent.

'Are you the detective in charge of the murdered prostitutes case?'

'Yes.' He wasn't going to argue the niceties of protocol at this stage. 'Who's speaking?'

The unknown woman ignored the question. 'I think there may have been another one you don't know about. Can you come to see me?'

'I think it might be better if you came to the station,' he replied. Accents like the caller's always got his back up. He was aware of it and tried to make sure it didn't affect his judgment.

'That is not practicable,' the caller said in a voice that had frost on it.

Timberlake sighed. 'What's your name and address?' he asked resignedly.

'Penthouse, Darcy Court. Do you know it?' It was like asking a resident of London SW1 if they knew Harrods.

'I think I've heard of it,' Timberlake said loftily. 'And your name, madam?'

'Lady Wadhurst.'

This time Timberlake *was* impressed.

Darcy Court was an apartment block as luxurious as anything in Monte Carlo or Zurich. The doorman wore a uniform that would have made Idi Amin envious, and the entrance hall was nearly big enough for five-a-side football. There were large, exotic plants in fancy pots, and at the far end from the main door was an enormous tank where tropical fish moved around with a dignified languor. Behind an ornate desk was a Chanel-suited receptionist with an elaborate hairdo. Her greeting to Timberlake was equivocal. Although he was smartly dressed in his usual Harrods-sale sports jacket and trousers, he clearly was not in the financial class of the Darcy Court residents, but at the same time he was very fanciable.

'Can I help you?' she asked in a tone that was on the warm side of neutral.

'Lady Wadhurst is expecting me. My name is Timberlake.'

The receptionist smiled and dialled a single number on a tasteful telephone. 'A Mr Timberlake is in the hall,' she said. After a moment she hung up without a further word. She turned to Timberlake. 'If you'll come with me, sir.'

She led him six yards to the three lifts. Timberlake felt that he could have found the way on his own, but made no comment. The young woman ignored one of the lifts where the door was already open and went to the far one and pressed the call button. The door opened silently. At once Timberlake noticed that there were only two buttons in the panel inside the door, even though Darcy Court had fifteen storeys plus the penthouse. Before he could step inside, the receptionist took a key from a tiny pocket in her suit and operated a lock beneath the two buttons.

'Press the top button,' she advised him gravely.

'Really?' he replied with mild astonishment.

Her smile remained as firmly welded on as Virginia Bottomley's at a press conference until the lift door cut her off from his view.

The lift opened on to a small entrance hall of the penthouse. On the walls which were covered with handmade Japanese straw paper were four paintings. Timberlake recognized them immediately: a Buffet, a Modigliani, a Murillo and a Braque. There was no question that they were originals. They helped to prepare a visitor for what he would find when he entered the apartment. It was not over-furnished, and the pieces looked like the sort of thing the Victoria and Albert Museum would like to get their hands on. The main room had floor-to-ceiling windows on three sides; double-glazed sliding glass doors gave on to a large patio garden, where a small fountain plinked away merrily. A balcony encircled the entire penthouse. Timberlake was led into the main drawing room by a servant of indeterminate title: a woman in her middle years wearing a simple black dress cut by a couturier who had probably come to a private arrangement with the Devil for his talent and got the better of the bargain.

The woman offered him a drink as she invited him to sit down.

He refused the drink, saying he preferred to stand and survey the stunning view. Over a period the tenant would have the opportunity to put his watch right by the Houses of Parliament clock, see the sunlight winking on the Thames, follow the flight of aircraft on their final approach to Heathrow, and admire Surrey's green open spaces.

'Her Ladyship will be with you in a few moments,' the superior servant said. This immediately evoked in Timberlake the memory of Madame la Comtesse Douairière Sophie de Gaillmont,* a titled woman with the autocratic attitudes of Ivan the Terrible.

Lady Wadhurst, widow of Howard Darcy de Bock, Lord Wadhurst, could not have been more different from her – in more ways than were apparent on the

*See *Written in Blood.*

surface, as Timberlake would learn with some astonishment. She figured frequently in newspaper gossip columns euphemistically called 'diaries', and in the glossy magazines which were stuffed with photographs of society people at functions, usually with other people's spouses or 'with a friend'. Her circle of friends was as high as you could get without being married to a royal, and she was on cheek-kissing terms with some of the less naff members of the family.

Lucinda, Lady Wadhurst, made an entrance with the easy self-assurance and appearance of someone who had come straight from Hardy Amies by way of a Helena Rubinstein beauty salon. If Timberlake had been a long-time reader of *Vogue* and *Harper's* he would have spotted her at once as a former cover-girl model. She looked a good ten years younger than her fifty years.

'Inspector Timberlake, do sit down,' she said and waved him towards a massive armchair. It was the sort of chair that folds itself softly around its occupant like a practised seducer. Even an active young man would find it difficult to stand up again without hauling himself to his feet by levering himself upright with his hands on the arms of the chair. Timberlake chose a mahogany chair with tapering, wave-moulded legs and a lyre back, which had gilded strings.

'Thank you for being discreet and not announcing yourself as *Inspector* Timberlake,' she said, smiling. 'It would have set the place buzzing with apprehension and gossip.' She looked at him directly. 'Are you always discreet?'

'I think so – when discretion is needed. But there have to be limits to a policeman's discretion.' The sub-text to that remark was, *Don't think you're going to get special treatment because of your position.*

'Of course. I've made enquiries about you, Mr Timberlake.'

He didn't ask who she'd asked about him. Her contacts with The Establishment must be considerable.

'You are well thought of by the people who matter. I think I can trust you.' Her face became grave. 'I have to.'

Timberlake remained silent and motionless.

'I make no excuses for myself, for what I do. I have all the money I need and more. I play bridge very well, my tennis is passable, and my charity work takes up some of my time. But . . . some years ago I felt the need to *do* something . . . something *outrageous*, amusing. Something . . . *risky*.' With a complete change of mood she asked, 'Would you like a drink?'

'No, thank you.'

Lady Wadhurst remained silent for a long moment, seemingly unaware of Timberlake's presence. At last she said, 'I have established a business of providing introductions.' She hurried on before Timberlake could say anything. 'Introducing young women to men . . .'

Timberlake managed to stop his jaw dropping with astonishment. There was no mistaking the implications.

'Men of the highest standing. Women of class and impeccable reputation. You would be astonished if you knew some of the women involved.' She gave a tight little smile that wasn't reflected in her eyes, and briefly glanced towards an escritoire that had *Debrett's Peerage* and *Who's Who* on it. Timberlake wasn't sure whether she meant him to notice her look.

'Why do they do it?' she went on. 'Pleasure, of course. Excitement . . . and again, the thrill of taking an enormous risk. It heightens other pleasures, as I'm sure you know.'

Timberlake nodded. His mind was racing.

'As for the men,' she continued, 'they all have enormous reputations to consider. What does an . . . archbishop, or a cardinal, or a president, for example, do for feminine companionship on a brief visit to London?' Her tone changed once more. 'Or in England a . . . chief of police, shall we say . . . or a cabinet minister well known for his forthright views on morality and family values? They must all feel totally confident that there will be no scandal, if they feel the need to . . . ' She shrugged. 'And as far as I am concerned, there is the delicious thrill of being privy to a hundred secrets that could bring down a government. And the power that goes with it.'

Timberlake was aching to ask Lady Wadhurst whether she accepted invitations herself.

She was more intuitive than he realized. She looked him straight in the eye and said, smiling once more, 'Only some heads of state.'

'I see,' Timberlake said. He felt it was a rather inadequate observation.

'One more thing, Mr Timberlake. My . . . fees for arranging the introductions: they all go to charity. I don't keep even my telephone expenses.'

'I see,' Timberlake repeated. 'Er, why have you told me all this?'

Lady Wadhurst looked distressed. 'I've heard nothing from one of my young women for three weeks. I have called her but she never answers her phone, and she hasn't called me. She has been with me for, oh, three years now, and this has never happened before. And with all these murders . . .'

'From what you've told me, I hardly think she's like the women who've been murdered in Terrace Vale. They're all fairly cheap street-whores from a relatively small area.'

'But Juliette – she calls herself Juliette Grande – has a flat in Terrace Vale, in York Gardens, which I believe isn't far away from where the murders have been.'

'Even so. From what you have told me, she's hardly likely to be taken for the sort of woman who has been—'

'Lady Wadhurst interrupted. 'I'm not going to say "I've got a feeling . . . " But I *am* intuitive—'

Timberlake was ready to grant her that.

'And I am worried – very worried – about her.' She was very convincing.

Oh, Christ, Timberlake thought. Could there be another one? 'Well, if you give me her address, I'll have a look there myself.'

'Oh, thank you,' Lady Wadhurst said. 'And if she is all right, that will be the end of the matter?'

'Unless there is evidence of something illegal or a complaint is made.'

She looked relieved. 'I don't think there's much chance of that. I really am most grateful.'

Timberlake considered her for a moment. 'You've successfully kept your activities secret this long. Why are you running the risk of everything coming to light now?'

In a low voice she replied, 'I can't just close my

eyes and forget her. I have my obligations to my young women. We are all friends, as well as . . . colleagues.'

In other words, Timberlake thought, *noblesse oblige*.

It was only when he was halfway back to the Terrace Vale nick that he began to think that although Lady Wadhurst had told him the truth, perhaps she hadn't told him the entire truth.

York Gardens was on the affluent side of one of Terrace Vale's invisible internal frontiers. The road was only a hundred yards from The Grove, but it might as well have been a couple of miles. It wasn't the most expensive part of the area, it was occupied by middle- and upper-management executives, successful professional men and well-heeled widows.

Juliette Grande had a flat in a 1930s four-storey block of flats which had been modernized and kept in good order. There were a number of ways Timberlake could have proceeded. First, he could ring the doorbell just to make sure that no one was in the flat. Then he could speak to the caretaker – if there was one – to see if he knew anything about Juliette Grande, and then ask if he had a key to the place. If that failed, he could make the same enquiries of the managing agents. If those approaches failed he could take a couple of uniforms with him and break in on the grounds that someone might be ill or dead inside.

He was in luck. A possibility he had not considered presented itself.

As he rang the doorbell of the flat an over-made-up middle-aged woman wearing a dark-blue overall coat over a green blouse and a voluminous dark skirt came down the stairs. She looked rather like a retired paratrooper in drag.

'I don't think she's there,' she said amiably. 'I haven't seen her for two or three weeks.' She introduced herself as Mrs Wiles, who 'did for' Miss Grande from time to time.

'You don't happen to have a key to the flat, do you?' he asked.

Her reaction satisfied him that she did. Mrs Wiles backed a couple of paces up the stairs, regarding him with deep suspicion.

Timberlake produced his warrant card. 'It's all right, I'm not a burglar,' he said.

Mrs Wiles was only fractionally mollified. It wasn't until he passed his mobile phone to her and had her call Terrace Vale nick that she was convinced of his identity.

'I wish everyone would be as careful as you,' he told her.

'My husband was a copper,' she said. 'Died four years ago.'

'I'm sorry. He sounds like a good one.'

She nodded, studied Timberlake for a moment. 'I remember you now. You was in the paper about that German bloke whose wife and mother-in-law got killed.'

'Have you been in the flat recently?'

She shook her head vigorously. 'Oh, no. I never go in without her calling me and fixing a date. I mean, if I walked in unexpected—' She looked around before lowering her voice and saying archly, '—she might have company.'

'Very thoughtful of you,' Timberlake said. He stood beside the door and waited.

Mrs Wiles pulled out from some recess of her skirt a large bunch of keys on a long chain, which looked robust enough to keep a destroyer safely secured to a dockside, and opened the door with something of a flourish. She was about to follow him into the flat, but he stopped her.

'Better not. Just in case . . . Wait there to lock up behind me.'

Before he entered the flat Timberlake called out a couple of times just to make sure no one was inside. He was pretty sure the place was empty because of a faint smell; not the unmistakable odour of a decomposing body, but a musty, stale smell of long-closed windows and doors.

It was unlike anywhere he had been before, yet within moments he had a strong sense of *déjà vu*, and not for the first time, but he could not place where he had experienced it before.

Timberlake went first to the main bedroom, where he knew he would get the best insight into Juliette Grande's character. It was luxurious and obviously feminine, with one unusual feature. Beyond the foot of the bed was a large-screen television set and video recorder.

The wall-length fitted wardrobe contained a score of ruinously expensive day and evening dresses: Versace, Armani, Lagerfeld and the rest. Equally fashionable underwear, tights, stockings and suspender belts were neatly folded in drawers. Bottles, jars and tubes of top-name makeup and perfumes covered the top of a wide dressing table, together with four real-hair wigs on stands. The rest of the flat was in the same key. The kitchen deep freeze was stacked with Fortnum and Mason provisions, the crockery was from Harrods and the cutlery from Goldsmiths' Hall.

The whole ensemble was like something from a James Bond novel, and equally characterless.

There were no personal documents in the flat: no address book, no diary, nothing with Juliette Grande's name – or anyone else's – on it. Timberlake noted the number on the telephone so he could check later on the calls that had been made.

Finally, dissatisfied with the lack of success on the disappearance of Juliette Grande, he set off for the nick. He had no idea whether the Terrace Vale killer had murdered Juliette Grande and disposed of the body, or whether she had simply gone off with one of her clients, or been knocked down by a car. The Hitchcock thriller *North by Northwest* nagged at him. Usually he was irritated by the thought of the attempt on Cary Grant's life by a crop dusting aircraft, when it would have been much simpler for someone just to drive up to him on the deserted road and shoot him. This time his memory of the film was of the sequence when a government secret agency set up a flat with clothes and personal belongings to establish the existence of a non-existent character. Maybe Juliette Grande doesn't really exist either, he guessed.

He was wrong. Juliette Grande was definitely a real person.

Chapter Fifteen

Timberlake reported to Detective Superintendent Harkness his visit to Juliette Grande's flat. He gave him the full background, including Lady Wadhurst's involvement. When he mentioned her name Harkness did not try to disguise his surprise.

'I've known her for some years and I never suspected for a moment . . . Good heavens.'

'I did promise her I would keep her name out of it if it was at all possible, sir.'

'Yes, of course . . . as long as you're absolutely certain he or she isn't involved in the disappearance.'

'Quite certain. There was no need for her to tell me anything.'

'I don't think there's any connection between the Grande woman going missing and the murders, do you, Harry?'

'Oh, no. They're different worlds.'

Timberlake was halfway home from the nick when he remembered with a shock that he had arranged to go to dinner with his wife that evening at a new French restaurant, with an eclectic menu, that had been warmly recommended by one of the heavyweight

Sunday papers. He had agreed to her suggestion with well-concealed reluctance. He would have much preferred to spend an evening at home to relax: he had been working long hours for some days without a break. Still, it was obvious that Jenny was making an effort to rebuild bridges, and he had to meet her at least halfway. He glanced at his watch. He could just about get to the restaurant in time.

An hour later he was sitting at a table on his own, still waiting. He had drunk half a bottle of Mouton Cadet and eaten enough bread dipped in some marvellous Ligurian olive oil to kill his appetite stone dead. For the past half an hour he had been getting more and more peevish despite the normally soothing effect of the oil and wine, and now depression was beginning to give his ill-temper an extra edge of discontent. The waiter's politeness and attentiveness only deepened the dark purple of his mood, and he was conscious of other diners' amused glances and whispers.

He knew that Jenny was subject to sudden emergency calls just as he was; and he could not deny to himself that he had sometimes kept her waiting. But he had always got someone to pass on a message. Well, almost always.

Eighty minutes after Jenny and Timberlake were due to meet the waiter came over and said quietly, 'Mr Timberlake? There is a lady on the telephone for you.'

There was no doubt who it was. Only Jenny knew where he would be. The station would have called him on his mobile phone, and asked for Inspector Timberlake.

Timberlake rose. 'Tell her I left half an hour ago,

and left no message.' This was one bridge that would not be rebuilt.

Just to be on the safe side, he called the nick on his mobile. No one had asked for him. It was not a good night for Harry Timberlake. He arrived home after having drunk just enough to make him indiscreet without making him incoherent. Jenny was exhausted and badly irritated after an operation which had not been life-threatening but one where everything that could go wrong did, including a student nurse fainting and scattering the contents of the instruments trolley all over the floor.

As a result of their evenings Timberlake and Jenny said things to each other that were insulting, unjust, immoderate and stingingly hurtful.

They sat in angry silence for what seemed a long time. Eventually the anger cooled, to become bitterness and finally sadness. Jenny was the first one to speak.

'We need to talk.'

'Yes.'

'This isn't working, is it?'

'No. I'm sorry. You see, this evening I—'

'It's not just tonight. It's been quite a while.'

'Yes.' He sighed. 'It's the job. Detectives should never marry. It puts too much strain on the wives.'

'You could say the same thing about doctors. Marriage is all right if you've got a husband – or a wife – who's willing to play second fiddle to the other person's career. But if you're both ambitious first violins, the marriage doesn't work.'

'That's rubbish,' Timberlake said sharply. 'There are lots of couples who have successful marriages where both partners have careers.'

'How do you know? Anyway, what's "successful"? Like—' She checked.

'Like ours was . . . at first? Then it's even sadder: the problem isn't with the jobs. It's us. We're both very much first violins.' He sighed again. 'So what can we do to save our marriage?'

'The first thing we have to do is decide whether it's worth saving,' Jenny said instinctively regretting it almost before she had finished speaking.

There was another silence, but different from the first one. It was as if they had just heard of the death of an old friend and could not come to terms with it. The deep toc-toc of the grandfather clock which had belonged to Jenny's parents seemed abnormally loud.

Timberlake was first to speak. Quietly, with a rare hesitancy in his tone, he said, '*I'd* like to save it.'

Eventually Jenny replied. 'The usual thing is a trial separation.' Timberlake shrugged. She went on, 'Look, one of us doesn't have to move out. This house is big enough, and I think we're both mature enough to live our own lives under the same roof. Separate lives?' He looked up, surprised. She added quickly, 'We can still be friends, though; we don't hate each other's guts, do we?'

'I don't.' He glanced at her again, and felt a sudden surge of desire, which he managed to quell.

Jenny turned away and poured herself a whisky. 'Want one?' He shook his head She was struggling to tell him something. At last she said, 'Look, there's something I haven't told you.'

Another man! was Timberlake's immediate thought.

'I've been invited to work in a New York clinic on an exchange visit. I've been doing a lot of specialist thoracic surgery recently and this'd be a marvellous chance to extend my experience.'

'And when will you be leaving?'

'If I go, it'll be at short notice. 'I've been putting off a decision, but I have to give an answer this week. If I don't go, there'll be someone to take my place, and they'll want to know as soon as possible.'

'How long will it be for?'

'Six months, initially. After that . . .' She made an indeterminate gesture.

For some time now life with Jenny had been difficult and abrasive, and there had been times when he himself had contemplated some sort of separation. But in the working-class background of his early youth there still had been a stigma associated with divorce or separation. The thought of his own marriage failing made him uneasy, even though his head told him that these days it was a commonplace.

Now the initiative had come from her, and there was a possibility – probability, really – that *she* was going to leave *him*, something else his strict, old-fashioned father would have found almost unthinkable. It was not easy for Timberlake to accept.

He rose slowly, like an old man. He felt that there was something he ought to say, but he could think of nothing better than, 'Well, that's that. Good night, then.' Somehow, it didn't seem adequate.

They slept in separate rooms, an arrangement they maintained by tacit agreement.

So the night was bad, but the next day was worse.

Timberlake had a medium-sized hangover and a bad bout of depression. He arrived at Terrace Vale nick looking uncharacteristically seedy and feeling awful. When Ted Greening noticed him he briefly wondered whether Timberlake had joined his over-indulgers' club.

'You're looking like something the cat dragged in, Harry,' Greening said with his usual gift for original metaphor.

'I'm just rather crapulent,' Timberlake admitted.

'Yeah, you look shitty,' Greening said, betraying his ignorance of the meaning of the word.

Timberlake moved on, reminded once again that the failings of great men are the consolation of fools.

He sat through the morning conference of the murder squads without saying much, his despondency aggravated by the general lack of progress in the various inquiries. Harkness glanced at him sharply once or twice, but didn't comment.

In addition to studying the reports on the prostitute murders, Timberlake was sneaking a look at some of the latest files on the Mary Docker killing, even though he was officially off that particular inquiry. Somewhere, he thought – he hoped – there would be something to open up the case against his prime – and only – suspect. There was nothing that he could see, and it was making him even rattier.

Towards the end of the day Timberlake found he was again concentrating on the Mary Docker files of witness statements and scientific reports. There was something there if only he could *see* it, he told himself. Then a line from *Henry IV, Part II* sprang to his mind:

Henry IV's remark to his son, the future Henry V, 'Thy wish was father, Harry, to that thought.'

'No it bloody wasn't,' he said out loud. 'He *did* it.'

Harry Timberlake looked at his watch and saw it was much later than he thought. He picked up the files and took them to the room where staff were working on transferring the handwritten and typed files to computer records. There were only two people left there, a civilian woman clerk and Sarah Lewis. He dumped the files in one of the In trays, and went over to her.

'What are you doing?' he asked.

'I'm knitting a Fair Isle sweater for my doberman,' she said tartly before turning to see who had spoken. 'Oops, sorry, guv,' she said. 'I didn't know it was you.' In a quieter voice she added, 'I'm just pissed off to the eyebrows with trying to read bad writing and lousy typing, and staring at the sodding screen. Much more of this and I'll be having Valium sandwiches for lunch. Christ! Look at the time! That's it for today.' She clicked the mouse pointer on Save, then, on Bak before switching off the machine and putting on the cover. She stretched luxuriously like a cat that has just woken up.

Timberlake was suddenly reminded of times they had spent together in bed. Because of work, and more particularly because of his present relationship with Jenny, the line of his sex drive had recently dropped off the bottom of the graph. Sarah's movements had sent it shooting up again, and she was quite aware of it. He was on the point of inviting her for a drink, or a meal, thought better of it, then asked himself, Why not? Before he came to a decision, it was made for him.

In a quiet voice so that the other person in the room did not hear, Sarah said, 'Any chance of a lift home, Harry? My car's in for a service.' Quite unnecessarily she added, 'You could come in for a coffee, or something.' They had both already understood and come to an agreement.

On the way to Sarah's home they stopped to pick up some Chinese take-away from a shop that Sarah said was markedly better than average. 'I just don't feel up to cooking tonight,' she said. Neither of them remarked on the fact that they had bought enough for two people. Timberlake also bought a bottle of Côtes du Luberon, which had been one of their favourites when they were year-long lovers.

She had moved since the last time Timberlake had been to her home. She had a one-bedroom flat on the fifth floor of an upmarket block, plus a garage space in the underground carpark. As her car was being serviced, Timberlake put his own car in Sarah's space.

Almost all the furniture had been changed from her previous place – 'I flogged the last lot with the flat,' she told him – which gave this visit a sense of novelty, even expectancy. As they ate, they took it in turns to talk about work, with a fair degree of bitchiness, which made them both feel a little better.

She said how fed up she was about not being able to follow up the drugs inquiry at the Abbot Perceval school, now she had a good lead.

When it was Timberlake's turn to whinge, his first

complaint was about the activities of the media. 'I've had it up to here with "Yorkshire Ripper II", "West London Ripper", "Son of Jack the Ripper" and all the rest.'

'Funny,' Sarah said, sounding as amusing as the sound of a coffin lid being nailed down, 'I've just been reading about Jack the Ripper.' She indicated a paperback on the table. 'Interesting.'

Timberlake picked it up and glanced at the publicity on the back cover before ploughing on. 'Journalists are all over the place, questioning the brasses, talking to local residents, getting underfoot, making our job all the more difficult as people start imagining things and making things up to please the hacks and get their names in the papers. If I see another quote from some brainless gasbag about a sinister-looking man with staring eyes, I'll . . . On top of that, Darren Webb's still running the Mary Docker case.'

'Maybe you'll get a break and be put back on it,' she said, trying to sound supportive.

'Sorry. You've got your own problems,' Timberlake said.

'I could do with a result,' Sarah said. 'I might have bagged a villain if that horrible turd Greening had left me on the cannabis inquiry at the school, but . . .'

Despite the intimacy of the moment, Timberlake was slightly ill at ease with her slagging off his own superior officer, even though he mentally agreed Greening was a steaming shit. He would not put it past Greening deliberately to take Sarah off her case to stop her having another success. Greening hated almost all foreigners and all good-looking men. He thought he hated women, too, but the truth was he was afraid of them.

'You might still get your result if I can fix something.' Timberlake said. 'Most coppers won't have anything like that if they're in the job until they're fifty-five. And you're still young. There's no telling what you might do.' Neither of them spoke for a while, as their respective hormones began to push thoughts of work from their minds.

After a while Timberlake said, 'I'd better ring home.' Not that she'd worry too much, but . . .' He picked up the phone and began to dial his home number, hung up halfway through and pressed 141 before dialling the number again. 'It's me,' he said. 'I'll be home very late. If there's anything really important, you can get me on the mobile.' He turned to Sarah. 'Answering machine,' he told her.

Although they knew that they were going to bed together, the moment of spontaneity had been back at the station and now they were both faintly embarrassed about breaking the ice. At last Timberlake said – a shade too loudly – 'Is your shower big enough for two?' It was.

He had almost forgotten how Sarah looked when she was naked, and once again it was almost like seeing her for the first time. He found the sight of her and the feel of her smooth, wet skin under the shower very arousing. She sighed deeply as he caressed her breasts, then moved one hand slowly down his body.

Rather shakily she said, 'God! I hope I can remember how to do it.'

Surprised, he replied, 'It's like riding a bicycle; you never lose the knack. Haven't you, er . . . ?

'I might as well have been in quarantine. I had the urge, all right, but there wasn't anyone I wanted to . . .' She looked away and said, not altogether convincingly, 'Besides, I haven't had the time. Then, after a while, I didn't miss it all that much. Finally, not at all, really. Well, not much . . . What about you?'

'Much the same. It's not all that great at home these days.' He stopped the conversation by kissing her with his tongue deep inside her mouth, with one hand on her breast. While the water still cascaded down on them he put his hands on her buttocks and lifted her off her feet. Instinctively she wrapped her legs round him. He thrust into her for a few moments, then pulled away.

'The floor's slippery. If we fall we might break something,' he said.

'Well, as long as it's only a leg or an arm.'

They were both highly excited by the time they got to the bed. Timberlake planned to delay his climax by trying to recall England's 1966 World Cup team, and then Fulham's team in their losing Cup Final against West Ham in 1975, but to his surprise Sarah had an explosive orgasm quite quickly, which set him off simultaneously.

He wondered whether she had been as sexually inactive as she had claimed, but before he could make the awful mistake of mentioning it, she said, 'God, I didn't expect *that* quite so soon.' There was no mistaking her sincerity. Anyway, what the hell, he thought.

Their second bout of lovemaking was slower, more leisurely and totally satisfying. They slept fitfully for about half an hour in each other's arms before they began again.

'Oh, God, I'd forgotten it could be like this,' Sarah said as he continued to press into her. '*Rwy'n du garu di*, I think,' she murmured with a deep sigh.

'What?' he asked dreamily.

'I said that's lovely,' she lied, then cried out as her body shuddered with another orgasm.

They slept a while, then he left her just before five o'clock.

When he got home, the pilot light on the answering machine was still blinking. He checked: it was his own message to say he would be late. He erased it from the tape.

His wife's bed had not been slept in.

Timberlake decided to have another couple of hours' sleep. When the alarm woke him, he felt weak, but otherwise marvellous. For the first time in quite a while, he felt sure he was going to have a good week at the nick.

He was in for the shock of his life; one that would fire a broadside into his carefully reasoned theories.

Timberlake entered his office and had hardly sat down when Molly Dobson followed him in. She was dressed in a Sloppy Joe sweater and jeans, and was carrying a large shoulder bag and a polystyrene cup of Terrace Vale coffee. For a moment he thought she had come collecting for a children's charity.

Molly Dobson was the 27-year-old fingerprint technician who had lifted prints from Vicki Stevens's flat. Timberlake also recognized her as the androgenous figure he had seen at Sharon Lester's flat. She was as slender as a twelve-year-old schoolgirl without looking anorexic, with an angelic-looking face and short dark hair. She could have been Audrey Hepburn's daughter. Even beery, sexist macho males who trumpeted they liked women 'with a bit of meat on them, something to get hold of . . .' would have been enchanted by her.

She sat down on the chair opposite Timberlake, put down the coffee, opened her bag and placed an official folder on the desk in front of her.

Molly Dobson gave a smile that would have softened the blackest heart. She said, 'There's been a right royal fuckup somewhere. The prints from the Vicki Stevens flat in The Grove . . .' She took a mouthful of the coffee, grimaced, and added, 'Your sodding cat needs killing.'

Timberlake partially pulled himself together. 'The fingerprints . . . How, exactly?'

'Well, either Vicki Stevens and Mary Docker, the victim at Holly Mansions, have the same fingerprints, which is about as likely as winning the lottery jackpot without buying a ticket, or they're one and the same person.'

'That's impossible,' Timberlake blurted before he could completely collect his thoughts.

'Bollocks,' the angelic waif retorted briskly. 'I'll say it again. Mary Docker left her dabs all over the Holly Mansion flat, and hers are the *only* ones in The Grove place. For a start, I got four separate matching prints from the two places, each pair with a minimum of twenty points of reference, and another two pairs with eighteen matching points. So Mary Docker and Vicki Stevens are one and the same. I'm not a detective, but even I can work that out. If it's buggered up your investigation, hard fucking luck. I suppose you know something about fingerprints.'

'I can tell an AA from a TT, and I know the difference between a CI, CM and CO,' he said coldly.

There are three basic patterns of fingerprints: Loops, Arches and Whorls: Timberlake was quoting from one coding system of fingerprint classification, in which AA means Plain Arch; TT, Tented Arch; CI, CM and CO stand for Inner Whorl, Meeting Whorl and Outer Whorl respectively. Normally he wouldn't have shown off like this, but the young woman had got under his skin.

Molly Dobson was unabashed. She grinned. 'Love fifteen,' she said cheerfully with a beguiling smile, and was briefly forgiven, until she said 'Aren't you a clever cock.'

She took two sheets of paper from the folder and handed them to Timberlake.

'Here's my report: one copy for you, one for old Iron Knickers.'

'Huh?'

'Detective Superintendent Harkness to you.' She rose to go.

'By the way,' Timberlake said, 'are you going to the Cheltenham Ladies' College Old Girls' reunion this year?'

Molly Dobson smiled again. 'Love thirty,' she said as she exited.

By the time the dust had settled in Timberlake's office after Molly Dobson had exploded her bombshell, many of the officers working for the murder squads had gone out on their enquiries. Detective Superintendent Harkness was still in the building, of course, as were Darren Webb, Nigel Larkin, Shylock Holmes and a few other detective constables. They gathered in the conference room, which looked as underpopulated as the Oval on the last day of a Test when England need 500-plus to win.

When Timberlake had briefed them on the fingerprint evidence there was a heavy silence. Harkness was the first one to speak.

'Well, it's quite possible that the Mary Docker murder is associated with the other killings after all. For the moment, at least,' Harkness said heavily, 'we shan't release the information that Mary Docker and Vicki Stevens were one and the same person. The media, and certain newspapers in particular, would have a field day . . .'

'Getting under our feet, interviewing everyone who knew her in either of her personas,' Timberlake interjected.

'Shouldn't that be "personae", guv?' Webb whispered.

'No.'

'And it could be useful to have that piece of information up our sleeves when we question any suspects,' Harkness concluded.

'What beats me,' Darren Webb said slowly, after recovering from Timberlake's snub, 'is how she managed to do her job at the factory and whoring at the same time.'

'She never worked in The Grove after two o'clock in the morning, according to Sharon Lester,' Timberlake pointed out. He went on 'Mary Docker, or Vicki Stevens, whatever you want to call her, was an extraordinary woman: the most extreme case of multiple personality I've ever come across.'

'Schizophrenia,' somebody said.

'No. Schizophrenia isn't split personality,' Timberlake said. 'It's severe disorder and distortion of thought and mood, social withdrawal.' He was only trying to be helpful; he didn't actually mean to sound like a clever dick. 'As Mary Docker she was a one-man woman, well-behaved, churchgoing, "kept herself to herself". As Vicki Stevens she was promiscuous – I know all prostitutes are promiscuous by definition – but apparently she was exceptional in actually enjoying the sex. And rather noisily, apparently.'

There was a muted cough or two and some shuffling of feet as one or two detectives tried to think up a funny reply, then thought better of it.

'Sir,' Timberlake said after a moment. 'I don't think it's necessarily true that the Docker murder is associated with the other killings. It might well be, but for the moment we don't know who the murderer killed. Did he kill Mary Docker, or Vicki Stevens?'

Chapter Sixteen

Harry Timberlake had a lot on his mind. It was true there was some sunshine as well as clouds: the Yardbird Charlie case had been thoroughly buttoned up, and he and his accomplices had been remanded in custody at the Magistrate's Court to appear at the Old Bailey. He had been caught bang to rights: the guns and drugs paraphernalia found in the Cairo Walk house would mean he'd be having porridge for breakfast for years. But Timberlake wanted more than that: he wanted a conviction for Dimi the Greek's murder.

Another stone in his shoe, as a goodfella might put it, was his disintegrating relationship with his wife, exacerbated by the explosive renaissance of his affair with Sarah Lewis. He might have dismissed this as a meaningless, albeit highly pleasurable, one-off exercise in nostalgia, but he had an uncomfortable feeling that it might be rather more than that.

More recently, there was the disappearance of Juliette Grande. Although he could put this case – if indeed it *was* a case – on the back burner of his mind, it was something he would have to deal with sooner or later.

And then there was the other, sharper stone in his shoe. Most of all, like Everest looming over the foothills of the other cases, were the murders of the prostitutes. Solution of those cases was as far away as ever.

Sarah Lewis had her problems, too. She was on her way home after a hard day at the keyboard transferring boring, probably irrelevant statements on to one of the computers at the nick. Her route normally took her nowhere near the Abbot Perceval Secondary Modern, but her car somehow managed to take her past it. 'What the hell am I going to see at this time of the evening?' she asked herself grumpily. No sooner had she formulated the words than she saw two figures coming out of the school gates. One was her snout, Jocko McLeish. The second was Alfred Herbert Gunter, a man with criminal convictions, including one for possession of cannabis with intent to supply.

He was also caretaker of the school.

As soon as she got to her flat she picked up the phone. She was on the point of calling Timberlake's home number, but changed her mind and dialled his mobile phone instead. He answered after three rings.

'It's me, Sarah,' she said. 'Where are you?'

'In the car, on my way home.'

'I need to talk to you. About the job,' she added quickly, in case he thought it was something to do with the night he spent at her flat. She didn't want to give the impression of being a possessive female, although Timberlake would know her better than that, anyway. There was a long silence. She wondered whether he had gone into a transmission blackspot.

'Are you at home?' he asked at last.

'Yes.'

'I'll be there in ten minutes.'

Sarah had tea ready when Timberlake arrived. She

thought it was a safe option, without the suggestive undercurrents of brandy or their favourite wine. He gave her a brotherly kiss on the cheek and sat on an upright dining chair. 'OK, Sarah, what's the problem?'

She told him about seeing her snout, Jocko McLeish, with Gunter, the caretaker. 'I can't just leave it, but if I report it and Gunter is supplying the stuff, Greening'll take the case out of my hands and grab all the credit himself. What should I do, Harry?'

He thought carefully for a moment before replying. 'It *could* be a coincidence that Gunter and your snout are involved.' He shook his head. 'It's much more likely the caretaker is dealing on a small scale, just to the kids at the school. If there was any sign of Class A drugs being pushed there I'd say the situation would be urgent, and you'd have to report it at once. But cannabis, well . . . another few days . . .' He added quickly, 'For God's sake don't tell anyone I said so. If you can keep an eye on Gunter in your spare time—'

Sarah snorted with derision. 'Spare time?'

'Yes, I know. Look, I'll see if I can fix something unofficially. If you can find where Gunter gets his stuff, we may be able to lay our hands on someone higher up the distribution ladder.' He yawned uncontrollably. 'Sorry. Sarah, if it's not too much trouble, could I have a coffee? I don't want to fall asleep driving home.'

She rose. 'Sure.' Impulsively she added, 'If you have to. Go home, I mean.' The possibility of anything more than asking Timberlake for advice simply hadn't crossed her mind when she first called him, and her own words took her by surprise. At once she felt her heart beat faster, and there was the familiar stirring at the pit of her stomach.

Timberlake looked at her for a long moment before taking his mobile phone from his pocket. He dialled his home number. 'It's me. I shan't be home till late. Don't bother to wait up.' There was more than a hint of sarcasm in the way he spoke the last sentence. He snapped the phone shut. 'Answering machine again,' he told Sarah.

Their last love-making had been passionate and fresh because they had been apart for so long. This time it was quite different, although none the less exciting and possibly even more satisfying; there was a comforting sense of total ease in each other's company, of warm empathy, as if they had been friends and lovers for years. Although he was no great fan of Samuel Beckett, Timberlake was reminded of a newspaper headline quoting one of his remarks. 'Sex without love is like coffee without brandy.' This unaccountable change in his feelings for Sarah during their lovemaking, and their relaxing together afterwards, made him wonder exactly what his relationship with Sarah was becoming. It made him slightly uneasy.

Just before he left her Sarah asked softly, 'Harry, where are we going?'

'For the moment, just with the current. Let's see if we like where it takes us.' Although it was as good an answer as any, it did nothing to quieten his uneasiness.

Timberlake arrived early next morning at Terrace Vale nick, before Detective Superintendent Harkness, and well before Ted Greening. He was in luck: Detective

Constable Benny 'Shylock' Holmes was at his desk as well.

'Benny have you got a minute?' Timberlake called out, and went to his office. Holmes followed him in. 'Shut the door,' Timberlake said. 'This is strictly between us, all right?' he went on. 'I need a favour.'

'That I knew when you spoke the first word, guv. You called me Benny. I'm always Shylock to everyone, except when they want something.'

'I never call you Shylock, Benny. This is totally confidential. There's something I'd like you to do, but if you say no, I'll understand and there'll be no comeback.'

Benny Holmes nodded.

Timberlake explained what Sarah had told him about seeing, Gunter, the caretaker at Abbot Perceval School, with Jocko McLeish. He was careful to refer to Sarah as DC Lewis, but wondered whether Benny had guessed what their relationship was. Well if he had, he was probably the least likely of the CID officers to gossip.

'DC Lewis has decided to keep observation on Gunter and the school in her spare time, but it's asking a lot of her to do it on her own. You were working with her at the beginning and I thought you might think it worthwhile to put in some unofficial, unpaid overtime. I think there's a fair chance you might get a result.'

Benny Holmes looked directly at Timberlake for an uncomfortably long moment. 'You got children?'

'No.'

'I've got two. If we can drop the hook on villains who sell drugs to kids . . . But, guv, one question: why you? Why didn't Sarah come to me herself?'

'She was going to,' Timberlade lied, 'but I told her it might carry more weight coming from me. It'd be a pity for both of you to miss getting a result because of . . . Well, you know who. Besides, you need someone senior in CID who knows what you're doing, and can help cover your backs if anyone asks where you are, or any flak starts to fly around.'

'Help, unofficially.'

'Unofficially, officially; whatever it takes.'

Benny sighed. 'OK, count me in. You're a hard man, guv.'

'You're right. You're right,' Timberlake said, straightfaced.

On his way out Benny Holmes nearly collided with Jeff Waters.

'That's it, knock me over, you great Nazi bully,' Benny said. In fact the two detectives got on very well together. They shared a common experience of racial harassment from other policemen, although it could have been much worse. Waters's intimidating physical presence discouraged too much liberty-taking, while Holmes's sharp wit could penetrate the thickest skin. Someone once said that slagging off Benny Holmes was like pissing into a strong wind.

Chief Inspector Ted Greening gave a long, bubbling, boiling-tar sort of cough. When it tapered off into a sort of intermittent wheeze, he instinctively pulled out his packet of cigarettes, then checked. He glanced across the desk to Doctor O'Shay, who was regarding him with amused pity. O'Shay was a former police surgeon who had known Greening since he was a detective sergeant. Greening was allegedly a private patient, although he never went as far as actually paying O'Shay.

The doctor got his moneysworth out of the relationship by being frank to the point of rudeness to Greening, a luxury he couldn't afford with his other patients.

'Well, what's wrong with you apart from what I can see and hear?' he asked in a strong Cork accent.

'I just don't feel right in myself,' Greening said plaintively. 'My nerves are all shot, and I can't sleep properly.' This was partially correct, for Greening did not sleep as nature intended. He regularly fell into something like a deep coma, induced by alcohol. He began to cough again, and this time defiantly lit up a cigarette. He drew in a lungful of smoke as desperately as a man dragged from the sea taking his first breath of air. Dr O'Shay pointedly got up and opened the window with a thump.

'Take off your jacket and roll up your sleeve,' he ordered.

'You're not going to give me a jab?' Greening asked anxiously.

'For getting yourself into this state I ought to give you a right hook. No, I'm just going to use my sphygmomanometer.'

'What the hell's *that*?' Greening said in alarm.

The doctor ignored him. 'Now put out that cigarette.'

Greening pinched off the burning end and put the three-quarter length cigarette back in the packet.

Dr O'Shay opened up the sphygmomanometer's case and proceeded to take Greening's blood pressure.

In disbelief he took it three times before saying, 'Jesus Christ.'

'Whassamatter?' Greening demanded.

O'Shay didn't answer the question; he wanted to frighten Greening into doing something about his health. 'Pull up your shirt,' he said. Using his stethoscope he began to listen to Greening's chest, and then his heart. 'Mother of God,' he muttered when the examination was complete.

'I'm not going to ask you to give up smoking and drinking; knowing you I might just as well tell you to flap your arms and fly. But . . .' He looked at Greening intently. 'Cut the fags and booze down by half. For a start. Right away. Otherwise . . . And lose a stone, *at least.*' He shook his head. 'I'm not joking: your blood pressure's a candidate for the *Guinness Book of Records*, there's more liquid than air in your lungs, and your heart's got more murmurs than a confessional. I shudder to think what your cholesterol level must be. D'you ever suffer from loss of breath? Stupid question, of course you do. Chest pains?'

'Bit of heartburn sometimes, you know,' Greening said with a ghastly smile.

'Pain go across your chest? Down your left arm?'

Greening shook his head. He didn't trust himself to speak.

'How're your waterworks?'

It took a moment for the doctor's meaning to sink into Greening's alarmed mind. 'Oh, you know. All right, I suppose.'

'Any trouble starting, or stopping? D'you dribble at all?'

'No, not really.'

'Hmmm. Well, if you have any trouble like that, come and see me right away.' With a wry smile he added, 'I can't afford to lose private patients.'

The irony was lost on Greening, who was feeling on the edge of panic. For once he looked almost pale, instead of his usual whisky-red.

O'Shay finally eyed him sympathetically. 'Look, Ted, if you like I can refer you to a consultant, National Health, of course. He'll recommend you have a medical board for retirement on health reasons.'

'For Chrissake don't do that, doc! I haven't got all that long to go now, and I want to get a full pension.'

'What would you like me to do, then?'

'Could you manage a sick note for a couple of weeks off work? Not for stress, though.'

O'Shay sighed. 'OK. I'll make it for influenza for, er, seven days.' He began writing. 'Come and see me again same time next week.'

'Sure, doc. And thanks.' Greening pulled his shirt back into position, more or less, and put on his jacket.

O'Shay held out the certificate, but held on to it when Greening tried to take it. His expression was serious.

'Remember what I said about losing weight and cutting down on smoking and drinking. I'm not joshing you, Ted. If you don't, you could keel over at any time, walking down the street, at the office, in the pub. The only pension you'll get is a widow's pension paid to your wife.'

Greening went pale again. His hands were trembling as he walked out of the surgery. He walked straight across the road to a pub and ordered a double brandy. It steadied his hands and nerves, for the moment.

'Oh, what the hell, what do doctors know anyway?' he said to the barman, who'd heard that from different customers more times that he could remember.

Timberlake was getting his paperwork up to date before the evening murder squad conference. For once the door to his office was closed. The Terrace Vale station had almost supernatural powers to produce strange sounds ranging from creaks to unidentifiable minor booms and bangs, peculiar smells of unknown origin and, most of all, draughts even when the air inside and outside the premises was still. It was as if all the sighs heaved by villains and police were stored up for a while by some paranormal force which then allowed them to escape slowly. One of these mysterious currents had been ruffling the papers on Timberlake's desk, and he had closed the window and the door of his office in a fairly vain attempt to stop it. There was a knock on the door. 'Come in,' Timberlake said rather irritably, barely looking up.

Molly Dobson, the civilian SOCO fingerprint expert, entered. She was carrying her usual shoulder bag, from which she took a file and put it on Timberlake's desk. 'Fifteen–forty,' she said. 'You're right again.'

His mind was still on the contents of the file of the Mary Docker case, and for a moment he was at a loss.

'Your Juliette Grande,' Molly went on. 'I went through her flat like you asked me, and there's no two ways. She's Vicki Stevens and Mary Docker. Same prints all over the place. She certainly got around, didn't she?'

'No wonder I had a gut feeling of *déjà vu* when I was in their flats,' Timberlake said, half to himself. 'Same style, same person. But three separate identities: one as an office worker, another as a low-life brass and the third as a very high-class call-girl.'

'I don't know how she managed it,' Molly said with the faintest hint of admiration in her tone.

'She worked only part time in the factory office, as Vicki Stevens the tart she went home earlier than the other women, and had maybe just three or four dates a month as a call-girl.'

'Even so.'

For a normally observant man Timberlake was particularly slow on this occasion. With something of a mild shock, for the first time since she had come into the office Timberlake really noticed Molly Dobson. Instead of her jeans and Sloppy Joe sweater she had on a dark blue trouser suit with a white blouse, but that was not what took his attention. She was wearing light, but effective makeup: mascara on her long lashes, a faint blush of colour on her cheeks and a light lipstick which enhanced her lips, all of which Timberlake found rather sensual.

He was going to tell her she looked very attractive, but kept the remark to himself. There had been a lot of justified complaints of sexual harassment in the police, and some imaginary; he didn't want to take any chances. Instead he said, 'You going to a party or something?' It was an oblique acknowledgement of her appearance.

She smiled. 'No.'

'Well, I'm very grateful,' Timberlake said. 'Finding out about Juliette Grande being Mary Docker could put an entirely new complexion on the case.'

'You were the one who told me to check.'

'You discovered that she was Vicki Stevens as well. That was the key to the whole thing.'

'If there're any more compliments flying round I'll have to start ducking.'

'So, thanks. I owe you one. A large one.'

Molly Dobson looked at him steadily. 'So what about a drink after work?'

'Sure. No, sorry. I've got the car.'

'One drink would be too much?'

'Uhuh. Personal rule.'

'Well, I eat, too.'

It was his turn to stare. 'Dinner?'

'Tonight?' she asked.

He laughed. 'All right. I'll pick you up. Eight o'clock. Where do you live?'

'My address and telephone number are in the folder.'

She rose, gave him a brilliant smile, turned and went out.

The door had hardly closed behind her when Timberlake said out loud, 'Christ, what the hell am I doing?'

He had little enough time to worry about it: the news he had to give to the conference pushed other thoughts out of his head.

When he had finished telling Detective Superintendent Harkness and the others the news of Juliette Grande/Mary Docker and his own thoughts on the implications, Timberlake concluded, 'So the problem is which one of the three women did the murderer kill? Mary Docker herself, Vicki Stevens, or Juliette Grande?'

'Your two alternative hypotheses are these, then, Harry,' Harkness said. 'First, Mary Docker was actually the intended victim, and the perpetrator was unaware of, or indifferent to, her other two personas. In other words, it was an ordinary, straightforward murder. Second, he – let's call the killer "he" for the moment – wanted to kill either Vicki Stevens or Juliette Grande, and killed Mary Docker to camouflage his crime and lead us in the wrong direction.'

'In the second case it presupposes our murderer knew of the multiple identities, which seems pretty unlikely.'

'I can see a motive for someone killing Vicki Stevens: a nutcase, for a start. Or, for example, a pimp to teach her a lesson. Or give the other girls who were holding out an object lesson,' Bob Crust suggested.

'If none of the prostitutes knew that Vicki Stevens was also Mary Docker, it wouldn't be much of a warning to the other women,' Nigel Larkin said brightly. 'They wouldn't know.'

One or two dark looks were aimed in his direction.

'What about Juliette Grande?' Bob Crust said. 'Could she have been the intended victim?'

'A high-class call-girl? Why go to all the trouble of tracking her to Holly Mansions and topping her there?' said Alistair McPhail. 'I can't imagine anyone having a motive to kill Juliette Grande and track her all the way to Holly Mansions to do it.'

'Oh, I can.' Timberlake said sombrely. 'I can.'

He looked at Harkness, who nodded agreement.

'I'll see if I can learn anything from one of my friends. It'll be difficult, but it's worth a try.'

Timberlake had second thoughts. 'D'you really think they might, sir?'

Harkness's expression was enough.

Chapter Seventeen

Molly Dobson lived in a coach house attached to a large Edwardian house on a busy main road in the nearby Castle area, on the other side of the river from Terrace Vale. A line of tall trees at the front of what had been a garden but was now a gravel-topped parking space for half a dozen cars did a fairly effective job of shielding the house from traffic noise. Timberlake arrived at five to eight in an upmarket minicab he frequently used. As Molly let him in she stood half-shielded by the door. When he saw her he was rather nonplussed to see she was wearing an ankle-length dressing gown. 'Am I too early?' he asked.

'No. Why?'

'Well . . .' He indicated her dressing gown.

She chuckled. 'I'm almost ready. It'll only take me a minute: I just didn't know what to wear. Where are we going? The Ritz, or Burger King?' She led him into the lounge, which was surprisingly spacious. The furniture was all good, but more the sort of thing he would expect in a middle-aged, rather stuffy couple.

'Neither, actually. A place near Sloane Square. Used to be a private house – mansion, really. Specializes in Italian food, although all the staff are French. There's English cuisine as well, if you're not keen on Italian.'

'Sounds great. How formal is it?'

He stood near a light and held out his arms sideways. He was wearing his second-best suit, another Harrods sale purchase.

She inspected him quizzically. 'Hmm. Little black dress, I think. D'you want a drink while I put it on? You'll only have time for a small one. I'm fast.' She smiled wickedly. 'I mean quick.' She turned and hurried upstairs.

Molly was as good as her word. In a couple of minutes she was back wearing a black dress, tights and court shoes. Her only jewellery were an antique ring on her right hand and a pearl necklace, which looked genuine to Timberlake's unpractised eye. She slipped on a large, handsome woollen shawl, picked up a small handbag and said, 'Ta-ra!' She looked quite special, light years distant from the casually dressed ragamuffin who first walked into his office.

As they walked to the waiting minicab Molly said, 'Ground rule number one. I'm a civilian, so I'm going to call you Harry.'

'Fine, Molly.'

They both smiled.

La Letizia was smooth. It was only Timberlake's second visit to the restaurant, but he was greeted – not too effusively – by name, and was asked, 'Your usual table, sir?' Molly was suitably impressed.

In the relaxed ambience of the restaurant Molly became communicative. She said that she preferred science to the arts, and was studying with the Open University for her M.Sc., which surprised Timberlake a little.

'Why?' she asked. 'D'you think that instead I should

be prospecting for a husband, so I can stay at home and cook and mend, and change nappies?'

'I didn't realize I gave the impression of being a dinosaur.'

'Sorry. I just get pissed- fed up sometimes by people asking me "Why aren't you married?" and some of them make things worse by adding, ". . . a good-looking girl like you".'

'So what sort of job do you want to do?'

'I don't know, yet. Science, of course. I'll see. In the meantime, I don't want a draggy husband hanging round my neck.'

'Oh, by the way, why all the effing and blinding the first time we met?'

'Coppers can often be real bastards with women. Effing them before they eff you can help keep them at arm's length.'

Briefly Timberlake wondered whether she was a lesbian.

She went on, 'Sometimes I wish I had a face like and old boot and a figure like a telephone directory.'

Timberlake laughed out loud. 'But not often.'

Molly Dobson laughed, too.

The restaurant had discreet background music coming from concealed, high-quality speakers. There was no Muzak, any more than there was ketchup on the tables. After a few bars of piano playing Molly Dobson looked up and said, 'Art Tatum.'

Timberlake stopped with a forkful of scallops halfway to his mouth. 'You're right,' he said after a moment.

'Of course I am,' she replied indignantly. "Willow Weep for Me". Unmistakable. Opens with a pure

Gershwin passage. Wait till you hear the end. Absolute fireworks.'

'I do know the recording,' Timberlake said, a little huffily.

'But have you *got* it? I have.'

He looked at her almost as if she had announced she had won the lottery. 'Can I borrow it some time?'

'No.' She smiled. 'But you can come and listen to it some time.'

'Great! Have a brandy?' Timberlake offered.

'Well, I don't know. One brandy and I'm nearly anybody's,' she answered. With perfect timing she added, 'I'll have a double.'

Sarah and Benny Holmes were seated in his small, nondescript Japanese car near the entrance to the Abbot Perceval Secondary Modern school, parked immediately under a street lamp so the interior of the car was in complete shadow. They were having sandwiches and coffee from a flask which she had prepared.

'Salt beef?' Benny asked, lifting the top slice of his sandwich. 'I didn't know you were Jewish.'

'I heard a rumour that you are.'

'Did I ever tell you the story of Shimon Meyer? For fifty years he always took dinner at Lou's café, and for forty years he always had the same waiter, Bernie. One day Shimon won a big prize on the lottery. He ordered a very special meal with wine that didn't come out of a bottle with a screw top. At the end he had a Monte Cristo cigar, and when Bernie asked him if he wanted coffee, Shimon said, "I'll have a demi-tasse".

' "A what?" Bernie said.

' "A demi-tasse."

'Bernie shrugged, walked away and came back with a big, thick mug filled to the brim. "I asked for a demi-tasse," Shimon said loftily.

' "So drink half." '

Sarah laughed, and nearly choked on a piece of sandwich. Benny thumped her on the back. She wheezed for a moment, then her breathing returned to normal.

'Thanks, Benny.'

'Oy, you all right? Such a disappointment. I thought that finally someone was going to die laughing at one of my jokes.'

Before Sarah could reply, Benny said quickly, 'There he is.'

The caretaker Alfred Herbert Gunter was coming out of the school by a side gate. He paused, and looked up and down the road. He seemed to stare right at the two detectives, but gave no reaction. It was obvious he had not seen them. He walked away from them; fortunately for Benny and Sarah, so they could follow him without having to make a U-turn which might have drawn attention to them.

Tracking Gunter was easy; he was clearly unaware that he was being shadowed. Whenever they came to a space between cars parked by the side of the road they pulled in for a few moments, never letting him out of their sight, before resuming their slow-motion chase. He led the two detectives to a main road on the fringes of the Peacehaven Hill area.

Finally Gunter turned into the doorway of a closed second-hand shop. He was not trying to hide, for the doorway was well lit by a fluorescent street lamp in front of the entrance. The detectives parked their car opposite, just out of Gunter's eyeline, but they could see his silhouette through the shop's side window.

Gunter looked at his watch.

'He's waiting for a meet,' Benny said softly, as if he were afraid Gunter could actually hear him.

Despite the fact that the seventy-year-old recording, even cleaned up and re-recorded on cassette, was scratchy and lacked depth, Timberlake was staggered by the brilliance of the performances of the musicians.

'The Art Tatum record was marvellous,' he said, 'but I prefer that last one, the "Black Bottom Stomp". Jelly Roll Morton was the outstanding piano player of New Orleans-style jazz, which I like more than swing anyway.'

'He wasn't better than Tatum.'

'They were different. Incidentally, the clarinettist on the Morton recording was Omer Simeon. Nobody – but nobody – at that time was a greater technician on the instrument. I remember I heard a radio programme a long time ago when someone described that last chorus of "Stomp" as totally controlled hysteria.' He finished the glass of wine he was holding rather precariously on his chest while he lay almost horizontally on Molly's sofa. 'How did you get into jazz, and get that collection of recordings?'

'My father. He was a jazz guitarist. Not a particularly good one, as far as I can remember, but he was music-mad.' There was something in her tone which warned him that she didn't want to talk about him.

She changed the subject abruptly. 'I've had a great evening.'

'So have I. The best one in a very long time.'

'It's late. Or lateish, anyway,' she said, more as a question than a statement.

'D'you want me to go?' he asked, not stirring.

'No. But won't your wife be wondering where you are? Maybe even worried about you?'

He gave a rueful laugh. 'No, to both. We're separated. *De facto*, if not *de jure*.'

'Honest?'

'Honest as the night is long.'

'So shall we go to bed?' she said, adding quickly, while Timberlake was still getting his breath, 'But get a couple of things right, Harry. I don't always go to bed on the first date, and sometimes not on the tenth, or twentieth. We had a super meal, and listened to some great music. Now we can enjoy something more if you want. If not . . .' She shrugged.

'I want.'

Their foreplay was leisurely but brief: they were both too excited to hold back for too long. Molly turned her back to Timberlake, arranging her legs so penetration was easy. Her orgasm was sudden and intense: her whole frame quivered and shook as violently as a wet dog's shaking itself dry. She made low sighs which she strangled deep in her throat. Timberlake was taken by surprise for he was still some way from reaching his own climax.

Molly lay still for some moments until her breathing returned to near normality. Without warning she turned rapidly, rose up and straddled him almost before he was aware of it, guiding his penis into her.

She rotated her hips and rose up and down on him with increasing force and rapidity. Her eyes were burning as she looked down at him, and he knew she was turning this into something of a battle, trying to make him come quickly.

He countered by using his old trick of mentally reciting the signals alphabet: *Alpha, Bravo, Charlie, Delta, Echo*, and right through to *X-ray, Yankee and Zulu*, but he remained fully conscious of the enormous pleasure she was giving him.

Molly realized he was deliberately resisting her. 'You bastard,' she said with a crooked smile, and increased her efforts.

He determined to hold out until the top of his head blew off. *Mellor, Cutbush, Lacy, Moore, Fraser, Conway, Mullery, Mitchell, Busby, Barrett* . . . 'But that's only ten,' Timberlake told himself. 'Who the hell . . . ? Oh, *Slough!* His other ploy of recalling the Fulham team of the 1975 Cup Final had worked again.

Only momentarily. *'Oh, hell! Oh, bloody, bloody hell!'* Molly screeched, uninhibited this time as she had a second orgasm. Timberlake groaned in ecstasy.

Molly collapsed beside him on the bed.

'There's nothing in the world like a good orgasm,' Timberlake said at last.

'Unless it's two orgasms,' Molly said, and giggled weakly.

'Want to try for your hat-trick?'

There was no doubt that Gunter was waiting for someone. He stayed in the shop doorway, moving from one foot to the other, glancing at his watch and occasionally poking his head out to look up and down the street.

'Maybe it'll be a no-show,' Benny said to Sarah. She shrugged.

Less than a minute later a Lexus saloon with dark windows came round the corner, slowed to a crawl, and stopped in front of the shop where Gunter was waiting.

'Thank Christ,' Sarah muttered. She snatched up her portable phone and spoke into it urgently. 'Come on,' she said to Benny.

They bustled out of the car and walked rapidly across towards the other car. As they reached the pavement they could see Gunter leaning through an open rear window. He took something from inside the car and put it in his pocket. Benny ran the last few yards, grabbed Gunter's neck and pushed him further into the car. 'Don't move!' he said, which was like telling someone with his foot in a bear-trap not to make a run for it.

Sarah, meanwhile, was trying to open the driver's door, but it was locked.

Somebody in the rear seat shouted, and the car began to move off, indifferent to Gunter's plight.

Round the corner roared a dark-blue unmarked van, a police siren whooping madly. As Sarah and Benny waved, it screeched to a stop radiator to radiator with the Lexus. A Ford Granada with a movable flashing blue light, its own siren making an off-key duet with the van's, came rushing up from the opposite direction and pulled up immediately behind the target vehicle, and to complete the operation a second unmarked car stopped alongside. Uniformed policemen piled out of the van, and plain-clothes detectives, pulling on baseball-style caps marked 'POLICE' with blue-and-white chequered bands.

'Bloody hell,' Sarah said. 'When I called in for backup I wasn't expecting to start World War III.'

Gunter looked catatonic. He didn't even move when Sarah reached into his pocket and took out a large plastic bag full of closely-packed dried leaves. 'What's this, then?'

There was no answer.

'I'm arresting you on suspicion of being in possession of an illegal substance,' Sarah said, and she went on to recite the standard caution.

She opened the rear door of the car. On the seat was a large briefcase. Beside it, sitting hunched up was a small Black man. He made no effort to stop her when she opened it, to reveal packets of what was obviously cannabis. Much more serious were small bags of white powder.

At Terrace Vale Sergeant Rumsden was doing a rare night duty as station officer when the small army of policemen clattered into the station. In the middle of the group were Sarah, Benny and their prisoners, who included the driver of the car.

'What've you got here?' he asked.

'Possession of controlled substances with intent to supply,' Sarah said nonchalantly, as if she were bringing in a couple of shoplifters.

'You know who he is, of course?' Rumsden said, indicating the man from the back of the car.

Sarah shook her head.

'That's Willy Manley. He owns the whores' flats in The Grove.' He glanced at the driver of the car, a wizened little man with facial skin like a moonscape. 'Well, if it isn't Wheelybin! How long have you been out, Wheely?'

'Fortnight. Honest, Mr Rumsden, I had no idea he was doing drugs. I was just a chauffeur, that's all. I—'

'Has he been cautioned?'

'Yes,' Sarah said cheerfully, at the same time as Benny said, 'All three of them, all neat and tight as a ballet dancer's trousers.'

Sergeant Rumsden and the custody sergeant proceeded with the tiresome paperwork once Sarah and Benny had given them all the information.

Sarah yawned enormously. 'God, I'm tired,' she told Benny.

'Can I give you a lift home? Hey, best of all, come to my place first and have some of my wife's Jewish Benzedrine.'

'What the hell's that?'

'Chicken soup. It doubles as Jewish penicillin. You know . . .' He exaggerated his accent. 'A little chicken soup won't do you any harm.'

'No thanks, I don't want to stay awake all night.'

'Chicken soup's also great for giving you a good night's sleep.' He smiled. 'Come on, I'll drive you home.'

When Timberlake arrived home he was surprised to see that there were lights on in the main bedroom and the downstairs reception room.

'Hello?' he called out as he entered the house.

'I'm upstairs,' Jenny replied.

'Is everything all right?' he asked as he went upstairs.

'Yes.'

He entered the bedroom, and stopped short. There were two jumbo-sized suitcases, closed and strapped up, and a third which she was packing with her clothes.

'What's going on?'

'I accepted the American offer. I'm leaving tomorrow.'

Timberlake felt his heart thumping, and for a moment he was short of breath. 'Tomorrow? Bit precipitate, isn't it?' he said at last. It was typical of him to use a word like 'precipitate' instead of 'sudden' when he was disturbed.

'Not really. I made up my mind a couple of days ago.'

'But you didn't think it was worth mentioning?'

'There didn't seem to be a lot of point. Besides, you were out so much. Or I was,' she admitted.

'I suppose you'd have left me a note if I hadn't come home tonight?' he said, careless of how bitter he sounded.

'That's been half our trouble, hasn't it?' Jenny said with a tinge of sadness. She waited a moment before going on with her packing. Timberlake stood watching, irresolute.

After a while he said in a neutral tone, 'You'll have a lot of excess baggage, from the look of it.'

'The hospital will pay for it.'

'I see. What time's your flight?'

'I have to be at Heathrow at ten-thirty in the morning.'

'Would you like me to give you a lift?'

'There's no need, thanks. The hospital are paying for Business Class, and I get a free chauffeur-driven car to the airport and from the airport at the other end.'

'Oh, right.' He didn't know what else to say.

'I've left a file with everything you need to know. I'll be staying at the hospital at first; I'll let you have my New York address as soon as I find a place. I may ask you to send on some more of my things when I'm settled in.'

'Yes, of course.' Timberlake felt an ominous hint of permanence in her remark.

'Mrs Czerska has agreed to stay on and come in to clean twice a week, if you want her to. You'll know what letters to send on and which ones to open and deal with. What else? Oh, yes. The garage will send someone to put my car up on blocks while I'm away – unless you want to use it.'

Timberlake shook his head. With an unsuccessful smile he said, 'If I turned up at the station in a series-5 BMW they'd think I'd gone bent.'

She, too, smiled unconvincingly. 'There's a meal in the fridge if you want it. You can pop it in the microwave, or eat it cold.'

Timberlake wasn't hungry. He felt as if he had a great stone in his stomach. There was yet another awkward silence. 'Can I give you a hand?' he asked.

'No thanks. I've nearly finished.'

'I'll take your cases down for you.'

'There's no need. The chauffeur will do that.' It sounded like a rebuff, which she didn't really mean.

'Well . . . good night, then.'

'Good night.'

He turned and walked to the door, where he stopped for a moment, half turned as if to say something, but turned away again and went out.

Timberlake called the Terrace Vale station on his bedside phone to leave a message for Detective Superintendent Harkness that he would be in late in the morning. It took him a long time to fall asleep, and when he did his sleep was fitful. He thought that Jenny didn't sleep much, either. He heard her go to her bathroom once, and down to the kitchen.

The morning light woke him up. He could hear Jenny moving round in her bedroom. He went into his own bathroom, shaved, showered and dressed quickly.

Neither of them felt like eating much: they had toast and coffee in silence.

The time dragged on slowly, then accelerated remorselessly. At a quarter to nine the doorbell rang, making them both jump. Timberlake opened the door to see the airline's chauffeur standing there. He saluted briskly.

'You're a bit early, aren't you?' Timberlake said.

'It can be a bit of a bugger getting to the M4 from here, sir, and there's no telling how the motorway can be, either. Better too early than never. Anyway, it's nice and comfortable in the First Class lounge, if madam's early.' He smiled cheerfully.

Timberlake could have strangled him.

At last the moment came and Jenny was ready to leave. At the doorway Timberlake said, for want of something better to say, 'Have you got everything? Passport, ticket, credit cards . . . ?'

She nodded, also trying to find the right thing to

say. She gave up and uttered, 'Well . . .' She stopped in the open doorway.

'So this is how it ends.' Timberlake said, a little hoarsely.

Jenny hesitated a moment before she answered. 'Not necessarily. It might even be the beginning of something . . . of healing.'

They stood facing each other, still as statues.

Jenny moved first. She stepped close to her husband, put her arms round him and kissed him on both cheeks, real kisses, not polite gestures. Then, instinctively they kissed each other full on the mouth. Timberlake didn't know what the hell to think.

Jenny hurried out to the car, where the chauffeur was holding open the door for her. She got in, and raised her hand in a half-wave to Timberlake, who had walked halfway down the path to the front gate.

As the car drove off, he turned sharply and walked into the house without turning. He didn't want to know if she was looking back at him.

Harkness was shocked when he saw Timberlake's face when he walked into his office. It was white and drawn; his eyes looked dead. Shrewdly he decided not to ask anything about Jenny's departure.

'There was a development last night. Sarah Lewis and Benny Holmes arrested a man who they suspected of selling cannabis to schoolchildren. They got his supplier, too, with a bag of what appears to be cocaine or heroin. It was Willy Manley.'

The implication was instantly obvious to Timberlake. 'Well, I'll be . . . You think he could be involved with the prostitute murders?'

'It's a possibility we have to consider. The incidence of drugs being involved in non-family-related murders is high.'

Timberlake nodded. 'So perhaps some of the girls found out that Willy was drugs dealing and were threatening to grass him up, or were causing problems.' He thought for a moment. 'He was brighter than I gave him credit for. It was shrewd, using a slightly bent operation as a cover for something very bent and nasty. If he'd run something overtly legitimate, like a florist's, or a couple of grocers' shops to launder his drugs money, we'd've been suspicious of him if he'd flashed lots of cash around. But letting flats to brasses was a perfectly good reason for him to have lots of readies.

'By the way, sir, any news from your contacts about high level "funny people" possibly disposing of Juliette Grande?'

'If she was threatening to blackmail some VIP or VIPs and had to be silenced, tracking her to her to Holly Mansions and killing her as Mary Docker to cover their tracks would be very much their style. But as far as I can find out they weren't involved. This time.'

'I'm not really surprised, but it was something that had to be considered.'

'You don't sound too disappointed, Harry.'

'No, sir. I know who did it all right.' Timberlake went on, 'What about Lady Wadhurst? She doesn't know what's happened to her, er, friend Juliette Grande.'

'You tell her.'

'There's one more thing, sir.' Timberlake drew a deep breath. 'I'd like to do another dig into Mark Sibley's background. I want to send two or three people to the airport and ask some of the AirAlbion crews what they know about him. After that, I want to get him in for a friendly little chat.'

Harkness stared hard at Timberlake, which even that experienced, hard-nosed detective found disturbing. 'Have you forgotten the other murders – *all* the other murders?'

'No, sir. But first things first. Mary Docker – not Vicki Stevens or Juliette Grande – was killed first. And we do have a prime suspect – the *only* suspect – in the Docker case.' Timberlake returned Harkness's icy gaze, although inside he was feeling much less confident than he looked.

'I hope you're right, Harry.' Harkness paused before saying very quietly, 'For your own sake.'

Chapter Eighteen

The celebration party was held at Fergie's Bar, the scene of some fair old police shindigs in its time. Large quantities of alcoholic liquor were poured down throats, enough cigarettes were smoked to cure several crans of haddock, and as the evening wore on the songs progressed from bawdiness to plain obscenity. If anyone else had sung them in public they would have been arrested.

Early in the proceedings 'For They Are Jolly Good Fellows' was sung in honour of Sarah and Benny for their success in feeling the collar of Willy Manley, which genuinely deserved extravagant praise.

For all the apparent good humour and *esprit de corps* there were inevitable faint whispers of spitefulness and jealousy. Terrace Vale's unredeemed racist element agreed that Benny Holmes's insistence that Sarah deserved all the credit for the arrests was typical Jewish phoney flattery. And that bloody tart Sarah wasn't a *real* copper; she wasn't much better than a fucking amateur who was dead lucky, the anti-feminists agreed.

'Still, I wouldn't mind giving her one. I bet she's had more bloody stuffing than a Christmas turkey,' a detective constable said as Timberlake happened to be passing. Timberlake staggered as if someone had bumped into him, and caught the detective on the instep with the edge of his heel, his full weight behind it. Timberlake apologized to his crippled victim and offered him a drink. It wasn't much of a gesture because it cost him nothing: everyone had put a tenner in the pot and could drink until the money ran out or the drinker passed out – whichever came first. Timberlake was nearly always a loser on these occasions because of his personal rule of not drinking alcohol when he had his car with him.

The chief of the drugs squad, Detective Sergeant Luke Mawdsley, and his men were others who weren't wholeheartedly happy about Sarah's and Shylock Holmes's success.

'You look as cheerful as the ghost of Hamlet's father,' Timberlake told Mawdsley. 'I'd have thought you'd be thoroughly delighted that Willy has been lifted in possession.'

'Yeah, that's OK – up to a point. But if we'd known he was dealing we could have let him run for a while and see where he was getting his shit.'

'But you didn't know it was him,' Timberlake pointed out. 'And probably you never would have, if Sarah and Benny hadn't nicked him.'

'Well, maybe we can get Willy to tell us where he was getting it,' Mawdsley said, still looking glum. 'But it's not very likely. If he grasses to get a lighter sentence he could still be got at in prison, and he'll know it. The other problem is, what with him and Yardbird Charlie facing long laggings there's going to be a power vacuum in the area. It's going to be very lively round here as villains fight among themselves to become top dog.'

'No pleasing some people,' Timberlake said.

Not long afterwards he managed a few words with Sarah without drawing attention to themselves.

'Great result. What's next? Nobel Prize?' he said.

She smiled. Without expression, she said quietly, so no one could hear, 'Go back to your office. I'll phone.'

Timberlake nodded, and walked away. A few minutes later he went out of his way to pass her as he made for the exit. 'Well done, Sarah,' he said. 'See you tomorrow.'

'You off, guv?'

''Fraid so. Got things to clear up.'

Five minutes later the direct line in his office rang. 'Your place or mine?' Sarah said without preamble. 'That is, if you want,' she added.

Timberlake thought for a few seconds. The idea of going back to his own house was unattractive; taking home another woman for a one night stand while his wife was away seemed tacky. The implications of this feeling did not occur to him. 'Yours,' he said. 'I'll be there in a quarter of an hour. That OK?'

'Great.'

When she went off for her shower after they had made love, Timberlake looked at her closely. She seemed even more attractive than when they had first become lovers years ago. There was something about her body, or her face, or how she walked, or something, which touched him deeply. Yet he was troubled by the question she had asked the last time they were together, 'Harry, where do we go from here?'

Unexpectedly he was hit by a crushing wave of *post coitus tristus*. Recently he had had sex with Sarah, Jenny, Sarah again, Molly and Sarah once more. He wondered if he was going from woman to woman for loveless love to try to fill an unfillable emptiness.

'Christ Almighty, what's wrong with you?' Sarah's voice shook him out of his gloomy introspection. 'You look like something on an autopsy slab.'

'Work. These murders. We've had God knows how many interviews and taken statements, and all for nothing.' He didn't mention the Mary Docker case.

'You're sure it's that? Or was I bad in the sack?'

He couldn't help smiling. 'Bad? You were marvellous. It was the best sex I've had with anyone all day.'

'I wish I could say the same about you. Never mind; you weren't too bad. Maybe you'll be better next time.'

They both laughed, and she fell on him on the bed, where they wrestled playfully; Timberlake's depression was forgotten and he felt his old self again.

At least, for the time being.

Next morning they were both up early: they each had an important day ahead of them. As they left the flat Timberlake realized that something in the living room had caught his eye without his being really aware of what it was, but somehow it seemed important. After puzzling about it for a while he thought he'd simply let his subconscious mind work on it.

The next day, with Timberlake present in the background, Sarah and Benny Holmes began their interrogation of Alfred Herbert Gunter. They played the elementary nice-guy/nasty-guy scenario, but with a twist. Benny, oozing bonhomie and fatherly understanding of a son's little peccadilloes, played the nice guy; Sarah was the nasty, threatening, hard-faced bitch who would cheerfully dump Gunter in an oubliette and throw the key into the castle's moat. Unfortunately it was all for nothing. Gunter told them nothing, because he knew nothing. His contact for marijuana was Willy, but the contact ended with him. Gunter had no idea of Willy's source.

Detective Sergeant Mawdsley joined the team interrogating William 'Willy' Manley. This interview went no better. While Gunter was silent because of ignorance, Willy was equally silent from knowledge – the awareness of what would happen to him if he gave the police one word of information. Mawdsley promised him he would fix it for Willy to go to a prison well away from London. Willy just laughed.

Timberlake had a try. 'You're looking at a long, long time in prison,' he pointed out. 'By the time you come out, there'll be a motorway or council flats where your houses in The Grove used to be. What'll you do then?'

Willy was fairly tense but outwardly unperturbed. 'I'll manage.' It was an easy guess that he had money stashed away somewhere.

'Don't forget the courts can seize money resulting from drug dealing,' Timberlake added.

'If they find any.'

'Don't be too optimistic, Willy. If you've got anything stashed away, it'll be antique paper when they let you out. We won't have pounds sterling; we'll have Ecus.'

'Forget it, Mr Timberlake. I'm not going to tell you anything. I've got my reputation as a trustworthy businessman to consider. I've got respect.'

'Respect? Come off it, Willy. You'd better think hard. The courts are getting very tough with drug dealers these days, and when the judge hears you've also been supplying marijuana to school kids, he's going to come down even heavier . . . if you don't help us.'

Willy gave a surprisingly cheerful smile. 'But he won't hear zilch of any school kids, man. I'm going to plead guilty, so there won't be any evidence given in court. And you'll hear the God-damnest plea in mitigation by the best QC money can hire.'

Timberlake mentally accepted that they wouldn't get anything about suppliers from Willy for a long time, if ever. 'Very well. Now, there are other matters I want to discuss with you.' He spoke slowly and clearly. 'You have already been formally cautioned, but I want to remind you that it may harm your defence if you do not mention, when questioned, anything which you may later rely on in court.' He gave Willy The Look.

Timberlake cleared his throat. 'I want to talk to you about the murder of several prostitutes operating in The Grove.' He studied Willy to see his reaction.

Willy's mouth fell open with shock, and he could not speak for several seconds. Timberlake was quite certain that the man's stupefaction was genuine. With a sinking heart Timberlake knew without a doubt that it was the shock of genuine surprise, and not of guilt.

The questioning was suspended for half an hour

for Willy to have a meal and something to drink. When it resumed there was a change in his attitude: it was evident that he had come to accept the realities of his position, although he still refused to give any information about his suppliers. Timberlake again pressed him briefly on the murders of the prostitutes, but it was just routine. Willy wasn't really worried, and said that if he could have access to his diary he might well be able to produce an alibi for some, if not all, of the times when the murders took place. Timberlake believed him.

For some time the murder squad's tempers were becoming frayed and morale was sinking. The enormous list of people who had been interviewed – some of them several times – had proved to be fruitless.

News media interest in the crimes came in cycles. There would be periods of relative calm; when other news was thin on the ground, the Terrace Vale murders would be highlighted again. Police competence was criticized and the Yorkshire Ripper and Fred West cases recalled.

Even Detective Superintendent Harkness was sometimes less than his equable self. Unfortunately for Timberlake, the morning he made up his mind to pressure Harkness about changing tack with their enquiries was one of the detective superintendent's more prickly days. As Timberlake began to outline his plan Harkness showed an unmistakable lack of enthusiasm that bordered on hostility.

'I was thinking that a new line of enquiry might

help to freshen up our ideas,' Timberlake said with an unusual diffidence.

After a moment Harkness said rather ungraciously. 'What do you have in mind?'

'Sir, we don't have a single credible suspect, or even a worthwhile lead in any of the prostitute murders. With the best will in the world, the troops are getting stale. Supposing we change direction and concentrate on the case where we do have a suspect – an odds-on suspect? We stand a much better chance of getting a result there, which would recharge everybody's batteries – and get the Press off our backs, for a while at least.'

'You mean Captain Sibley and the Mary Docker killing. Are you suggesting that Sibley committed all the other murders as well?' said Harkness in a voice like ice cracking.

It was the first time Timberlake had heard him be so acerbic. In previous cases when he had worked under Harkness, the senior man had always seemed iron-nerved and unaffected by any pressures or disappointments. Now Timberlake realized that the stress of these unsolved murders was getting to him at last. Somehow that gave Timberlake back his own confidence.

'No, sir, of course not. But Sibley . . . Look, I've been thinking a lot about this case. It all fits. First, Docker's killer got in without forcing an entry, breaking that window lock was just to mislead us. It had to be someone who Docker knew and wasn't afraid of. Or someone with a key. Second, he got the probable murder weapon from the kitchen drawer. It must have been someone who was familiar with where things were in the flat. Third . . .' He paused for emphasis.

'Docker apparently wasn't bothered by seeing a naked man walking into her bedroom. The bedclothes were hardly rumpled. If she had been scared, or shocked, she would have made some movement. I mean, with who else other than her lover would she behave like that, naked on a bed, without creating some sort of fuss or resistance?'

'She was a prostitute and a call-girl. It could be anyone.'

Timberlake sensed that Harkness was beginning to come round to his line of thought: he sounded much less critical. It increased Timberlake's confidence.

'No, sir. At Holly Mansions she was neither. She lived completely separate, compartmentalized lives.'

'Wait a moment. How do we know *he* was naked?'

'Remember, he took a shower *after* the murder. The scientific report said leuco-malachite green showed there were traces of blood on the bath, the tiles and the shower attachment. And it's pretty obvious *why* he was naked.'

'To make sure he got no blood on his clothes.' Harkness nodded thoughtfully. 'He wouldn't be the first murderer to do that.'

'Right, sir. Fourth, Mary Docker herself was naked in or on the bed, her nightdress on a chair. She was obviously preparing to make love with him. Fifth, the murderer took her completely by surprise. The sheet showed she hardly moved on the bed when she was brutally stabbed. After all, he was the man she least expected to attack her. Maybe she wasn't killed by the first couple of blows, but when the man she loved suddenly produced the knife he was hiding behind his back she must have been paralysed with shock, and it was too late to protect herself when the fatal blows were struck.'

Harkness was silent for a long time. 'The motive?' he said at last.

'I can think of two or three, but I can't be absolutely sure of which one . . . yet.'

'So what do you intend to do?'

'First, have some quiet enquiries made among the staff of AirAlbion – the training captain, other pilots, cabin staff . . . Find out what we can about him. After that, I'll bring him in for questioning. Have a real go at him. With your permission, sir.'

'I'm sorry, but at the moment we don't have enough to justify asking him to assist us with our enquiries.' He uttered the cliché with a wry smile. 'Let's see what the enquiries among the airline staff turn up, although I must say I'm not very sanguine about that. Anything else?'

Timberlake debated with himself whether or not to answer. He found something of a compromise. 'Yes, and no.'

Harkness waited.

'Nothing concrete,' Timberlake went on. 'But I've been looking at the files again. I *know* there's something there if only I can put my finger on it.' He shrugged. 'And I've seen or heard something recently that has rung a very distant bell, but . . .' He shook his head. 'To paraphrase Donne, the bell isn't tolling for me. Yet.'

The first detectives chosen to make the enquiries at Heathrow were Darren Webb, Nigel Larkin, Alistair

McPhail and Bob Crust. Timberlake also wanted at least one woman officer on the operation. He would have liked to ask for Sarah Lewis, but he was afraid that some of the others might pick up signs of his relationship with her, particularly the sharp-eyed Harkness. He went to see Sergeant Rumsden.

'Anthony, I need a very bright WPC as a CID aide for a few days, to make some delicate enquiries.'

'Oh, no, Harry, you're not going to do it again.' Rumsden groaned in mock agony. 'Look what happened to the last one you nicked for CID, the Welsh Rarebit. You ruined a perfectly good woman constable who'd make someone a good, bed-warming wife, by turning her into a hard-nosed detective who'll probably end up as a vinegary dried-up old maid. She's started to show the first signs already.'

'D'you think so?'

'You ought to know,' Rumsden said, looking directly at Timberlake.

This almost threw him off balance, but Timberlake knew Rumsden was too perceptive for him to be this wrong about Sarah Lewis.

'Why should I?' Timberlake said in a neutral tone.

'Well, you see a lot of her.'

Now he knew what the crafty Rumsden was fishing for, and he was glad he hadn't picked Sarah for the team. He put on a convincing puzzled expression.

'She works for your lot, doesn't she?' Rumsden added.

'Oh. But I'm interested in her work, not her marriage prospects,' Timberlake said deprecatingly, hoping like hell that he sounded nonchalant. 'Now, what about my aide?'

Rumsden looked at him. 'There's a new WPC who was transferred here three weeks ago from North Horden. Anne Beacham. She did a lot of CID aide work while she was there.'

'Why was she transferred? Any special reason, do you know?'

'Well, I did have a word with her sergeant there. Apparently there was a . . . er . . . personality clash with a new chief inspector there.'

'That doesn't sound much of a recommendation for her to join my lot.'

'The new chief inspector is a woman.' He looked significantly at Timberlake. 'I suggest you have a word with Beacham.'

Timberlake wondered why Rumsden wanted to get rid of her, but decided to see her anyway.

When WPC Beacham reported to Timberlake's office, he was inclined to turn her down right away. She was attractive enough to model for a recruiting poster, or front a television crime programme. She had an air of dumb-blondishness, but as Timberlake questioned her he discovered she was quite bright. In addition, it soon became evident she could exude a near-palpable aura of sexuality that could cause severe softening of young men's brains. Timberlake guessed that Rumsden probably thought Anne Beacham might be better out of the way where she couldn't cause some distraction to his uniformed troops.

That same evening Timberlake introduced Anne Beacham to Darren Webb, Nigel Larkin, Alistair McPhail and Bob Crust, before briefing them for the

Heathrow inquiry. He explained that he wanted as much background information as they could dig out of AirAlbion aircrews and cabin staff about Captain Mark Sibley.

'But this must not, repeat, must not, be heavy-handed. Darren, you'll be in charge at Heathrow, although you'll all have to exercise a certain amount of individual initiative. I'll see the senior captain myself, or training captain, whatever he's called.'

He stared hard at each of them in turn with an intensity that made them ill at ease.

'Now, remember; just because you're away from the area, keep in mind this is a murder inquiry, not a few days' skive. And I don't want there to be any distractions. Understood?'

Everyone understood all right. No one looked at Anne Beacham.

Shortly after Timberlake got home to his dark, empty house, the phone rang. It was Sarah Lewis.

'Hello, Harry. Feel like having a drink?'

He hesitated before answering. 'I could really do with one, but to tell you the truth, Sarah, I'm too beat, blown out and burnt up to come out.'

'You forgot "buggered".'

'That's because I'm knackered.'

'I'm a great pourer-outer, bach. Get the corkscrew. I'm on my way.' Her phone went down before he could tell her not to come.

In the event he was glad of her company.

They ate and drank very little; and the sex, although more than merely satisfactory, had more of friendship than passion in it. Timberlake found himself slightly bemused by this; it set him wondering how their relationship was developing.

Later, Sarah said, 'I hear you've got Bitchy Anne as a CID aide.'

Timberlake let that pass. 'Yes, I'm sorry. I would have preferred to have you on the inquiry, but I thought people might start being suspicious about us. As it is, Sergeant Rumsden was dropping some pointed hints earlier today. I think I managed to put him off the scent.'

'I suppose the men with Beacham are walking round with their tongues hanging out. For a start,' she added.

'Oh, yes. But I warned them to keep their mind on their work.'

Sarah laughed. 'You needn't have bothered.'

'Why not?'

'She's a bull dike – and aggressive with it.'

'You're kidding.'

'I'm not. She's got a reputation. *And* she came on strong to me in the women's loo.'

'Good God. What did you do?'

'I told her if she didn't stop it I'd knee her in the bollocks.'

It was Timberlake's turn to laugh. 'Very ladylike.'

'But effective. That's why she left North Horden.'

'How do you know?'

'I've got a friend there. She was the only other WPC with me at detective school. Apparently Beacham misread some signals and tried it on with the new woman chief inspector.'

'Well, we'll see how she does on the inquiry. I don't care about her sexual orientation.'

'Talking of which,' Sarah said, 'what do you suggest this time? North-south or east-west?'

'Did you know,' Timberlake said some time later when he had got his breath back, 'that in San Francisco in the 1880s, enormous numbers of Chinese girls were imported to become prostitutes, and some newspapers carried small ads from bordellos saying that while White girls were north-south Chinese girls were east-west?'

'In the yellow press, I suppose. No, I didn't know, and I can only thank you very much for sharing that with me. You lying sod.'

'Actually, it's true – the advertisements, I mean. There were even serious articles discussing the alleged anatomical anomaly.'

'Now I know you're lying.'

'I'm not. But have it your way.'

'Don't I always?'

Captain Trevor Perowne was the senior pilot and training captain of AirAlbion. His nickname – never used in his hearing – was Eva. To Timberlake's surprise when they met, he wore half-moon spectacles on a solid chain round his neck. Later Timberlake learnt from him that he was not licensed to fly without the spectacles, and he always carried a spare pair in a strong case in his pocket.

Perowne was a shortish man with a thin body but a full round face. His nose was as stubby as a Pekinese dog's and his eyes were so wide-spaced that Timberlake had the unexpected thought that he looked almost as if he were wearing a stocking mask. His AirAlbion uniform had a few campaign medal ribbons that Timberlake didn't recognize, headed by the rose-pink and pearl-grey bordered ribbon of the OBE without a central pearl-grey stripe, signifying that it was the civilian version, plus the red and white diagonal-striped Air Force Cross.

They had met in Perowne's office in the airline's building at Heathrow. The office was not nouveau-riche luxurious like the office of Gus Tennant, AirAlbion's PR executive, but old-money opulent. The furniture could have come from a Pall Mall club's reading room, apart from the pictures, which were mostly of modern aircraft. There were two exceptions: one was a reproduction painting of Icarus plunging to earth after the wax on the wings he had made for himself had melted. Timberlake looked quizzically at Perowne.

'Just a reminder,' he said. 'My father was an RAF pilot. He always said there were two kinds of pilot: the bold ones and the old ones. Icarus was one of the bold ones. I'm the other kind.'

'As an occasional air passenger I'm glad to hear it.'

The second was a photograph of a light aircraft with RAF markings: one that Timberlake didn't recognize.

'What is that one?' he asked.

'D.H. Chipmunk. It was the first aircraft I even flew in. I was in the Air Cadet Corps, and I was taken up in one on an Air Experience flight. Gipsy Major 145hp engine; top speed 138mph' He smiled. 'My car's got a more powerful engine and could go faster. And as a matter of interest – or not, according to taste – the Duke of Edinburgh earned his wings in one of those.'

Perowne went on to tell one or two anecdotes about

his early flying days which helped unstiffen the sense of guarded formality in the meeting.

Timberlake began as casually as he could with the usual preamble that this was simply a routine enquiry. The moment he mentioned Mark Sibley's name Perowne barked, 'What's he done?' He stared at Timberlake with an intensity that nearly matched anything Timberlake himself or Harkness could have managed.

'Nothing that we know of,' Timberlake replied, mentally justifying the lie with the use of 'we'. He *himself* knew Sibley had murdered Mary Docker, but 'we', the police as a whole, didn't.

'Don't take evasive action with me, Inspector. I'll be straight and tell you what you want to know if you'll be straight with me.'

'That's a refreshingly unusual attitude, Captain.'

'If Sibley's done anything badly wrong I'm not going to cover for him. If he hasn't, the truth won't hurt him.'

'I wish more people thought the same way.' Timberlake looked at Perowne for a long moment. 'In complete confidence?'

'Of course.'

'His fiancée was murdered.'

'I know. We all do.'

'Statistically, the majority of murders are done by members of the family, or by someone close to the victim. Well, unlikely as it may seem, we have to make the usual routine enquiries about Captain Sibley.' He waited, but Perowne gave no reaction. 'What's he like?'

'Fit, keeps in shape, sails through his biannual medicals. Good pilot, not quite above-average rating, but better than plain average. Loves flying. Has his own light aircraft. Uses it to commute to work sometimes when he's had a few days off.'

'*Commutes?* From Knightsbridge?'

Perowne laughed. 'No, near Land's End. He's got a holiday cottage there. Flies from St Just aerodrome.' His voice softened. 'I envy the lucky sod. He's got a lovely little Cessna. That's *real* flying; you can *feel* the elements. You're not separated from the air by hydraulics and computers . . .'

'I'm not trying to recruit pilots, Captain. What sort of *man* is he?'

'Good God, what a question! Still, I know what you mean. Well, all airline pilots have to be fairly stable people.' There was a note in his voice that prompted Timberlake.

'But . . . ?'

'He can be . . . excitable, sometimes. On the ground, that is. There haven't been any complaints, official or otherwise, about his behaviour in the air.'

'Does "excitable" mean "bad-tempered"? Or "violent" even?'

'It means *excitable*. I'm not Humpty Dumpty, inspector.'

Timberlake blinked. Then he remembered Humpty Dumpty's often-quoted remark: 'When *I* use a word, it means just what I choose it to mean – neither more nor less.' He grinned.

Timberlake changed tack. 'I take it that Captain Sibley was badly affected by his fiancée's murder.'

'Yes. He tried to hide it, but it was obvious he was in a bad way. He was very twitchy and preoccupied, naturally enough. The company doctor insisted that he take a fortnight's sick leave, and Sibley added on a fortnight's leave he was owed.'

'Did Sibley have any other women friends?'

'Not as far as I know. Mind you, I have heard rumours that aircrew staying overnight when they're abroad have occasional affairs.' Perowne said this with a perfectly straight face, apart from a minimal twitch of his lips.

'Really?' Timberlake said with mock surprise.

'He had a reputation for being something of a ram when he was operating out of Manchester, but he soon settled down when he came here. Why do you ask about other women?' Perowne asked.

'We have to consider the possibility of Mary Docker's killer being a jealous rival.'

The interview went on for a while longer, but Timberlake learnt little more. Still, Captain Perowne had given him one nugget of information that might lead to a rich vein.

The members of the team who had been making less official enquiries of AirAlbion returned with a heterogeneous collection of opinions about Sibley that were as mixed as a bag of liquorice allsorts.

Pilots and male chief stewards had a wide range of adjectives to describe him. Timberlake noted them down: 'honest', 'proud', 'straightforward', 'all-round good egg', 'fond of himself', 'crafty', 'good pilot', 'unsociable', 'conceited', 'decent', 'neurotically inclined', 'something of a woman-chaser'.

Stewardesses and a few of the reception area staff were equally as diverse in their opinions: 'charming', 'smarmy', 'high opinion of himself', 'stand-offish', 'very bright', 'kind', 'egotistical'.

The detectives looked at each other with a certain amount of confusion when they heard the conflicting descriptions.

'Any of you want to change your mind?' Timberlake asked.

'They're not our opinions, guv,' Bob Crust said. 'We don't know the geezer. It's what the airline people said.'

'True. Thanks, Bob. Well, in other words, he's a closet complex character,' Timberlake summarized with unintentional alliteration.

'What did *you* think of him?' Harkness asked Timberlake.

'The first couple of times we met, I found him quite personable and very convincing. But now I know him for what he is.' No one asked what that was. 'I think he may be suffering from – from mild schizophrenia. They can be damned convincing.'

Timberlake went on, 'Sibley isn't on the national computer, but Captain Perowne mentioned something that might give us a new lead. Sibley used to operate out of Manchester before coming to London. I think I'll have a word with Manchester to see if their files have anything about him that didn't get as far as court. You never know,' he added with an air of optimism he didn't really feel.

Detective Sergeant Horatio 'Raich' Burbank – his father was a fanatical Sunderland supporter and named his son after the celebrated Horatio 'Raich' Carter –

returned Timberlake's call to Manchester City Police in less than quarter of an hour.

'Yes, we've got a card on Mark Sibley,' he said. 'He had a couple of unofficial cautions. The super didn't think it was worth taking him to court.'

'What had he done?'

Burbank's answer made Timberlake jump as if he had jammed his fingers into a live thirteen-amp electric socket: it set off enormous synaptic activity in his brain. In a second of inspiration all the elements of the Mary Docker inquiry came together to form a critical mass: everything became clear to him. It was like a star shell bursting.

There were only two problems.

The first was the matter of proof.

The second was, would Harkness think he had lost his mind?

Chapter Nineteen

Although he was tired, Timberlake could not sleep. This was not unusual with him; frequently his body became more tired than his mind; this time it was different. On the other occasions it was because he was still mentally searching for the solution to a problem. Now he knew the answers – who, when, where, how and why – but persuading his senior officer he was right and finding the necessary proof to secure a conviction were still out of reach.

He got up, made some hot chocolate and went into the lounge. He was used to being alone in the house because of the odd hours he and Jenny worked, but now she was a continent away, he had access of an acute sense of loneliness. He went to his racks of jazz cassettes recorded from his precious collection of long-play and 78rpm discs and took one at random without looking at the title. It wasn't the happiest of choices.

He recognized after no more than a couple of bars that it was Billie 'Lady Day' Holiday, with her incomparable 1941 recording of 'All of Me'. He had forgotten that the next song on the tape was 'Strange Fruit', which was the one most closely identified with her own tragic life. This version was made before the famous 1949 version, when her addiction to alcohol and drugs had roughened her voice and ruined her life. It threw him halfway down into a dark pit of depression.

The telephone rang. Timberlake guessed it would be the nick. No one would be making social calls at this time of night, and then it hit him forcibly that he *had* no social life anyway, with almost no real friends. He picked up the phone as if it were made of lead.

'Hello,' he said uninvitingly.

'It's me. Molly. I'm feeling a bit on-my-own-ish. God! Is that Billie Holiday I can hear in the background?'

'Yes.'

'Can I come round for a drink? Or would you like me to call in and take you on to my place?'

Timberlake thought for a moment. 'Where the hell are you?'

'About twenty yards down the road from your house.'

'It may sound like a stupid question, but what the hell are you doing there, and at this time of night?'

'Sitting in my car. I'm on the mobile. I was called out to a break-in, and on my way home I passed your place and saw the lights on. So . . .'

As Molly entered the house she said, 'Christ, do you always meet women at the door in your pyjamas? Or are you trying to tell me something?'

Timberlake asked her if she had eaten.

'Not really. There was a bag of crisps in my car.'

'I'll make you something while you have a shower, if you want one.'

'I'll eat first, if that's all right.'

He made her a large silverside and tomato sandwich with nearly half a baguette, which she devoured to the last crumb, she also despatched a solid wedge of a cheesecake he had bought at a supermarket.

Molly went to the sofa and slumped into it with a sigh of relief. She was in working clothes: jeans, tee-shirt and cardigan. She slipped off the cardigan and asked, 'D'you mind if I loosen my trousers? I was so bloody hungry I ate more than I should have done.'

'Sure.' He grinned. 'Where's the elegant young woman who came with me to *La Letizia*?'

She smiled back at him. 'In here somewhere.' She undid the top button of her jeans and pulled the zip down an inch or so, no more, and pulled out her tee-shirt. Idly he thought that she had a pretty navel.

'Where was the break-in?'

'A factory office in Sanderson Street,' she said, trying to sound casual.

'Uhuh.'

His house was on her way home from Sanderson Street to the Castle district like Ireland is on the way from England to France.

Molly could read his mind like an open atlas. She shrugged. 'So I'm a rotten navigator.'

'And a worse liar,' he said, smiling again. 'Listen, Molly, it was great the other night. You know. And I'm very fond of you. Tonight, though – well I'm feeling pretty damned depressed, one way and another, and I'm really grateful for your company, honestly, But I'm afraid I'd be a disappointment to you if we went to bed together.'

'What's wrong with good old friendship, Harry? Now, if you don't mind, I'll have my shower.'

After Molly had been in the shower for a while she shouted out for him. 'Harry! There's no towel!'

Freud would have said it was no accident: Timberlake had deliberately arranged it, albeit subconsciously. When he had gone to make sure the shower was all right, he had taken his used towel and put it into the linen basket, but he had forgotten to put out another one.

He took a bath towel from the cupboard over to the shower cubicle. Molly had the door wide open.

Timberlake's immediate reaction on seeing her was that if naiads had really existed this is what they must have looked like, their hair shiny as sealskin, their bodies sparkling with the clear river water. As he looked her up and down, her nipples became instantly erect. For a moment, just a moment, she was a heart-stopping sight. She began to giggle and broke the spell.

'What's up?' he asked.

'*That* is. Either button up your dressing gown or put a zip on those pyjama trousers.' She began to sing, not very tunefully, '*Friendship, friendship, what a beautiful friendship* . . .'

Five minutes after they got into bed the phone rang.

'If that's your nick, tell them you've just resigned from the force and they can take a running jump,' Molly said.

It was Sarah Lewis. Timberlake was faced with the problem of not sounding too off-hand with her, while not seeming to be too intimate with someone else while Molly was lying beside him. He was holding the phone to the ear nearer Molly's side. Assuming a casualness he was far from feeling, he moved the phone away from that ear, rubbed it vigorously and changed the phone to the other side. Molly was not fooled, but at least she could hear only his side of the conversation now.

'I'd love to, but I need an early night. I'm in bed already . . . ' He gave an almost perfectly convincing chuckle. 'No, of course not. Chance would be a fine thing . . .'

Timberlake started as Molly began moving her hand gently in his groin. He tried to move away without making too much of it. Molly was having difficulty in suppressing her laughter. He somehow managed to keep his voice steady.

'Nothing, I was just turning over in bed . . .Who do I know who'd be in bed with me? . . . Her? That over-acting actress? I haven't seen her since that time when I was in hospital . . .'* He simulated a prodigious yawn. 'I'll ring you tomorrow, OK . . . ?' He hung up.

'Your wife?' Molly asked.

'No.'

'I don't suppose it was your mother?' she said disingenuously.

'It was an old friend.'

Molly showed not the least sign of pique, and increased her manœcuvres in his groin. 'Well, shake hands with your new friend.'

Timberlake made no effort to make direct comparisons, but he admitted to himself that if it wasn't the very best sex he had ever had, it was far from the worst.

*See *Elimination*.

As they lay together afterwards, half asleep, he began to wonder how deeply he was beginning to involve himself. He said out loud without meaning to, 'What the hell have I done now?'

Molly was more awake than he was. 'If you can't remember, I'll show you.'

Which she did, emphatically.

'The *annus horribilis* is back with us,' Alistair McPhail greeted Timberlake as he walked into the murder squad room the next morning.

Timberlake looked puzzled. 'Now what's happened?'

'He's back. The horrible arsehole. DCI Greening.' There were some sniggers from other detectives within earshot.

'That's either pig-ignorant, or a lamentable attempt at humour,' Timberlake snapped. The prospect of putting his new theory about Sibley to Detective Superintendent Harkness was making him tense, and a largely sleepless night had done nothing to calm him. And although he shared McPhail's and practically everyone else's assessment of Ted Greening, Timberlake had a strong sense of propriety concerning junior ranks being publicly rude about their seniors, even if they *were* horrible arseholes.

A matter of seconds later there was one of those coincidences which defy all the laws of chance and probability. Ted Greening walked into the room saying, 'What a bleeding *annus horribilis*.' It got as big a laugh as any of Woody Allen's five-word one-liners.

Greening, who meant to explain what a rough time

of it he had suffered during his extended sick leave, was at a total loss to understand the reaction to the beginning of his sad story. What could have been an embarrassing moment was averted by the arrival of Harkness.

'Good morning, sir,' Greening said, and shot out again. He still avoided Harkness like a vampire trying to dodge a silver bullet.

The Greening incident temporarily lifted the gloom that weighed heavily on the murder squad detectives, but not long afterwards it descended again. For what had seemed an eternity everyone had been working hard, the files of interviews had become monstrous, and all for no result whatsoever.

'The big problem is one of geography, sir,' Timberlake suggested. 'It's a busy area, with a lot of punters. There's an Underground station just round the corner from The Grove; a man can sneak in, have the woman he wants, then sneak out again without drawing attention to himself. There's not much kerb-crawling there, cars are few and far between. And anyway, not all the women were killed in The Grove.'

'Yes, I think we've all seen that problem,' Harkness said with a voice that would sharpen knives 'The only answer is good, old-fashioned policing: boring, tedious, thankless legwork. It will get us there in the end.'

At the end of the conference Timberlake went up to Harkness. 'Can I have a few words, sir?'

'Of course.' He signalled for him to follow him into his office.

When they had settled Timberlake took a deep breath. 'It's the Mary Docker case and Sibley, sir.'

'Really,' Harkness answered. His ironic tone was unmissable.

'As you know, sir, the team made enquiries about him at Heathrow, and I spoke to the training captain myself. Now, here are the comments that were made by the people we contacted.' He showed him the list of adjectives Sibley's colleagues had used to describe him.

'Interesting,' Harkness said, this time not at all ironic.

'So he's complicated, and different people have different views of him. But . . . there's one trait that's mentioned several times in different terms. "Proud, fond of himself, conceited, high opinion of himself, egotistical". And the senior captain said he was something of a womanizer.'

'Fortunately, that's not a crime – yet. And there's one characteristic that isn't mentioned at all. No one said he has a sense of humour,' Harkness pointed out.

Timberlake stared at him. 'I hadn't noticed that. But it fits in with the pride, conceit. egotism and the rest.'

'Anything else, Harry?'

'One more thing, sir. He was originally stationed in Manchester. I gave the CID there a ring. They had a small file on him. Although he had no convictions or charges, he'd been given a couple of cautions. Kerb-crawling.'

There was a long silence. Eventually Harkness said slowly, 'Yes. I can see what you're thinking. It's a possibility – just, and at least it suggests a motive. But there's still no hard evidence. The CPS wouldn't consider it for a minute. What do you suggest we do about it?'

'On the basis of what the AirAlbion people said about him, and the information from Manchester, as I said before, I'd like to have him in here for an interview,' he said firmly. Before Harkness could say anything, he added, '*Please.*' Then, po-faced, 'To ask him if he'd be good enough to help us with our inquiry into the murder of his fiancée.'

'Supposing he doesn't agree to come in voluntarily?'

'Oh, he'll come all right. By now he must think he's bombproof. And there's that egotistical strain in his character. He thinks he's too clever for us.'

'Delusions of mental superiority aren't unusual,' Harkness said, 'and they can be a dangerous trapdoor.' Timberlake got the message about stones and glass houses.

After a long pause Harkness added reluctantly, 'All right. But be careful. Be very careful. As you've suggested, Sibley's no unintelligent petty criminal.'

'That's what I'm counting on.'

Harkness looked at him sharply, but made no comment.

After he left his chief's office Timberlake took a couple of deep breaths. The meeting had gone better than he had expected, although it was clear that Harkness had strong reservations about his tactics. Back in his own office he picked up the phone and dialled a number.

'Captain Perowne, please,' he said. While he waited to be connected he dared not think too long about Harkness's reaction if he knew what he was up to now, and even more importantly, what he planned to do. If his scheme went wrong it could destroy their relationship, and blight his own career.

Sibley acceded to the polite, almost off-hand request to come to Terrace Vale to help with enquiries. Timberlake immediately launched into preparations for the interview that were meticulous to the point of approaching the almost obsessional, but everything he did had a firm psychological basis.

'I'd like Jeff Waters in with me when I do the interview, sir,' Timberlake told Detective Superintendent Harkness.

'Why him, and not Sergeant Webb?'

'Sibley keeps fit and is rather proud of his physical condition. As you know, that can give a suspect a sense of superiority over his interrogator. If big Jeff Waters walks into the room, it'll put a small dent in Sibley's mental armour. And Jeff will just stay silent, sitting there.'

'Would you like me to be present?' Harkness said, knowing the answer in advance.

'With respect, sir, I'd rather you weren't. Your presence would diminish my authority in Sibley's eyes. I was hoping you'd watch the interview over the video link.'

Harkness looked long and hard at Timberlake. He knew exactly what he was thinking.

For his next arrangements Timberlake called on Sergeant Anthony Rumsden.

'Tony, Captain Sibley is coming in for an interview at three o'clock tomorrow. I want you to make sure that Interview Room A is kept free for me from two o'clock onwards.'

'Sure, Harry,' said Rumsden, exercising his *droit de* senior sergeant and Terrace Vale character to use Timberlake's Christian name. 'But why so early?'

'Sibley is very sharp. He could well arrive early to throw us off balance. Or late, for that matter. Now, who does the odd maintenance jobs about the building?'

'Stan Brackett.'

'Is that his real name, or a nickname?'

'It's his real name.'

'What's he like?'

'He's a first-class workman: does an honest job.'

'Can he keep his mouth shut?'

'Except when he's eating, which is pretty frequent.'

'Will you get him in? I need him to do a couple of small jobs for me.'

'Private or official?'

'Let's say private, for the moment.'

Stan Brackett weighed nearly 300lb, of which two or three pounds were his camel thorn hedge of a beard, and he looked as if he was wearing a full set of an American footballer's protective gear. He was a former butcher who gave up chopping meat to become a self-employed builder, decorator, electrician and general handyman. His hobby was weight-lifting. Brackett could break down front doors just by leaning on them.

Timberlake, accompanied by a curious Rumsden, took Brackett into Interview Room A. He pointed to the four chairs, two of each on either side of a plain table.

'I'd like you to do something to a couple of the chairs. First of all, cut six centimetres off the legs of one of them, and put non-slip pads on the feet.'

Brackett looked monumentally unsurprised. 'Uhuh,' he said.

'After that, put gliders – those flat, shiny button things – on the feet of the others.'

'That all?'

'For the moment.'

'Right. I've got me tools in the van. I'll just nip down the road and pick up the gliders.'

While Brackett was out, a puzzled Rumsden asked 'What're you up to, Harry?'

'I'm sure you know the difference between strategy and tactics.' Rumsden nodded sagely. 'My strategy is to thoroughly unsettle Sibley from the moment he gets here.' Even under pressure Timberlake rarely split infinitives, although he grudgingly admitted that there were occasions when it was permissible. 'One of my tactics is to put him in a chair he can't move easily. You'd be surprised how this can rattle someone being interviewed when he tries to change position. It's a common enough practice in a lot of big firms when they're interviewing candidates for a job.'

'You really think it makes any difference?'

'I'm sure of it. And making my chair higher than his – even two inches – will add to his discomfiture. They're not much on their own, but the highest wall is made of single bricks.'

'Supposing he picks your chair?'

'He won't. I'll see to that. And something else, Anthony. When Sibley turns up and asks for me, call me "sir" on the phone, and be extra respectful. Warn whoever else is on the desk with you. It's all part of what the book calls enhancing the investigator's status.'

'What book?'

'*Police Interrogation.** It's worth its weight in gold.'

Captain Mark Sibley arrived for the interview two minutes early. At least he wasn't trying any mind games, Timberlake thought. Whether that was a good or bad thing from Timberlake's point of view could be argued either way. It could mean that Sibley was not expecting to be subjected to an aggressive interview, and so could be taken off balance. Alternatively, it could mean that he was totally confident of his own invulnerability and would be hard to break down.

Sergeant Rumsden performed his role perfectly, almost standing to attention when he called Timberlake's office. 'Detective Inspector Timberlake? There's a Captain Sibley here to see you, sir . . . Very good, sir.' He hung up the phone. 'The detective inspector will send someone down to show you the way. If you'll wait just here.'

Three minutes later the massive Jeff Waters arrived at the desk. Rumsden gave a nod in Sibley's direction.

'If you'll come with me, please, Captain Sibley,' Waters said.

He led Sibley to Interview Room A.

There was a table with three chairs, the single chair against the wall and with its back to the door. A fourth chair was by the door, well away from the table. Waters preceded Sibley into the room, stopped by the table

***Police Interrogation* by Superintendent John Walkley M.Sc.

and turned, blocking Sibley's progress. It seemed a perfectly natural movement.

'Have a seat, sir,' he said.

Inevitably Sibley took the single chair.

Almost without exception suspects and interviewees will take the single chair when they are presented with this layout of the furniture – particularly people who are frequent visitors to police stations. Timberlake had taken no chances: he had rehearsed Jeff Waters in the manœcuvre.

Waters sat opposite Sibley and stared impassively past Sibley's head.

At Timberlake's entrance, followed by Police Constable 'Rambo' Wright, Waters rose and moved back from the table. Wright stood by the door.

Sibley stood up, a little awkwardly because his chair wouldn't move easily, when Timberlake offered his hand for the briefest of handshakes. 'Thank you for coming in, Mr Sibley,' he said neutrally.

Timberlake placed on the table two buff-coloured files with a broad diagonal red stripe and CONFIDENTIAL: RESTRICTED marked on the covers. He took the chair next to Jeff Waters, took it round to Sibley's side of the table and sat next to him. Waters was still standing. Timberlake nodded to him to sit down.

'Why is he sitting there, instead of opposite him?' Detective Sergeant Darren Webb whispered, as if Timberlake could actually hear him.

In the observation room Detective Superintendent Harkness, Webb, Detective Constable Nigel Larkin and one or two other detectives were watching the screens of the closed-circuit television operating in the interview room.

'So he can see him – all of him,' Harkness said in his normal voice. 'So he can observe all his body language, from his head to his feet. Suspects who lie know that anyone questioning them will be looking at their faces for clues, and they don't know that hand and leg movements can be just as revelatory. If they're sitting on the other side of a table, their legs and hands can't be seen.'

'What about those two files, sir?' asked Larkin. 'What's he got in them? I don't recognize them as our sort of covers anyway.'

'Props. They're to reinforce Inspector Timberlake's image of authority and power.'

'D'you reckon that sort of thing works, sir?' asked Detective Constable Alistair McPhail, with a marked tinge of Caledonian cynicism in his tone.

'I *know* it does, from controlled observations in a number of cases.' Harkness turned to the detective at the remote control of the cameras. 'Put one camera close on Sibley's face, and leave the other showing the whole of the table area.'

Timberlake smiled coldly at Sibley and said, 'If you don't mind, it'll save time if we record this interview. We won't have to keep stopping while Detective Constable Waters takes notes. We'll give you your own copy of the recording, of course.' He reached out and turned on the twin-cassette recorder. In a matter-of-fact, almost bored manner he went through the usual preamble of giving the place, date and time of the interview, and the names of the officers present. 'Now, if you'll please give your name and address, Mr Sibley.' Again Timberlake deliberately did not call him 'Captain'.

Timberlake had given a lot of thought to how he would open the interview. Unfortunately he was compelled to caution Sibley first, which would weaken – but not destroy the shock effect of his first question. His first sentence was enough to put Sibley off balance.

'I must tell you that I suspect you of murdering Mary Docker. You do not have to say anything, but if, when questioned, you do not mention something that you later rely on court, it could harm your defence. *Did you kill her?*'

'Of course not. Have you lost your reason?' Sibley replied with apparent calm after a few seconds. 'I *loved* her. I wouldn't have harmed a hair on her head.'

'He lied!' Harkness said. 'He kept a straight face, but look his pupils are enlarged. Then did you notice how he folded his arms? The classic defensive gesture. And "have you lost your reason?" and its variants, playing for time, are typical lie indicators. Finally, he said too much.'

'I don't know what has possessed you, inspector, but I'll just remind you that I was in Glasgow that night: I have an alibi for the time poor Mary was murdered.'

'Oh, no you don't,' said Timberlake. Slowly he picked up one of the files, and took out a single sheet of paper. 'We've checked. There are three flights to

London – two British Airways and one British Midland – after 8 p.m., the last one getting in at half-past ten. You could have returned to Glasgow on the 11.55 p.m. overnight train back to Glasgow, which gets in at 6.40 the next morning. That would have given you ample time to kill her and be back in time to pilot your own AirAlbion aircraft to London. Here are the times.'

He pushed the sheet of paper a few inches closer to Sibley, who ignored it.

'Let me put a scenario to you, Mr Sibley. You phoned Miss Docker to say you were coming to see her, and arrived at her flat late on Friday night. Either she let you in, or you had a key. She was pleased to see you, and went back to wait for you to join her. You went to the bathroom, stripped, then passed by the kitchen where you took a carving knife, concealed it behind your back, and entered the bedroom. Mary Docker was lying in bed, totally unsuspecting. You walked to the bed, and suddenly – so suddenly she was too shocked even to put up her arms to protect herself – you stabbed her . . . and went on *stabbing her . . . stabbing her . . . stabbing her* . . . forty-three times in all.

'There was a great deal of blood; you yourself were heavily splashed with blood. You went straight to the bathroom where you took a shower, and cleaned the bath, the shower curtains and the walls. Not well enough, though. We found traces of blood in all those places and on the shower taps.' Timberlake stared remorselessly at Sibley. 'Do you take a lot more showers these days? Scrub your hands a lot?'

He leaned forward, closer to Sibley, so that his face and upper body were less than a foot away. Sibley tried to move his chair back a little, but the non-slip pads would not let it budge easily. He assumed a nonchalance by brushing some non-existent specks off his jacket. This was a mistake: it was another sign of unease.

'Are you all right, Mr Sibley? You don't look very well.'

'I'd like a glass of water.' Sibley's voice was badly unsteady.

'Constable, fetch Mr Sibley a glass of water. Interview suspended at' – Timberlake noted the time – 'while PC Wright fetches Mr Sibley a glass of water.' He switched off the twin-deck tape recorder.

'Asking for a glass of water, or a cup of tea, or a cigarette – or to go to the lavatory – are all typical delaying tactics. I'm now convinced that Sibley killed Mary Docker,' Harkness said. 'Every gesture he's made confirms that he is lying when he denies it. But . . .'

'Proving it,' said Darren Webb. 'Unless the guvnor gets him to cough.'

'Unlikely, I'm afraid,' Harkness said. 'At least, this time.'

Sibley put down the empty glass.

'Interview resumed at' – Timberlake noted the time again – 'Present are myself, Detective Inspector Timberlake, Detective Constable Jeff Waters, Police Constable Wright and Mr Mark Sibley.'

'Am I under arrest?' Sibley asked.

'No,' Timberlake said.

'Then I think I'll go now.' Sibley tried to get up, but had difficulty in moving his chair back. 'I shall make an official complaint about this interview, your harassment and your totally unwarranted suggestions. I loved Mary deeply, and—'

'I'm sure you did,' Timberlake said. 'In your fashion.'

Sibley managed to get away from the table and turned towards the door. He stopped, turned back. 'What possible motive could I have for killing her?' he said, his voice almost steady again.

'That's a mistake!' Harkness said. 'He should have left while the going was good.'

'Motive? Jealousy and wounded pride. Rage at what you considered to be a betrayal, when you found out that she was a prostitute, found out she was making a fool of you, a sort of triple cocu. Your massive self-esteem couldn't take that.'

Sibley gripped the table with both hands to steady himself. His knuckles were white. After a moment he sat down heavily.

'That's preposterous! It's *disgusting*! You're sick!'

'You saw her by chance when you were on one of your kerb-crawling expeditions. Or maybe when you were in the house with another whore.'

'I'm not a kerb-crawler! And I've never been near The Grove!'

Jeff Waters noisily drew a deep breath. There followed a heavy silence in both the interview and the observation rooms.

Almost in a whisper Timberlake said, 'I didn't mention The Grove.'

Sibley was good. He gathered himself and after swallowing once he said, 'I just assumed you were referring to The Grove. It's notorious in this part of London, and it's been in the papers often enough.'

Timberlake nodded. 'You say you're not a kerb-crawler?'

'Of course not.'

'*Not even in Manchester?*'

There was another long pause. 'That was a long time ago. It was when I was depressed and feeling lonely. I'm going now. You'll be hearing from my solicitor about your absolutely outrageous behaviour.'

Sibley struggled to his feet with as much dignity as he could muster, which wasn't much. 'And I want my copy of the recording of this monstrous interview and your disgusting remarks.'

'Interview terminated,' Timberlake said, adding the time. He switched off the recorder and gave Sibley one of the cassettes.

'Wait for me just outside the door,' Timberlake told the other two policemen, 'and leave it open.' When they were outside he said softly to Sibley, almost into his ear. 'I know you did it, and—'

'Prove it!'

'Oh, I shall, I shall. What you did to that poor girl makes me burn. Every criminal makes at least one mistake, and I'll find yours. You can bet your life on it: I'm paid to be patient. I'll have you, Sibley, for Mary

Docker's murder . . . *and for the murders of those other prostitutes. I know you did those, too.*'

'What the hell . . . !' Harkness exclaimed. He started to move towards the door, stopping just long enough to say, 'Tell Inspector Timberlake I want to see him in my office. *At once.*'

Timberlake had never seen Harkness so angry. His had red patches over his cheekbones which stood out against the unusual whiteness of his face; his lips were compressed into a thin line.

'Inspector Timberlake, I demand an explanation.' Although his voice was low, it was sharp as a stiletto.

Timberlake was scared; nevertheless, he didn't hedge or try to pretend he didn't know what Harkness meant. 'Sir, I hate Sibley for the savage murder he did, and I'm going to get him for it. It wasn't a crime of passion; that had had time to atrophy. It was cold, premeditated murder, without a grain of extenuating circumstance. It made me lose my temper and blurt out the bit about the other women. Still, if I may say so, I don't think it has done any harm. It shook him, and brought him closer to cracking. It could jolt him into making a false move. But I'm sorry. It was unprofessional.'

'That's not what concerns me primarily, although it was bad enough. You said you knew he'd murdered the other prostitutes, too. What in God's name makes you think he committed *those* murders?'

Timberlake took a deep breath. 'I've thought about

this a lot. I'd noticed a book on the Jack the Ripper murders—'

Harkness stared at him with something like horror, as if he thought Timberlake's mind had begun to fail him.

'It was a relatively recent book,* in which the author pointed out – for the first time in more than a hundred years – that all the Ripper's victims knew each other and lived close to each other . . . Apparently that hadn't ever occurred to anyone other than the girls' killer. The writer's theory was that the women were murdered because they all knew something about the first victim, something that might have led to the identification of the killer . . . or killers, in the Jack the Ripper case.'

Harkness was now looking a little less thunderous.

Timberlake pressed on. 'I should have cottoned on sooner. We had a case like that here, you'll remember – the Neumann–Newman affair† – where Newman killed women who might have seen him and broken his alibi. Well, I'm sure that when Sibley saw Mary Docker whoring as Vicki Stevens, he realized later those other prostitutes could have seen *him* in the area. So . . .'

'Why would they connect him to her?'

'The newspapers at the time of the murder. They were full of photographs of Mary Docker and her fiancé, Captain Mark Sibley. You can just imagine the women: "Look! That Mary Docker's our Vicki Lester!" And one of them, "Here, isn't that the geezer who was looking for business round here last week? . . ."'

***Jack The Ripper: The Final Solution* by Stephen Knight.
†See *Elimination*.

'Sir,' Timberlake went on, 'all the prostitute killings had nothing of the usual serial murderer's *modus operandi*: they were at different times of day, had different methods and absolutely no traces of the killer. No fibres, no saliva, no sexual interference, and so no semen, nothing. The only common factor was that they were all prostitutes. The killer was a cool operator performing skilful executions. Above all, he was intelligent, like Sibley.

'He did make one mistake; unfortunately it isn't *the* mistake that will let us get him. If he'd killed Vicki Stevens on her own patch down The Grove, we'd eventually have considered it as simply one of a bunch of serial murders by some psychopath who had something against prostitutes. But he didn't: he killed Vicki Stevens in her real persona as Mary Docker. And only Sibley could have done that.'

'It's all possible, of course, but you're creating a very large scenario on the basis of some very fragile hypotheses and unsubstantiated guesswork.'

'And gut feeling. Oh, yes – and something else.' Timberlake produced the second folder he had in the interview room. He took out a sheet of paper. 'Here's a list of the dates of the murders, and the dates when Sibley wasn't on flying duty.'

Harkness didn't have to look at the list. He sighed heavily. 'Why didn't you come to me with this?'

'Sir, I was going to, after the Sibley interview. It wasn't my intention to accuse him now. But, as I just said, I lost my temper with the bastard. I'm sorry.'

Harkness stared at Timberlake as if he could see right inside his brain. He didn't know whether Timberlake was telling the full truth. For that matter, Timberlake didn't know himself.

'Well, the situation is simple, Harry.' He smiled wryly. 'All you have to do now is find that one mistake Sibley made.'

Chapter Twenty

As Timberlake walked into the house the answerphone was signalling that someone had called. He pressed the Play button, whoever it was who had called had just hung up when they heard the recorded message. He dialled 1471.

'You were called today, at 15.03 hours. We do not have the caller's number. Please hang up.'

Timberlake pressed the phone rest, released it and left the phone off the hook. He switched on his mobile phone and put it on the table next to where he was going to work.

After he had changed into pyjamas and dressing gown, he put on a long tape he had made from some of his cherished vinyl records of jazz pianists: 'Tad' Dameron, 'Bud' Powell, Count Basie and Thelonius Monk. He turned the sound down so the music wasn't too distracting. He went into the kitchen and made himself a couple of sandwiches and black coffee strong enough to have satisfied Proust. He took them through to the lounge on a small tray and started to go through the Docker case files. His head began to ache, and he wondered if he needed glasses now.

The shrill ringing of his mobile phone made him jump. He picked it up irritably.

'Yes?' he snapped.

'Harry, you all right?' It was Sarah Lewis. 'You sound strange.'

'Sorry. The phone startled me.'

'You looked a bit humpty at the nick. There's nothing wrong, is there?'

'No, not really. Not at all, actually.'

'Would you like to come over? Or I come to you?' He reflected for a long moment, torn between anxiety to get on with his re-reading and the desire to have some company.

His silence prompted Sarah to add, 'We don't have to go to bed if you don't want. Just for company. You know. But if you don't want to see me . . .'

'No, no; it's not that, Sarah. I was trying to make up my mind whether I should concentrate on some work I've brought home.'

'Have a break, for Christ's sake, Harry! Wind down a bit.' She said firmly, 'I'm on my way. I'll make you something to eat. I bet you haven't had anything.'

She banged the phone down before he could say, 'I've already eaten.' He looked at his tray. The sandwiches were untouched, and the coffee even looked stone cold. He'd had no idea how long he'd been working. He got up, took the tray into the kitchen and guiltily threw the sandwiches into the rubbish bin.

Sarah Lewis, wearing a shirt and jeans, arrived with a carrier bag full of Chinese food. 'I decided I couldn't be bothered to cook, and anyway, I'm too hungry to wait. My treat.'

Timberlake made another pot of coffee, while Sarah set out the meal on a side table. Because they were both rather hungry, they were a little sloppy with the chopsticks they usually preferred. As she was leaning forward Sarah accidentally dropped a small ball of rice from her chopsticks down the front of her shirt. She was reaching for it for it when Timberlake said, 'No, I'll do that.' It took him quite a while to get out the last grain, and he searched long and diligently to make sure he hadn't missed any.

The advantage of a Chinese take-away is that you don't need to do any washing up if you eat from the containers it comes in. The table was cleared in a matter of minutes and they settled down to their Blue Mountain coffee and Rémy Martin on the long leather sofa Timberlake had bought in the winter sales.

'What's all that?' Sarah asked, pointing to the files on the main table. Timberlake explained to her.

'I thought you'd been through them a couple of times already. At least.'

'Yes. But I'm still sure there's something there I've missed. There *must* be. I don't want to believe that Sibley committed an error-free crime – crimes, actually.'

'Could I give you a hand?' Sarah asked tentatively.

Timberlake was caught painfully on the horns of a dilemma. Maybe he hadn't been seeing the wood for the trees, and Sarah's fresh approach might spot something he had overlooked and so pass him the handcuffs to put on Sibley. On the other hand, he wanted to get Sibley *himself*: it was a personal thing. He pushed aside the thought that he wanted all the credit, and did not want to have to share it with Sarah – or anyone else.

Still uncertain of his answer, he turned to look at her and was overwhelmed with desire when he noticed that her shirt was gaping open where he had unbuttoned it to get out the rice.

'You did say we didn't *have* to go to bed?' Timberlake asked with patently false nonchalance.

'Uhuh.' Sarah tried to keep all emotion out of her voice.

'Good. The sofa's a virgin. We can do it right here.'

Quite soon Timberlake thought that he had made a bad mistake: he had been caressing and kissing Sarah for some time as he sat beside her without any stirrings in his groin. He closed his eyes and lay back for a moment, without stopping his caressing: at least he was enjoying that. He became aware of a strange sensation. He looked down. Sarah was breathing her hot, alcohol-perfumed breath on his penis.

It worked as rapidly as a spray of Kwik-Start on a car engine on a winter's morning.

For a while, at least, he was able to clear his mind of his personal and professional problems. Now as he lay against the back of the sofa, pleasurably exhausted, with the naked body of the Welsh Rarebit sprawled unselfconsciously beside him, he wondered how he really felt about her. Sure the sex had been great – it was even funny, with the squeaky sound of the leather sofa as they moved. Afterwards he *liked* her. But . . . but . . . He had a niggling feeling there was something lacking. Come on! he told himself. Most of the elements were there for him to be able to believe it was love, whatever the hell that was. He smiled wryly as he thought of Antony's words to Cleopatra in Shakespeare's play: 'There's beggary in the love that can be reckoned.'

Companionship! That's what it was he was looking

for. Sarah was a marvellous sexual partner, she was amusing, understanding and a good mate. But not a *companion*, in his understanding of the word. Maybe I should settle for what there is and stop looking for perfection, he thought.

He suddenly felt very thirsty. Slowly, so as not to wake the drowsy Sarah, he disengaged himself from her and padded barefoot to the kitchen to get a drink of water. He drank a whole tumblerful in one go, and returned to the lounge.

Halfway to the sofa he stopped as if he had been pole-axed, and stood looking vacantly into the distance. Abruptly he jerked into action and went to the table where he frantically riffled through the files. He pulled out two documents and studied them intently.

Sarah stirred, yawned, looked at him and asked, 'What're you doing?' He held up a hand, and she had sense enough not to persist.

After he had read both documents twice, Timberlake gave a broad, broad smile. He stood up, drew a deep breath, and in a voice that made Sarah sit bolt upright with shock he shouted, 'I've got the bastard! *I've got him!*'

Detective Superintendent Harkness finished reading the two documents for the second time. He leant back from his desk.

'You're right, Harry. Until now the case against Sibley – your case – has been entirely circumstantial, but this puts a completely different aspect on it. This' – he tapped the papers – 'has transformed an abstract concept into a solid reality.'

'You took the very words out of my mouth,' Darren Webb whispered, but not softly enough for Harkness's sharp hearing. He speared Webb with a brief glance.

Timberlake, Darren Webb, Nigel Larkin, Jeff Waters, Alistair McPhail and other members of the murder squad were at the morning conference the next day. Timberlake had explained what he had found in the files, and put the evidence before Harkness.

'It was extraordinary that no one picked this up before,' Harkness went on. 'But these things do happen, and the pieces of information were buried rather deeply. Well done, Harry.'

'I was a bit lucky,' Timberlake said, not meaning to sound falsely modest. 'Something jogged my memory, and—' he shrugged.

Darren Webb, trying to make up for his earlier faux pas, said, 'Sibley really took a big chance establishing that alibi. If the night train back to Glasgow had been delayed for some reason, he could have been stranded right in the brown stuff.'

'Remember how some of the AirAlbion people described him? Conceited, fond of himself . . . The bastard is so arrogantly self-satisfied he thinks he's bomb-proof and doesn't make mistakes,' Timberlake said bitterly.

'There's more to it than that,' Harkness said. 'I shouldn't be surprised if he waited some time for everything to be right for him to commit the murder and fake an alibi. He made sure there were no engineering works on the London–Glasgow line and the weather was good for flying.'

'I hadn't thought of that,' Timberlake admitted. 'God, that makes it worse, the degree of premeditation . . . waiting for the perfect opportunity. No wonder he killed her so savagely, having to keep the lid screwed down on all that rage boiling up inside him.'

'Yes. But let's forget the speculation and get on with things,' Harkness said. 'First, we get in the witness to check on the original statement. I'll do the interview myself. We don't want there to be any suggestion that you used any undue influence to reinforce the statement, although I must say it seems very clear-cut as it stands.

'As soon as the statement is confirmed, I suggest we send a couple of unmarked cars round to his home, in case he's there and somebody from the airline rings him up to ask what's going on. If he's flying, we can meet him at Heathrow or wherever when he comes back. Or warn the police at the airport he's on his way to,' Timberlake said.

The vital witness was at home when Darren Webb and Nigel Larkin called, and agreed to return to Terrace Vale nick with them right away. On the way there the two detectives very carefully avoided mentioning the Mary Docker case: they didn't want a clever defence lawyer suggesting at any subsequent trial that they had planted ideas in the witness's mind.

After fifteen minutes' intensive questioning by Detective Superintendent Harkness, the original statement was confirmed. 'Cast in bronze,' was how he described it. 'So let's do it,' he said. 'Jeff, lay on the cars to go to Sibley's flat. Harry, you get on to AirAlbion and find out Sibley's duties. And I don't have to tell you to walk on eggshells when you speak to them.'

Timberlake called Captain Trevor Perowne on the training captain's direct line. From his experience of the man, he decided that eggshell-walking would be counter-productive, likewise pussy-footing and prevarication. 'Hang on a moment,' Perowne said in answer to Timberlake's enquiry about Sibley. 'Ah, yes. He's in the air now, due to land at Gatwick at 14.10 with an Airbus on a holiday charter flight from Nairobi. Let's see . . . at the last contact it's some thirty-five minutes behind schedule. His new ETA is 14.45. Probably delayed by some silly passenger bumbling about in duty-free.' He waited a moment and said with heavy irony, 'Would like me to raise him on the radio and tell him you'll be waiting to see him?'

Timberlake played the game, 'Er . . . on reflection, I rather think I'd prefer not. Don't want to worry him while he's flying.'

A noise something like a chuckle came from Perowne's end.

Timberlake looked at his watch. 'Five to twelve,' he said. 'Time enough to get there and set things up, if you'll fix things with Airport Security, sir?' he asked Harkness, who nodded agreement.

'I'll take Darren, Nigel and Jeff Waters with PC Wright as a uniform, if he's available. We'll go in two cars, led by a patrol car with a motorway horn, just to be on the safe side in case there're any traffic problems.'

'I'll contact the Sussex police to warn them you're on your way,' Harkness said.

'Right, let's move,' Timberlake said. He looked round. 'Where the hell's Nigel got to?'

'Here, guv,' Nigel Larkin said brightly. 'I was on the phone to Traffic. There are no holdups on the motorway.' He beamed, as if he had personally shunted all the traffic to one side.

Timberlake and the other two detectives stopped at the front desk, where Sergeant Rumsden was writing something in the incident book.

'We want a couple of cars, one with a motorway horn, Tony.'

Rumsden turned to a key rack and handed over two sets of keys.

'And d'you know where Rambo is?'

'Right behind you, guv,' Rumsden said calmly.

Timberlake swung round. Rambo Wright and WPC Hall had just come into the station for refreshments.

'How do you do that?' Timberlake asked Rumsden.

Rumsden looked suitably modest. 'Rubbed my magic wand.'

'Dirty old sod, and on duty, too,' came an anonymous voice from the area behind Rumsden. All the constables at their desks were working hard, heads down.

'Grab yourself a take-away burger,' Timberlake told Rambo. 'We're off to Gatwick. We'll meet you in the yard.'

'What about me, sir?' said Rosie, who could smell action in the air like a warhorse smelling cordite. 'I'll be left without a partner.'

Timberlake hesitated for a moment. 'All right. You can come, too. I'll take the first car with Rambo, and

DC Larkin. Sergeant Webb will be in the second car with Jeff Waters and Rosie. Right, move!'

'Gatwick, eh?' said Rumsden. 'Going on your hols, Harry?'

'Better than that. To bust Sibley,' Timberlake replied, stopping just short of licking his lips.

The journey to the airport was uneventful. Any motorists who hadn't noticed the blue lights and flashing headlamps were sent swerving out of the right-hand lane by an occasional blare of the motorway horn. Rambo Wright smiled to see brakelights of cars ahead go on when drivers cut their speed to the legal limit the moment they were aware of a police car coming up behind them. 'Bit more interesting than bumbling about in traffic round Terrace Vale,' he said.

Timberlake hardly heard him. When they set off he felt a surge of adrenalin which made his perceptions and reactions keener as he closed in on his quarry. He unashamedly exulted at the thought of nailing Sibley at last.

Without warning, his feelings changed dramatically. As the car neared Gatwick he became conscious of the sound of jet engines, followed by the sight of massive aircraft climbing away from the airport towards him. His earlier excitement unexpectedly drained away, leaving him unaccountably depressed. He was jolted when the reason for the swing in his mood came to him: the airport activity reminded him of the morning when his wife Jenny left him to go to America. It was inexplicable. He was on his way to arrest a clever, cold-hearted murderer, and yet he was preoccupied with thoughts of a woman he had once loved but who had left him and was 3,000 miles away. He shook his head in disbelief.

'Did you say something, sir?' Rambo asked.

'No. Just thinking.'

The two cars drove up to the main entrance of the South Terminal, where two uniformed security guards and a tall, lean man with close-cut iron-grey hair, wearing civilian clothes, were waiting. The man in mufti would have been unmistakably ex-Army even if he'd been on a beach wearing bathing trunks. When the three men saw the police cars arrive they approached the leading vehicle.

'Inspector Timberlake? I'm Colonel Tim Wilkinson, Head of Security. Your superintendent called and briefed me.'

'Good of you to give us your co-operation.'

'One of my men will lead you to where you can park your vehicles right beside the terminal, and then bring you all to my office for a quick conference.'

Timberlake opened the meeting by saying, 'I take it my superintendent has told you we've come to arrest an AirAlbion pilot who's due to land soon?'

'Yes. Captain Sibley. I don't know him personally, I'm afraid. I've checked: his aircraft's due to join airport control in thirty-seven minutes.'

'What's the usual procedure for aircrew after landing, colonel?'

'They come out of their own exit at the front of the aircraft and get into a crew bus which brings them to a special entrance into the terminal. There's a security man on duty in a booth, and he opens the remote-control doorlock when he identifies the crew. From there the crew take the lift to the briefing room. After the briefing – debriefing, actually – most of them go to the staff carpark behind the hotel and drive on to the A23. Some take the train.'

'Where would be the best place to arrest him?'

Wilkinson reflected. 'I should say at the entrance to the briefing room. All aircrew report there after a flight. There'll be less fuss: it's away from the public area so you won't get mixed up with any civilians.' He pronounced 'civilians' as if it were the name of a microbe.

'That sounds fine,' Timberlake said. 'If you don't mind, we'll have a discreet look at the crews' entrance to the building before we go to the briefing room. Just to check.'

'As you wish,' Wilkinson said, rather frostily.

Timberlake got the impression that he was the sort of man who expected everyone to follow his advice without question, which came as if it were being handed down on stone tablets. Wilkinson's attitude awakened in Timberlake a certain antipathy to ex-army officers in senior security posts. When Wilkinson looked at him Timberlake had the uncomfortable feeling he could hear unspoken thoughts. 'I suppose you wonder what I was doing in the army before taking this job?'

Timberlake was wrong-footed, and had to admit to himself that the man was brighter than he gave him credit for. 'Not really.'

'I was with Army Intelligence in a special unit.' He further caught Timberlake by surprise when he gave an unexpectedly charming smile as he said, 'If Army Intelligence isn't a contradiction in terms. Or maybe an oxymoron.'

Timberlake was won over. 'Well, we have a Criminal Intelligence unit.'

Wilkinson led the police group through the main entrance to the South Terminal and through a minor maze of corridors, down a lift to the special staff entrance from the airport apron.

'Can we go outside?' Timberlake asked.

'I'll have to get you yellow jackets before you do. Obligatory on the airfield.'

'Well, perhaps we'll have a look at the briefing room first.'

Wilkinson turned and led them to the lifts and up to the briefing room.

When Timberlake saw the layout he said, 'You were right, of course. This is the better bet. We'll wait just inside the door, and take him as he comes in. Then we'll quickly whisk him back into the corridor to avoid as much fuss as possible with the other aircrew. That's if it's all right with you?' he added politely.

'Of course. Would you like any of my security staff to give you a hand?'

Timberlake hesitated. 'As a backup in the corridor, perhaps. Sibley's a cunning, resourceful man. And ruthless.' A thought struck him. 'The fact they're there won't spook him?'

Wilkinson shook his head. 'I shouldn't think so. Security guards can be anywhere at any time.' He took out his personal radio. 'CSO Wilkinson here. What's the ETA of that AirAlbion charter from Nairobi? And which stand will it go to? Over.'

There was a short period of silence broken only by the frying-bacon sound of static from the radio before it squawked into life.

'Received. Call me when it's on final approach,' Wilkinson ordered. He turned to Timberlake. 'He'll be switching radio contact from Air Traffic Control to airport control in twelve minutes, and when he lands he'll go to Pier 4 at the North Terminal.'

'Does that mean we have to go over there?'

'No. Don't worry. There's only one briefing room, and it's in this terminal. You've got time. Would you like to come up on the roof and see his aircraft land? You'll be able to watch him get out and make his way over here.'

Because of their open spaces aerodromes always seem to have strong winds, and when Timberlake and the others came out on to the roof of the South Terminal, Rambo Wright and Rosie Hall had to grab at their caps. Tim Wilkinson pointed out the North Terminal and the so-called pier where Sibley's Airbus would finally park. A small, automatically controlled, driverless train rumbled and clicked towards them from the distant terminal on a raised track.

'What's that, sir?' Nigel Larkin asked.

'Shuttle service for passengers between the two terminals,' Wilkinson replied.

'Is there any possibility that Sibley will take it?' Timberlake said.

'No. Aircrew always stay apart from the paying customers. The aircraft to the crew bus is about as far as any of them want to walk, as far as I've ever noticed.'

Time was dragging its feet for Timberlake. Twice he looked at his watch disbelievingly to see how little time had passed. He realized how tense he was when

Wilkinson's radio suddenly came to life again and startled him.

'He'll be touching down in a couple of minutes,' Wilkinson announced after listening to the call. Timberlake turned towards the lift, but Wilkinson touched his arm. 'There's no hurry.'

The Airbus came out of the sun as it approached the airport's single runway towards the South Terminal. It then changed attitude, its nose coming up as it passed over the end of the runway before it began to sink under control. The main undercarriage wheels touched down, giving off smoke from the heated tyres like a gigantic Formula One racing car under too-enthusiastic braking. Slowly the aircraft tilted forward until the nose-wheel met the runway. Several seconds later the watchers on the roof heard the delayed sounds of the sudden roar of the engines as Sibley slowed the plane's descent, followed by the screech of the tyres, and another roar as the four engines' thrust was reversed to help it brake.

Timberlake took a pair of expensive, compact zoom binoculars from his pocket.

'I haven't seen those before, guv,' Darren Webb said. 'How long have you had them?'

Timberlake didn't answer. He was following the course of the Airbus as it rolled down the runway, turned off left across Taxiway 2/Emergency Runway and threaded its way to Pier 4. The noise of the engines finally died.

'There's the crew bus,' Wilkinson said, pointing out a single-decker coach scuttling towards the aircraft.

'Shall we go, guv?' Webb enquired.

'As soon as I see Sibley get on the bus,' Timberlake told him.

The delay before Sibley appeared began to fray Timberlake's nerves. His hands could not hold his binoculars steady enough for him to see properly, so he moved forward to rest his elbows on the roof parapet.

Sibley was the last one of the three aircrew to come down the ladder, by which time Timberlake had managed to regain full control of himself.

Timberlake's heart thudded in his chest. Right dead centre in his binoculars Sibley was staring directly towards him as if he, too, had binoculars and was studying Timberlake just as intently as he was observing Sibley. The pilot stayed motionless for a few seconds that lasted an age before he got into the bus. Common sense told Timberlake that it was all an illusion. He was too far away from Sibley for the man to have seen him as clearly as he had seen Sibley with the help of the binoculars. But it was an unnerving moment, and the exercise of logic failed to dispel completely Timberlake's sense of disquiet.

Wilkinson, Timberlake and the other policemen entered the briefing room and stayed just behind the door. Timberlake was still haunted by a sense of foreboding that things could go wrong.

Two crews from other airlines came into the room before two men in AirAlbion uniforms arrived.

Two! And Sibley was not one of them.

Timberlake spoke softly but urgently to Wilkinson. 'Ask them where Sibley is.'

Wilkinson nodded and joined the two men. 'Isn't Captain Sibley with you?'

The senior officer of the two replied. 'He left something on board and has gone back for it. He should be along in five minutes. Is anything up?'

'No, just a personal message for him,' Wilkinson said off-handedly.

'Something's gone wrong. Sibley *knows*,' Timberlake said softly but urgently to Wilkinson, his voice barely under control. 'Can you contact the aircraft to check if he is there?'

Wilkinson stepped out into the corridor and gave some terse orders over his radio. While he waited for a reply Timberlake felt an urge to bite his nails, or to have a cigarette, although he hadn't smoked for years. Trying to reassure himself he said, 'How the hell *could* he know?' Not realizing he had spoken out loud.

Wilkinson's radio came to life. He listened to the brief message.

'Well?' Timberlake asked.

'My people checked with the bus driver and the ground crew at the aircraft. Sibley hasn't been back.'

'So where the hell has he gone?'

'If he *has* twigged and is marking a run for it, to the carpark, sir?' Nigel Larkin suggested, speaking for the first time after an unusually long silence for him.

'Well done, Nigel,' Timberlake said.

'*Staff* carpark,' Wilkinson said.

'How many exits does it have?' Timberlake asked.

'Just the one. But the staff on the gate won't necessarily recognize Captain Sibley.'

'I will, sir,' suggested Rambo Wright.

'Right. Move! Wait! Give me the car keys – just in case.' He wondered what on earth had made him say that.

'I'll have one of my men take you,' Wilkinson said

to Rambo as he signalled to one of the security guards. 'Right. I think our best move is to go back on the roof and observe from there.' He started to move, then stopped. 'Damn,' he said, and took out his radio again.

'Control room?' he said. 'CSO here. Broadcast a general alert to guards on all the perimeter gates to check the passes of everyone leaving the airport in a vehicle or on foot. Detain a Captain Mark Sibley of AlbionAir. Call me if he's sighted.'

'God!' Timberlake exclaimed. 'I've just thought – what about the railway station?'

Wilkinson turned to the second security guard. Pick up two or three more men from the guardroom and get over there. Check anyone in uniform.' He spoke to Timberlake. 'He won't have had time to change.'

'Darren, you'd better go, too, as you know him by sight.'

Darren Webb looked to be on the point of arguing, but changed his mind and settled for, 'Right, guv.'

The remaining four men – Timberlake, Tim Wilkinson, Nigel Larkin and Jeff Waters – returned to the observation roof. Timberlake surveyed the aerodrome and sighed. Nigel understood. He said sombrely, 'Big, isn't it, guv?'

Wilkinson's radio was ominously quiet. Timberlake gave Wilkinson the look.

Embarrassed Wilkinson said, 'There could be some perfectly simple reason for Sibley's disappearance, if that's the right word.'

'For instance?' Timberlake said tetchily.

'Oh, I don't know. Stuck in a lift somewhere? Stopped to talk to someone?'

Timberlake shook his head. 'The rest of the crew

weren't held up. So why didn't he go to the debriefing with them?'

'Are you sure he's making a run for it?' Wilkinson insisted.

'Positive,' Timberlake lied.

'But suppose you are right, and he is on the run. Why now? Why not a week ago, when he could have had time to make proper arrangements? And where could he go, anyway?'

'People in his position don't think about that. You see, his egoism made him absolutely certain he'd got away with murder. But I managed to force a few cracks in his defences, start to erode his self-confidence. God knows he's had more than enough stress to affect the balance of his mind, maybe even push him to borderline psychosis. Somehow he's found out I've come here to arrest him, and it's tipped him over the edge. In his present mental state he's liable to do anything now.'

Wilkinson turned away without saying anything.

There was nothing Timberlake could do now other than wait until someone came up with a sighting of Sibley. He took out his binoculars and looked across at the AirAlbion Airbus still in its place at Pier 4. A number of vehicles were grouped round it: a fuel tanker, a catering van with the ready-prepared in-flight meals, a honey wagon, and a couple of engineering vans.

'Would the next crew let him on board the aircraft?' Timberlake asked.

Wilkinson shrugged. 'Perhaps. But they wouldn't let him fly with them, even as a passenger, without the proper authority.'

Timberlake was disappointed. He slowly swung his

binoculars, then suddenly stiffened. 'Those small aircraft to the left of the North Terminal. What are they?'

'They belong to small charter companies, business organizations, some private individuals . . .'

Captain Perowne's words came back to Timberlake, loud and clear: *'He loves flying . . . Has his own light aircraft. Uses it to commute to work sometimes when he's got a few days off . . . a lovely little Cessna.'*

As he watched, the propeller of one of the little aircraft began to turn. Timberlake thrust his binoculars into Wilkinson's hands.

'That one with the propeller turning. Can you tell me whether it's a Cessna?'

The urgency in Timberlake's voice stopped Wilkinson asking any questions. After a moment's scrutiny he said. 'Yes, it is.'

'Can you find out if it's Sibley's?'

Wilkinson spoke rapidly into his radio, while still keeping the binoculars on the Cessna. 'CSO. Put me through to the General Aviation Terminal . . . CSO here. Who is the registered owner of Cessna—?' He read out the registration letters on the side of the aircraft. 'Sibley,' he said to Timberlake. Then into the radio again, 'Has he filed a flight plan . . . ? Thanks.

'It's your man. He hasn't filed a flight plan.'

Timberlake turned and ran for the lift from the roof, calling to Jeff Waters, 'Come on!'

'What're you doing?' shouted Wilkinson.

'I'm going to get him!'

'My men'll do that!'

Timberlake ignored him and continued running, closely followed by Waters. The two policemen got into the lift just in front of Wilkinson, who barely managed to stop the doors shutting in his face. He tried to operate his radio during the descent but the shaft was a transmission blackspot.

'Where the hell do you think you're going, Inspector?' Wilkinson bellowed.

'My car. I'll stop the bastard!'

'Don't be stupid! You can't go charging about on the airfield! Christ knows what bloody havoc you could cause with aircraft taking off and landing!' Wilkinson continued to shout at Timberlake to stop as he fell behind the other two men.

Timberlake thanked his stars the police cars were parked right next to the terminal. He unlocked all the car doors with the remote control, and got behind the wheel. Jeff Waters ran round to the passenger seat just as Wilkinson arrived, wrenched open a rear door and fell inside. He said something but his words were lost in the sound of the racing engine and tortured tyres as Timberlake accelerated away towards the runway area.

He aimed the car roughly in the direction he had last seen Sibley's aircraft. Airport workers stopped what they were doing and looked, their mouths open, when the police car, its blue lights flashing and loud horn blaring, hurtled past them. Gathering speed, he drove past the short Pier 1 on the left side of the South Terminal, the great tailplanes of two aircraft towering above the car. To his right two Boeing 747s and three 727s were parked by the longer Pier 2, some of them with engines running. Timberlake and Waters had never been as close to the exhausts of aircraft jet engines before, even inside their car, the volcanic roar and banshee screech sounded terrifying.

As Timberlake turned right at the end of the pier towards where he had last seen the Cessna, an aircraft tractor slowly emerged from the other side of the pier, towing a 747 tail-first to manœcuvre it into position to taxi out. There was no possibility of the tractor braking sharply with nearly 300 tons of aircraft behind it. Timberlake swung his steering wheel viciously and as the tail of the car began to slide out he put on a reverse lock to send it into a four-wheel sideways drift which took it just past the nose of the tractor.

Waters clenched his teeth so firmly his jaw ached, while his right foot was pushing his foot hard against the floor of the car on an imaginary brake. Wilkinson was so involved with using his radio he was unaware of what was happening until the last moment and the shadow of the aircraft's massive wing passed over the car.

'Christ, are you trying to kill us all?' he said frantically.

'No, I'm trying not to,' Timberlake replied. He slowed briefly and looked round. 'Where's the fucking Cessna gone?'

'There, sir,' Waters said, pointing. 'Going away from us, about 300 yards along the taxi-track. Wilkinson, in the back seats, was talking rapidly into his radio. In his rear-view mirror Timberlake could see blue lights flashing as airport security cars took up the chase behind him.

'Tell your people to keep off,' Timberlake said. 'He's my man.'

'And this is my aerodrome,' Wilkinson snapped back. 'Besides, they're not after him – they're after you.'

Timberlake weaved in and out of the private aircraft then turned left to take the car past the control tower.

'I've lost the bastard!' Timberlake cried.

'Turn right!' Waters barked at him.

Timberlake yanked the steering wheel round just in front of the fire station. The doors were open and he could see a couple of firemen leaning against their machines, looking as startled as everyone else the police car had driven past.

As the car came on to Taxiway 2, Timberlake could see the Cessna taxying at speed away from him along the parallel Taxiway 1/Emergency Runway.

'Can he take off from there?' Timberlake asked Wilkinson.

'Yes, but not in that direction; that's downwind,' Wilkinson said, breaking off from giving orders on his radio. 'He'll have to turn and come back this way. There's a turnoff from this track on to the other one about 200 yards ahead. You can get on to his track and block him off.'

No sooner had he said that than Sibley slewed his Cessna round in a 180-degree turn that almost made the undercarriage collapse, and straightened up in line with the emergency runway. As it came into the wind it rolled forward slowly before gathering speed. As it rolled past Timberlake's car he caught a glimpse of Sibley's white face and staring eyes turned towards him.

Timberlake glanced at the grass area between his own taxi-track and the Cessna's wider one. Without any warning to the others he swung the steering wheel and ran on to the grass. The second he was on it he realized that the grass concealed deep ruts running parallel to the taxi-track. The car bucked wildly, and Wilkinson hit his head on the roof as he was flung out of his seat. His radio fell somewhere beneath his feet.

'Let him go, you bloody maniac!' Wilkinson yelled. 'Where the hell can he run to anyway?'

Timberlake ignored him; it was doubtful that he even heard him. He had managed to get the car running in the ruts but was having difficulty in getting out of them and on to the same track as the Cessna. Eventually the vehicle bounced on to the concrete, where it gained rapidly on the aircraft. It was touch and go whether it would reach the Cessna before it managed to get airborne. Timberlake was crouched over the wheel as if he were urging the car to go faster.

Fifty yards . . . thirty . . . twenty . . . fifteen . . . Timberlake could see the aircraft's elevators move down as Sibley tried to get it off the ground. The Cessna bounced a couple of times off the runway and back again . . . and then there was the most shattering, earthshaking, rumbling roar like a hundred peals of thunder.

Chapter Twenty-one

'Operational reasons' is the euphemism for what airlines call all sorts of unplanned changes and general cockups that cause aircraft to be diverted from their normal bases to a different aerodrome. Occasionally a Concorde lands and takes off from London Gatwick instead of London Heathrow. For operational reasons.

Although the chase of the Cessna had been brief in clock-measured time it had seemed interminable when measured by heartbeats. Timberlake was unaware that Wilkinson's planned call to the control tower to stop all aircraft landing and taking off had been aborted when the car's last gigantic leap had shaken his radio from his hand. At the very moment that the car closed on the fleeing Cessna, a Concorde was taking off beside them, its engines savagely assaulting their ears as they increased from a rumbling roar to a cataclysmic sustained roar like a volcano erupting. The earth shook.

The three men in the car and the one in the Cessna were momentarily disorientated, their heads ringing and their senses scrambled.

By the time Timberlake had at least partially recovered his wits, he could see that his car had crashed into the tailplane assembly of the Cessna, damaging it so comprehensively that the aircraft was impossible to control.

Sibley leapt out, his face contorted as he stared at Timberlake for a second before turning to run off in the general direction of the private aircraft park. Behind him Sibley left his Cessna, its airscrew turning over slowly, standing half on the taxi-way, half on the grass, like a wounded bird.

The first to move from the car to chase Sibley was Waters. His method of capturing the fugitive was simplicity itself. He stretched out a foot and tripped Sibley, then fell on him when he sprawled on the grass to knock his last remaining breath from his body. By the time Timberlake arrived, Waters had already handcuffed Sibley's hands behind his back and was hauling him to his feet. The bedraggled, dirty man with a wild expression was worlds away from the suave, sophisticated man Timberlake had visited in his luxury Knightsbridge flat.

'Well done, Jeff,' Timberlake said before turning to Sibley and saying in a nearly level voice, 'Mark Sibley, I am arresting you for the murder of Mary Docker, also known as Vicki Stevens and as Juliette Grande. You are not obliged to say anything, but it may harm your defence if, when questioned, you do not say something which you later rely on in court. Anything you do say will be taken down in writing and may be used in evidence. Do you understand?'

Sibley nodded.

'Please say yes or no.'

'Yes, yes, I understand!'

*

On the journey back to Terrace Vale, Rambo Wright drove the first car, with Timberlake and Jeff Waters on either side of the handcuffed Sibley in the back seat. As the cars left the airport – to the great relief of Tim Wilkinson and his staff and Flying Control – Sibley craned his neck to watch an Airbus take off. In the distance, some 1,500 feet higher, another aircraft was on its final approach to land.

'All that's over for you, Sibley,' Timberlake said. 'No more head in the clouds. Feet on the ground.'

Sibley turned his head slowly to look at Timberlake. He had dead eyes in a bloodless face.

By the time the police and their prisoner got back to Terrace Vale, Press and TV reporters were already beginning to congregate at the station. The two cars had to thread their way through the small crowd to get into the station yard. Sibley had a coat over his head.

Once Sibley had been booked in, Detective Superintendent Harkness took Timberlake into his office and closed the door. The senior officer's face was white and set. The expression in his eyes made even the case-hardened Timberlake quail inwardly.

'I don't know if you realize the storm you've aroused with your cowboys and Indians antics at Gatwick. I've had calls from the Assistant Commissioner Crime, the BAA Security people at Gatwick and at Holborn, not to mention the Home Office and others. I think I can save you from any actual charges, by talking to one or two people – thank goodness I'm on reasonable terms with the Commissioner and the Home Secretary – but you're going to have a lot of explaining and apologizing to do. And frankly, I'm extremely annoyed – *extremely* – that you've put me in the position of having to defend you.'

'I'm sorry, sir. The circumstances were . . . unusual.' Timberlake felt that the word was limply inadequate, but it was the best he could do for the moment. 'I was carried away in my enthusiasm to arrest Sibley. I'm sincerely sorry.'

'That's the second time you have behaved unprofessionally. If there is a third occasion, the consequences could be serious for you, Inspector.' Not, 'Harry'.

Captain Mark Sibley remained in hospital, under guard, for three days. He had no physical injuries to speak of; but it was to ensure that he was mentally fit to be taken back to Terrace Vale for questioning. The interview took place in the same room, with the same cast list and conditions, as before – with one difference. This time Sibley was accompanied by his solicitor, Corin Chester-Garonne. He was a man in his late sixties built on over-generous lines, with a shock of white hair, a soft but penetrating voice and a nose like the late W. C. Fields'. He was celebrated, not only for his formidable abilities and seeming over-politeness, but also for the hourly rates plus the imaginative expenses he charged. These were not unrelated to the fact that he drove a gold-coloured Bentley Muldane. He was not a good driver, but other road users always took good care not to damage this impressive vehicle.

Timberlake began the recorded interview with the usual preamble of giving the date and time, and a roll call of those present. Then he said, 'Mr Sibley, You have already been cautioned. I remind you that you are not obliged to say anything, but it may damage your defence if, when questioned, you do not say something you later rely on in court.'

'Thank you for reminding my client,' said Chester-Garonne smoothly, 'but I think he can rely on me to protect his interests.'

'Mr Sibley, why did you try to avoid arrest from Gatwick Airport?'

'I've not been able to get the awful death of my fiancée out of my mind, and your wild stories about her only made things worse. Then your unfounded suspicions about me only exacerbated my condition.'

Chester-Garonne nodded his approval of the statement. When Sibley continued the solicitor's lips moved almost imperceptibly as he mouthed what he was saying.

'All these factors were taking me nearer and nearer to a nervous breakdown.'

'I'm sure you understand that, Inspector,' Chester-Garonne said gently.

'But you were flying aircraft. Weren't you putting your passengers at risk?'

'Flying, and concentrating on the job in hand, helped me to forget those problems. But in any case, I had already decided that was to be my last flight. I had made up my mind to take sick leave and seek medical treatment.'

'So why run away?'

'When I saw you observing me from the terminal roof, and I noticed two police cars which didn't belong to the airport . . . well, it was too much for me. I just . . .'

He made a helpless gesture with his hand. 'It was too much for me.'

'How is it you noticed me on the roof of the terminal?'

'My attention was drawn by a bright flash when the sunlight was reflected from your binoculars. Then I made out the figure of that black officer. He's very big.' He gave a wan, brave smile. 'I have excellent long sight.'

In different circumstances Timberlake would have felt inclined to applaud Sibley's excellent performance. 'I see. Didn't it occur to you that running away would look very suspicious?'

'By then I'd been driven beyond normal, rational thought.'

'Are you feeling well enough to continue?' Chester-Garonne murmured solicitously.

Sibley gave another wan, brave smile. 'Yes, thank you. I want to clear all this up as quickly as possible.'

Timberlake could have strangled him. He still had a clear picture in his mind of Mary Docker's butchered body. Nevertheless, he managed to maintain a neutral attitude. 'Nevertheless, if you are innocent of the murder of Mary Docker, why did you try to escape?'

'I've told you, in so many words, that I didn't know what I was doing.'

'I think my client has made this point quite clear, inspector,' Chester-Garonne said. 'And I'm sure you've read the report of the psychiatrist who examined Captain Sibley at the hospital.'

'I've read that particular psychiatrist's opinion, yes.' Timberlake could have added that anyone could find one eminent psychiatrist who would declare that a patient was as mad as the March Hare, and who would also declare that the same patient was as sane as the three times multiplication table, but he was aware that Chester-Garonne knew it as well as he did.

'Very well. Now, in your earlier statement to me you said that on the night of the Friday, the 22nd of November, the night of Mary Docker's murder, you were in Glasgow. Is that correct?'

'Yes.'

'Do you mean that it is correct you said that, or do you mean that is correct that you *were* in Glasgow that night?'

'Both.'

'However, I pointed out to you that it would have been quite possible for you to arrive in Glasgow in the afternoon, return to London, murder Mary Docker, then return to Glasgow in time to fly back to London.'

'Yes. But I didn't. You can check my credit-card accounts. You'll see that I didn't buy any air or rail tickets.'

'Oh, we've done that – just as a matter of routine. But we didn't think you'd be naive enough to make that mistake. However, we did find something interesting.'

Chester-Garonne's only reaction was to allow his eyelids to drop a fraction. Sibley stiffened slightly.

'The 11.55 p.m. train from Euston to Glasgow Central . . . It's an overnight sleeper. No ordinary compartments with seats. One passenger, a man, bought a first-class ticket and paid for a sleeping compartment with cash. All the other sleeping compartments were paid for by credit card or cheque. That's most unusual. Curious, that.'

'What is your point, Inspector?' Chester-Garonne asked.

'Somebody didn't want to leave traces of his journey.'

'Well, it wasn't me,' Sibley said, a trace raggedly.

Chester-Garonne gave him a look which shouted, 'Shut up.'

'In any case,' the solicitor continued, 'I can think of a number of reasons why a man might pay cash.'

'For example?'

Chester-Garonne shrugged. 'A gambler who had won a lot of money and didn't want to leave a paper trail for the Inland Revenue. Or' – he smiled – 'an adulterous Scotsman who didn't want his wife to find out he'd spent a day, or two, in London.'

'You obviously have a more exciting life than I do, Mr Chester-Garonne.'

The atmosphere in the interview room seemed to have relaxed a little.

Timberlake closed the file in front of him with something almost like a sigh. 'So,' he said a little slowly , 'just to make sure I've got everything straight, you say you were in Glasgow on the night of Friday the 22nd of November, when Mary Docker was murdered?'

'Once again, yes,' Sibley said, more confidently.

'Then can you explain to me how you left your fingerprints on a tumbler on the draining board of her kitchen *that night?*'

After a long pause a white-faced Sibley said, 'It must have been from my last visit – the previous Wednesday, I think it was. Or maybe the Thursday. I've made no secret of the fact that I frequently visited Mary at her flat and stayed overnight.'

'All the crockery and glasses were washed and dried on the Friday morning. We have a positive statement from Mrs Freda Phillips, made two days after the murder, when her memory was fresh,' Timberlake emphasized, 'and confirmed again this week. She is quite certain she put everything into the dishwasher and back into place before she left at Friday midday.'

'She must be mistaken,' Chester-Garonne said positively. 'And in any case, this interview is now concluded. My client is clearly tired; he has only just come out of hospital after a long period of depression caused by the death of his fiancée, and all the traumatic experiences at the airport. I am advising him to say no more at this point.'

Timberlake stood up and announced for the record the time of the end of the interview. He took one of the cassettes from the tape recorder and handed it to Chester-Garonne.

'PC Wright, take Sibley back to his cell, please.'

'Yes, sir.' Rambo stood by Sibley as he somehow got to his feet.

'Don't worry,' Chester-Garonne said with a hearty confidence that he was very far from feeling. 'I shall see you at the magistrates' court tomorrow. Say nothing further until then.' He shook Sibley's hand, which was limp and sweaty.

As Sibley left the interview room Chester-Garonne said, 'Oh, inspector, I shall be representing Captain Sibley when he brings an action against you for the damage you caused to his aircraft. I shall also insist to your superiors that you be charged with criminal damage to it. Good day, sir.'

When he had gone, Timberlake looked up at the closed-circuit TV camera, and smiled. 'He's good, isn't he? Mind you, at five hundred an hour he bloody well should be.'

Chapter Twenty-two

Detective Chief Inspector Ted Greening was always pleased whenever Terrace Vale managed to put away a major criminal. It was not pride of achievement or the look-good factor for the station's crime statistics that delighted him. His enjoyment was simply because the success meant a party in the local pub where everybody put £10 into the kitty. His share was drawn from him like a tyro phlebotomist getting blood from someone with deep-seated veins. Still, Greening could easily manage to get through more than £10-worth of drinks in a session, not counting the spillage in the latter part of the evening.

When he was in the brief stage of alcoholic affability, between anxiety to drink his moneysworth and dyspeptic irritation, he approached Timberlake.

'Good collar, Harry,' he said.

'Thanks,' Timberlake said, doing his best to avoid sounding ungracious without encouraging Greening to stop and chat with him.

'For once the sodding DPP got it right. Sibley's brief had a fucking nerve trying to get the charge reduced to manslaughter on grounds of provocation or diminished responsibility or whatever.' He took a heavy gulp of whisky. 'Life. He was lucky. Bastard should have been hung.'

'Hanged,' Timberlake said, automatically. Fortunately Greening didn't hear him very well against the noise in the bar; the tobacco smoke on its own was practically thick enough to muffle a trumpet.

'Topped. That's what he should have been. Wan' another drink?' He was always generous when it didn't cost him anything.

'No thanks, Ted. I'm knackered, what with the Press conference and TV, and all that.'

'Oh, yeah.' Greening's bonhomie began to leak away rapidly. Timberlake, against his own wishes, had already developed a high profile with the media after his success with the Yardbird Charlie murder – a case that he had become involved with almost by accident while working on the Mary Docker case. Now the Sibley trial, with all its involvements of prostitution, multi-personalities, high-life call-girls, the chase at Gatwick and the rest, had set off a feeding frenzy among the media. Some of the more lurid tabloids had dubbed Timberlake 'Supercop'. He hated it – apart from any other reason, he remembered what had happened to the politician they called 'Supermac'. The mania had increased when Harkness, who paid rich tribute to Timberlake's major part in the investigation, said that with the conviction of Mark Sibley, there would be no further action in the cases of the murdered prostitutes Sharon Lester, Poppy 'Marilyn' Monroe and Suzanne Oliver. The implication was obvious.

Greening had tried to divert some of the media attention to himself, with very little success, and it had made him jealous. He stamped away and consoled himself with another large whisky.

Timberlake made his way to the door, suffering pats on the back, congratulations and lewd remarks with good humour. 'Sorry, everybody,' he said at the door, 'but I'm totally creased. My get-up-and-go has got up and gone. I'm off. And thanks.'

He waved as he went out the door, cheers and applause spilling into the street after him. At the nick he had the duty sergeant find him a car and driver to take him home.

Timberlake collapsed in an armchair and sat there without moving for ten minutes. The reaction after the tumultuous day left him badly depressed. Thoughts about loneliness and loss forced their way into his mind despite all efforts to keep them away. There was only one remedy for his gloom: he got up and moved over to his hi-fi system, but before he could pick a record, his mobile phone rang.

'Yes?' he said wearily.

'It's me,' said the unmistakable voice of Sarah Lewis. 'Any chance of a coffee?'

'If you make it.'

'Done, bach.'

Two minutes later she knocked at the door.

'You were quick. Where did you call from?'

'My car, just round the corner.'

They had quickly fallen into their own comfortable pattern of behaviour by the time they got to bed, with friendship as important as sexuality. Despite Timberlake's earlier tiredness and depression, the sex turned out to be much more than adequate, with Sarah's cries and fingernails urging him on.

'God, I'm thirsty,' Sarah said as she lay back, glistening with perspiration and not bothering to cover herself with the rumpled and displaced sheets. 'Get me a glass of water, darling.'

Timberlake groaned theatrically, but got out of bed and moved slowly towards the kitchen. On the way he noticed for the first time the indicator light blinking on the answerphone by the door. It was as difficult to resist as a ringing telephone. He switched the machine to play.

His wife Jenny's voice was as clear as if she were standing next to him in the room, instead of 3,000 miles away. In an even, assured tone she said, 'Harry, I have to speak to you. Be at home tomorrow night at nine o'clock your time. It's important.'

Instantly he knew what it was she was going to say. His heart sank more than he ever would have guessed.

He stood motionless for a long moment. He didn't hear Sarah calling from the bedroom.